THE ENCANTO

Arthur Swan

The Encanto is a work of fiction. Names, characters, business, events and incidents are either products of the author's imagination or used fictitiously. With the exception of public figures, any resemblance to actual persons, living or dead, is purely coincidental. Any opinions expressed belong to the characters and not the author.

This work is dedicated to all the creatives in LA who dare to
dream and dare to share their vision,
all those who sacrifice in pursuit their passion.

Prologue

Although the men were paid through a shell corporation, they all knew where the money came from, and they never expected to see the man in person.

Someone said officials had been bribed to clear the area surrounding Chichén Itzá where, below the central pyramid known as Temple of Kukulcán, ground penetrating radar had revealed a sealed-off passage that led to a secret chamber.

The men tunneled through coralline dust and limestone rock day and night for a week. When they finally reached the passage, they were ordered to stop digging, return to the surface, and wait.

The stadium lights surrounding the dig site and the makeshift runway created a dome of light like a giant bubble, breached only by the pyramid, its massive stone steps ascending into the black void of the night as if they went on up forever.

The men kicked around between the tunnel entrance and the runway until finally one of the diggers marched up to the foreman, Malcolm, and asked, "What the hell is in that chamber?"

Not a new question. Nor was the answer. "No idea," Malcolm said. They were paid not to ask. They were paid exorbitant wages to come here on short notice and work around the clock. What could possibly be worth so much?

The archaeologists—there were three among them—had described all kinds of Mayan ruins and artifacts. Interesting, but not worth venturing into the passage and jeopardizing their bonus.

At two a.m., a Pilatus PC-24 touched down. *Evan York's plane*, Malcolm thought, though he doubted it actually contained Evan York.

The man who emerged from the plane had dark stubble. He was thin, average height. Hair cut short at the sides, parted, and styled back into a wave. Not old or young. Not Evan York.

It was Niles Anderson, York's representative, whose first words were to remind them, again, of the agreement they had signed: *no one was to enter the chamber.*

Niles nodded toward the plane. "Evan York."

Malcolm nearly stepped back. "Evan York is here in person?"

He was. Evan York was on the plane. And he waited there while the men returned to the tunnel to disassemble the remaining wall of white ostra stone that sealed the entrance to the passage.

Malcolm was curious too, of course. He had hoped to see something. But the passage was too long, too narrow. The light diminished quickly, as if swallowed by the darkness in the passage. An absolute wall of blackness cloaked the chamber.

The men stared into it and then looked toward him. He knew what he had to do. Evan York was up there in his private plane, waiting for them to finish. Malcolm ordered the men back to the surface and followed them out of the tunnel.

Outside, they lined up like soldiers as another man, who was not Evan York, emerged from the plane. He was younger and brawny with a shoulder holster strapped over his pressed white shirt. His neck bulged against the collar. He looked them over, nodded to Niles, and waited at the bottom of the stairs…

Evan York stepped out.

He wore tan cargo pants and a long-sleeve, athletic shirt that seemed tailored to his broad shoulders. Malcolm had seen pictures, of course, but pictures failed to capture the spry energy coiled in every step Evan York took. He was sixty-seven but looked fifty-five, maybe fifty. His white hair was coifed back. His smile, genuine. His teeth, perfect.

He was often described, by the media, as *present, effervescent, charismatic and irresistible*, and it was clear why.

One by one, he shook their hands. Malcolm's palms were sweating from the humidity and the heat. Evan York maintained his smile. He looked Malcolm deep in the eye as if he knew him, not just who he was but who he wanted to be—the best part of himself.

Evan York gave a slight wink. "It's Malcolm, right?"

Malcolm choked on his words and barely managed to nod.

Evan York stood back and addressed them all, in his upper-class, British accent. "Really great work, guys. We're going to double the bonus."

Malcolm straightened. Who cared about the chamber? All he cared about was getting hired again, doing another job for Evan York.

At the tunnel entrance, Evan York removed a hard hat from the rack. Niles reached for a hat too, but Evan York placed a hand on his shoulder.

Niles paused, slumped. He stepped back beside the bodyguard.

Evan York donned the hat and entered the tunnel alone.

Once he was out of sight, Niles ordered the men to pack up. Malcolm glanced at the tunnel. No point in asking.

"Another crew is on the way," Niles said. "By tomorrow afternoon there will be no trace we were here."

—

It was a squat, single-story building. There was no sign, not even an address stenciled on the bare stucco. Just an aluminum door with a two-way mirror reflecting harsh sunlight and the Latino man on Lincoln Boulevard. He had gelled hair, a white shirt, and black pants. He moved an orange cone aside and motioned the black sports car, a brand-new Tesla Roadster, into the swath of red curb in front of the building.

The man who unfolded himself from the Roadster was Evan York. He left the door open for Ernesto to valet and frowned at the nondescript building. Next door was an artisanal water store. Across the street, parked beside a carwash, a pink van advertised Topless Maids $99. North of the carwash was Checks Cashed and a Starbucks.

The door to Starbucks swung open. A bearded hipster cruised out with a four-pack of grandes. He was wearing jeans, a black t-shirt, and a red cape. It was Halloween. Evan had almost forgotten. The hipster slid on a pair of black shades and gawked at the Roadster pulling away. Then at Evan.

Evan turned toward the mirrored door, hoping he hadn't been recognized.

Niles, his COO, held the door open. His gray shirt accentuated his all-day five o'clock shadow.

"I'll have a macchiato," Evan said, "plus whatever you want."

"We've got better beans here," Niles said. "Trust me. I'll have an assistant make you one."

"Never mind," Evan said. Niles didn't get it. Evan liked Starbucks. He hated that he couldn't just go in without his personal detail and a big fuss, so he was having his own Starbucks installed at his house. His own friendly baristas, espresso machine, his own milk frother.

Inside the building was a narrow lobby flanked by white doors. A thick, dull paint coated the cinderblock walls. The floors were rustic, unfinished wood. Evan had asked Niles to lease this place because there were too many people in the Santa Monica office lurking around, looking to get involved in things. This project required absolute secrecy. No leaks.

"Does Luis Luna have it?" Evan asked

"He's got something," Niles said, "but he'll only show it to you."

It was crazy, the stunts people pulled to get a meeting with Evan. But this time his hopes were up. Despite the bad phone photo, Luis Luna appeared to have the artifact Evan had been searching for.

Evan followed Niles into a narrow hallway. On the left was the room full of Mayan artifacts Evan had purchased. Many were fakes, but even the real ones were worthless to him.

"Amelia is asking about the procedures," Niles said. "She needs to know what to do after we put the test subjects to sleep?"

A sleep study was the cover story. Like everyone else, Amelia was unaware of the artifact and the ritual, which Evan would have her add on as some kind of coordination test. Even doctors stopped asking questions once there was enough on the table.

"I'll fill her in after I talk to Luis." Evan wished he knew more than what he'd gleaned from the wall paintings in the secret chamber. In the ritual they depicted, two men were lying down, each with one hand on a device. Their eyes were closed. He assumed they were sleeping, but who knew? There weren't subtitles.

At a turn in the hallway, Niles slowed. "This is crazy."

"Yes, it is, Niles, my friend. Indeed, it is."

He passed Niles and turned down the hall as if he were familiar with the place. He knew that by "crazy" Niles meant "a waste of time" which was worse. Though no one said it to his face, of course, everyone thought he was wasting his time. Why wouldn't they? They had no idea about the legend he was pursuing. But so long as the checks cleared, no one complained.

But crazy ideas had made InGenetics into a Fortune 500 in less than four years. Evan loved making big bets on crazy ideas, riding the thin line between bankruptcy and his island in the Caribbean. It took vetting. Deciding which ideas to pursue, who to listen to, who to ignore. Everyone had eyes and ears, but few actually observed. Listening had made Evan rich.

And this legend, far-fetched as it was, sounded like the real deal. Luis Luna's voice had trembled as he explained how his mother brought the artifact, which he called the Encanto, from Guatemala. Something about his story rang true. The Encanto might just be the object depicted in the ritual, the object missing from the chamber below the Temple of Kukulcán. Certainly, it was worth Evan's time to find out. If the legend was true, it would blow away everything else at InGenetic.

Evan had offered Luna five hundred thousand for the Encanto, though he'd gladly pay more. If the device actually worked, it was worth all the money in the world.

Niles sprinted past Evan and stopped a door on the left. He pulled his phone. "I'll have Amelia bring the first test subject—"

"Let me talk to him first." Evan waved him aside. "He's alone, right?"

The test subjects made Evan uneasy. If there was any chance the Encanto worked, letting a third party in on the secret was risky. Although they had signed an NDA, in the words of Ben Franklin, *three can keep a secret, if two of them are dead.*

Evan raised his hand to knock.

What if Luis held back? The Encanto was useless without knowing how to use it. The wall paintings depicting the ritual left a lot of questions unanswered.

But Evan knew how to get what he wanted. *Be prepared. Give yourself options.* He turned back to Niles. "Give us twenty minutes, and if I'm not out, knock on the door and say there's a problem."

"What kind of problem?"

"Just follow my lead."

"If you tell me what's going on, I can prepare some contingencies."

Evan trusted Niles as much as anyone of his staff, but this was too preposterous even for Evan to admit out loud. He first had to prove it to himself. "You'll be the first to know."

Evan entered. As he glanced back, Niles was trying to peer in behind him. Evan closed the door.

Luis Luna slid to his feet from the left of two hospital beds. It was a windowless examination room, with high-end monitoring equipment and all kinds of cords, dials, and screens. Bolted to the wall was a medicine cabinet. To the right of the door was a chair.

Luis wore a brand-new dress shirt, still creased from the package and bloused around the narrow belt line of his jeans. He had a round face with deep lines grooved into his forehead. Probably forty-five, possibly fifty. His teeth were stained and worn. Before shaking Evan's hand, he placed an object wrapped in a royal blue cloth on the far bed.

Evan's phone chose this moment to buzz in his pocket. Intending to decline the call, he pulled his phone out, but it was Ashley, his daughter. She was the one he was doing this for.

"I have to take this," Evan said.

Luis nodded.

Evan turned his back and answered the call. "Baby-love! Mind if I call you back?"

"Of course." Despite the extra layer of cheeriness infusing her voice, her disappointment was obvious. "So, does it work?"

"I'm checking it out right now." He wasn't about to say anything within earshot of Luis, and until he knew for sure, he had to wait. InGenetic was successful, wildly successful, yet so far it had failed to achieve anything memorable enough to capture her interest. He yearned to tell her how the Encanto could change the world. If it worked, she'd be proud of him. She would want to get involved.

"I'll call you back in one hour, I promise." He would make it up to her. He'd make up for all the times he had focused on work instead of her.

He ended the call and turned to Luis. "Alright, let's see it."

"What about the money?" His Latino accent was thick but clear.

"I'm good for it." Evan smiled. He knew the score. Once he issued payment, Luis Luna would vanish. But first, Evan had to learn everything Luis knew about this *Encanto*, and everything his mother or friends might know. "Give your account number to Niles."

"I need to get paid today."

Evan shook his head. "It will take some time to verify you're not selling me a fake. If you're telling the truth, the deposit should hit your balance in two days—a week at the most."

Luis's shoulders sagged. "That's not soon enough."

Evan shrugged. "Sorry to hear that." As he turned and reached for the doorknob, he forced himself not to glance at the blue cloth on the bed. "Didn't mean to make you drive all the way down here for nothing."

"Wait," Luis said.

Evan turned back.

Luis's face had tightened into a pained expression. "My mother... she has cancer."

"Sorry to hear that." Evan repeated, trying to mean it, but if not for the cancer, Luis might never have stolen the Encanto from her.

"Just promise me you'll pay as soon as you can. She needs treatment."

"Not a problem. We'll prepare a document of intent. Hospitals don't expect payment the same day." Evan would have Niles find out about this treatment and maybe pay for it. A hospital could consume the five hundred grand in a matter of hours, and Evan wanted Luis to walk away with a life-changing sum.

Luis bit his lip. His hands trembled as he picked up the cloth bundle from the bed and slowly unwrapped it. He held it out in the nest of cloth, just beyond Evan's reach.

It was a white stone, three inches in diameter and unnaturally round, aside from a flattened area at the bottom and top shaped like a tear. Coral-like holes spiraled around toward the bottom. The stone was pumice, probably, and mounted on top was an elongated *S* of chiseled obsidian with a head with nostrils and fangs, and a forked tongue. The feathered snake deity, Kukulkan. It matched, almost exactly, the wall paintings in the sealed-off secret chamber below the temple. This *was* it. What he'd been searching for. *The Encanto.*

"*Beautiful*," he said. "Beautiful." He reached for the device.

Luis pulled back. "You don't want to touch it."

"What does it do?"

"Do? You didn't tell me it has to do something." Luis held the Encanto off to the side.

"Relax. You'll get paid." Evan held out his open palm.

"Careful," Luis said. "It's really fragile. Just hold it by the cloth, okay?" He rewrapped the stone. Inhaled. Placed it gingerly on Evan's palm.

As he released it, his shoulders relaxed.

"Do you know where it came from?" Evan asked.

"Guatemala, like I said."

Over the phone, Luis had relayed the story of how his mother had smuggled the Encanto across the Mexican border only to keep it hidden in a drawer. Like an emergency fund. A drawer! An insane place to keep it, given the risk of fire or robbery. It could have been lost forever in shoddy apartment where Luis lived with his mother and daughter. Had she brought it along on the arduous journey across Mexico just because it might be valuable, or because she knew of the ritual?

She had to know. She must. And *if* she knew the ritual, then she must have tried it. Of course she had. And if she had performed the ritual and it didn't work, then why keep the Encanto?

And the way Luis was acting, she must have told him. Maybe not everything but he knew something about it. That was for sure. Evan's confidence surged. He couldn't wait to show Ashley.

"I mean, where is it from originally?" Evan said.

Luis shrugged. "You tell me."

Evan studied the feathered snake. It was a thousand years

old, maybe two thousand. "This is Kukulkan, the Vision Serpent. He acted as a messenger between the king and the gods."

Luis furrowed his brow. "What gods?"

Was he trying to play Evan for a fool? "Mayan. There are legends of Mayan technology that surpassed ours."

"Like what?"

Evan had eyes. He'd seen how Luis held it like a hot potato. *When they play dumb, you play dumber.* Play right into the natural human tendency to correct mistakes.

"It's an ancient GPS," Evan lied. It did sort of look like a compass, though it was more—so much more—if the legend was true. "It can point to any city in the Mayan Empire."

Luis made a thickened sound in the back of his throat. He looked doubtful, and for good reason. Ancient Mayans had only Earth's magnetic field to work with. Aside from the poles, it would have been impossible for the snake to point at any particular location.

Luis said nothing. He set his jaw like he'd arrived at a decision. *Had he bought the GPS-lie?*

Evan's heart thrummed. What if he was the one living person in the world who understood the true purpose of the Encanto? The only one who had seen the paintings in the sealed-off chamber below Temple of Kukulkan?

He lifted the Encanto from the cloth. It was a work of art. An amazing piece of craftsmanship, especially given that the Mayans had no access to metal tools. It felt surprisingly light. Must be hollow inside. He turned it over. The little holes spiraled into a ring on the bottom.

He turned it back upright and traced a finger along the jagged edges of the black snake.

"No!" Luis grabbed his hand. "Don't."

Evan hadn't planned on turning the snake-dial until the test subjects were sleeping with their hands on the device, like in the ritual, but why not test it? "If it breaks, you'll still get paid. Don't worry."

"It's not that." Luis swallowed. "It… My mother says… it contains an evil spirit."

Evan hadn't seen or heard anything about a spirit in any of the legends. Maybe she'd invented a story to scare Luis away from messing with it. Maybe, for some reason, she didn't trust him?

"You mean like a ghost?"

Luis glanced at his feet. "I don't know."

"Have you seen it?"

"No."

"Have you seen any evidence of one?"

"No."

"What did your mother say?"

Luis glanced down and to his right. "She said it killed my father."

"The spirit in the stone? You believe that?"

Luis's jaw clenched. "No. He was a dirty cop. He got himself killed by the army."

Evan nodded. He understood. She wanted her son to think highly of his father, to spare him the truth. And if Luis didn't believe her, there was her granddaughter to think of. Hell, maybe the old woman even had convinced herself, preferring to blame a ghost for the sins of her dead husband.

So then why all his nervous energy around the Encanto? "What do you believe?" Evan asked.

Luis blinked rapidly. "I don't know... Look, I made a mistake." He reached for the device. "I never should have taken it from her."

Evan backed away.

Luis lunged toward him, his eyes dark. Determination on his face, and... something else. Sweat beaded on his upper lip. He was afraid.

Evan turned, shielding the Encanto with his body. No way would he surrender it. It was finally his.

Evan had an idea. Maybe Luis would calm down if he thought the Encanto was useless. If Evan just twisted the black snake, nothing should happen. In the wall paintings both men were holding the device. And it seemed like they had to be sleeping.

And Evan wanted to turn the dial. The chiseled snake looked so easy to turn. Its bulging eyes seemed to dare him.

Twisting the snake was the right thing to do, the only thing. A need. He *had* to turn it.

And yet still, he hesitated. Why? Because of Luis? No.

With his forefinger, he flicked the head of the black snake.

Luis grabbed the Encanto, and they both clutched the device. Both afraid to pull harder. Both refusing to let go.

The snake spun clockwise, like a well-oiled compass. Half a turn.

Then, abruptly, it stopped. The tail pointed at Evan. Its head, the forked tongue protruding from its open mouth, at Luis.

Luis gulped.

Within the device, something clicked. A sound like two stones slamming together with the force of a spring. Evan pictured an ivory pistol, its hammer cocking.

Searing pain shot through his palm.

He screamed and nearly dropped the Encanto. He examined his hand. In the center of his palm was a puncture, no bigger than a pinprick but reddening. Something had stabbed him from the base of the white stone.

And it burned. It burned all out of proportion.

Luis had backed up to the wall beside the medicine cabinet, his eyes darted around the room.

Evan showed him his palm. "It stabbed me."

Luis gave no indication that he heard Evan at all.

Evan looked around. "I don't see any ghosts. Do you?"

Luis snapped into action. "I need that money as soon as possible." He lunged toward the door.

Evan casually blocked it. He couldn't let Luis leave. Not after they had started the ritual. Evan's palm still stung, though not as bad as before. But what if? What if, sometime after Luis left, the results of the ritual came to fruition? It would be an amazing experience. He hadn't planned on trying the ritual himself, not the first time, but now that they had started it, he hoped it *would* work. And he had to take precautions.

There was a knock on the door. Niles, and not a moment too soon.

Evan opened the door and stood to the side, letting Niles block Luis from exiting.

Niles glanced from Luis to Evan. "Problem. One of the test subjects cancelled."

Evan made a show of rolling his eyes. "For fifty grand just to sleep, you'd think they'd show up. We only needed them to nap for an hour."

Luis's eyes widened. He glanced from the Encanto, in Evan's hand, to the beds.

"I know," Niles said without missing a beat. He'd had years of practice following Evan's lead. "Especially since we're paying in cash."

Luis rubbed his cheek. "Fifty grand? Just to sleep?"

"The FDA won't approve our drug therapy without a study," Evan said. "It's a small price to pay if we can beat our competitors to the market." He could almost see the wheels turning in Luis's head. The best way to get someone to do what you want is for them to come up with your idea on their own.

Luis squinted. "What's the drug do?"

"It helps you sleep."

"You can't be telling him this," Niles said. "He hasn't signed the NDA."

Evan winked at Luis and smiled. "I trust him." He went to the medicine cabinet, removed the unlabeled spray bottle, and brought it over. "It's all natural. You just spray it on your skin, and it triggers sleep hormones in your body."

Luis tried to look doubtful but couldn't quite stop his lips from curling into a smile. "What are the side effects?"

"None that we're aware of," Niles said.

Luis scratched his head. "I guess I can help you out, but... I'm going to need a hundred grand."

Evan gave Luis his best smile and slapped a hand on his shoulder. "That's great, Luis. You'll be helping a lot of people desperate for this product."

"I'm going to need that in cash," Luis said. "Today."

Niles raised his hand. The closest he ever came to protesting. "That—"

"Is no problem," Evan said. If they didn't have the cash,

Niles would figure out where to get it. He always did.

"I'll call Amelia," Niles said.

"That won't be necessary. I'm going to do the trial, too. Right here with Luis."

Niles's hands shot up in protest. "You? Uh—"

"It will be great advertisement." Evan smiled and glanced at Luis. "Excuse us for a second."

He ushered Niles into the hall and closed the door behind them. Niles glanced down the hall as if hoping for backup.

"Can I count on you?" Evan asked.

Niles straightened. "Absolutely." He seemed to forget whatever protest he was about to make.

"Call Dimitri." Evan's personal guard followed orders without question and would come as fast as he could, but he was at the estate in Palos Verdes, and with the 405 always jammed, he might not get here in time. "Get Ernesto in here too. He's discreet, right?"

Niles's eyes widened. "Of course, but—"

"I'm not to leave this room without the secret password." Evan glanced behind him at the door. Niles leaned in close, and Evan whispered, "Excalibur."

"You got it," Niles said.

"Luis is free to come and go as he pleases. In fact, I want you to go in and wake him up in an hour."

"O-kay." He obviously wanted to ask why but knew there was no point. Evan wasn't going to explain.

Evan returned to the examination room, sat on the bed by the door, and rolled up his sleeves. He squirted each forearm three times with the cream. Passed the bottle to Luis. Rubbed the cream into his skin.

He felt exposed. He was taking a big risk here. No telling how Luis would react. What if Evan's safeguard with the password didn't work? He needed Luis to trust him completely. And more money, at this point, would only raise his suspicion.

"Come work for me," Evan said.

Luis applied a meager squirt to one arm and smeared it lightly. "Doing what?"

Evan smiled. The half-squirt was more than enough to

induce an overwhelming drowsiness.

"What's your current line of work?"

"Maintenance."

"We need maintenance. Who's your employer?"

Luis clenched his jaw. "An apartment."

Was he undocumented? "I'll talk to Niles after our little nap. We've got all kinds of openings. If you need a work permit, we can get that no problem. If you're qualified, we'll sponsor your H1B."

Luis's lips tightened. He nodded. "What if I can't fall asleep?"

Evan shrugged. "Then it doesn't work. Not your problem. We'll do a blood test and try to figure it out."

Luis laid back on the bed beside Evan's, seeming satisfied to close his eyes and ask no more questions.

No need to bother with the motoring equipment. Evan dimmed the lights and rolled onto his side. He watched Luis's regular breathing, wondering how he'd spend the windfall after his mother's cancer treatment.

Evan had long ago passed the point where money could change his life. He had more than he could spend in many lifetimes. Money was just a tool now. Useful, but not everything.

He closed his eyes and exhaled, feeling a certain sense of nostalgia, and loss, for the time in his late twenties when he sold his first company. To be young, suddenly rich, but still anonymous. To be able to walk into a Starbucks without personal security and an entourage of assistants.

Because of him, Ashley had never experienced life as a normal human being. He had failed to provide her this privilege—but maybe now he could.

Gray

Gray was quitting, so the incessant din of his coworkers clicking away on their workstations no longer made him feel hopeless. In fact, he felt sorry for them. He almost skipped down the aisle between the cubes and then up the three steps to the raised platform where Brad lorded over them from his all-glass corner office, the only office on the floor.

Brad was sitting behind his oversized desk, which was also glass, staring at his phone, as usual.

Gray knocked on the door.

Brad slapped the phone face down and leaned toward his monitor. "Just a minute."

Behind him on the glass wall, he'd mounted a large digital clock—the kind you'd normally see at a sports event —so that the engineers coding away in the cubes below merely had to look up to see the red numerals marking the time: 2:07:31, 2:07:32. Behind the clock, LA sprawled eastward, the buildings ascending like an irregular staircase to downtown, where the tallest cluster of gleaming monoliths was still dwarfed by the backdrop of mountains. The peaks clustered with antennas and towers.

Brad clicked his mouse and punched his keyboard. His thin, colorless hair, spiked up with some kind of gel, always looked wet. His face was unnaturally tan, his cheeks flat, and his eyes were too small for his face. His mouth twisted into a bothered expression whenever someone came up to his office uninvited, and now was no exception.

He motioned for Gray to enter, making a performance out of the next four keystrokes.

I quit, Gray wanted to say. He couldn't wait to see the look on Brad's face. But first, he had to tell Claire. "I need to leave a little early."

Brad blinked as if the request was outlandish, way beyond anything anyone had ever requested throughout his vast career as a supervisor, which was all of two years.

"I need to take my kid trick-or-treating," Gray added. Which was true. It would be Mindy's first time, and Gray was looking forward to it, but it wasn't until six.

"O-kay," Brad said. "How early?" Surprisingly, he passed up the opportunity to remind Gray, yet again, about the sprint, the arbitrary milestone Brad had probably invented himself in order to pressure the team into working unpaid OT.

Gray glanced over his shoulder. Below Brad's office, the arrayed cubes were occupied, all except for his. The thought of returning to his desk made his throat tighten.

"Now."

Brad's eyes widened. He stared at his watch. Then, as if his watch might be mistaken, he checked his phone and turned in his chair toward the digital display behind him.

2:07:47. 2:07:48. 2:07:49.

Wasted seconds clicking by.

Gray could agree with Brad on this, because every second he spent standing there was time he could be painting. Creating art was a need. The food of his soul. Without it, he was hardly human at all, just a code-writing robot. This job was standing in his way. He couldn't take it.

Brad swiveled back to face Gray, his brows raised. "You're coming in this weekend, right?"

"Maybe Sunday," Gray lied.

Brad's brows slammed together. "You know the sprint is due Wednesday."

There it is, Gray thought. *2:07:58. Almost thirty whole seconds without mentioning it.* "My stuff is basically done."

"It's in code review?"

"Not yet." No point in submitting any earlier than he had to just so some stickler, of which there was one on every review, could eat up all the available time with an endless stream of unnecessary changes for Gray to implement.

Brad exhaled a long breath. "Do what you've got to do, I guess… but you're the only one leaving early."

Brad's little jabs used to anger him, and so did his insinuation that this was all a contest to see who could put in the most hours, but now he just felt sorry for his coworkers, most of them single men (or "goldmines" as he'd overheard Brad refer to them on occasion), who would no doubt toil for decades before realizing they were going nowhere.

In his performance review, Brad had said Gray needed to focus on priorities, basically implying (though not in a provable way) that Gray's family had cost him a raise. Well, he was focusing on priorities now: *his* priorities. Brad could think whatever the hell he wanted. *What's the worst he can do?*

If Brad fired him, it would be a favor. If he was fired he could collect severance, and he wouldn't have to worry about convincing Claire that he could quit his job to become an artist and yet still, somehow, continue supporting her and Mindy and Tyler. It would all be out of his hands.

Gray pulled out his phone, careful to obscure the lock screen from Brad. "It's Claire," he lied. "I'm already late."

Lifting the phone to his ear, Gray turned his back on Brad. "On my way."

He descended the office steps and strode past the cube farm to the little hallway with the elevator. He pressed the down button for the next to last time.

Saul

Would a cloud be too much to ask? The afternoon sky had thinned out and surrendered to the relentless sun. Saul parked on Lincoln Boulevard near the mob of looky-loos pressing in around the barricades on the sidewalk. Behind the crime scene was a carwash with faded fin-toppers that might have looked stylish in the sixties.

He left the engine running for the AC. In front of him was a pink van advertising *"Topless Maids $99"* and then a squad car. Beside it, Hernandez was talking to the uniforms. She was five foot two and lithe. She only saw him as a partner, but Saul was hoping for more.

He couldn't bear for her to see him heave his huge belly out. If she would just get in here with him, they could crank up the AC and talk like human beings. Forget all the politics and procedure of the LAPD.

He motioned her towards his car, but she looked away.

He flashed his lights.

Useless signal against the sunlight. He sighed. Grabbed his trench coat from the backseat. Climbed out of the car and put it on. It did little to hide his girth. If anything, the coat made him more conspicuous.

Instantly sweating, he tried to ignore the murmurs from

the crowd, the mouths gaping open, all the phones pointing at him as he plowed his big belly toward Hernandez.

She glanced at him from the corner of her eye but continued joking with the uniforms, as if unaware of his approach. Her skin was perfect. She would look twenty-five if not for the clump of gray hair always falling across her forehead.

"What's the status?" he asked.

"Where you been, *Barker*?" She trotted out her Chicana accent, pronouncing the *P* in his last name like a *B*. She was pissed.

"Traffic's a bitch," he said.

She pointed inside his coat. "Is that the evidence you were looking for?"

He glanced down. A dollop of ketchup stained his shirt. He hadn't noticed it escape his burger. He should have told her he was going to the Castle for lunch. She knew he belonged to the clubhouse for the Academy of Magical Arts, but she had no idea how much he loved going there. The ornate wood and crystal chandeliers. The deliberate lack of windows which made it feel like stepping out of LA and back in time to an alternate world where the air seemed to spark with possibility.

He'd only lied because Hernandez was working through lunch, and what if, like his ex, she hated magic?

He buttoned his coat over the stain. They needed to focus on the case. At least Saul did. Not that Lieutenant Levy had actually told him in so many words, but she'd called Hernandez with the assignment instead of Saul when he was the lead detective, or he was supposed to be. If Levy had demoted him, she should have at least told him, but Saul wasn't surprised. She was passive-aggressive and still held a grudge against him for the Brown shooting. Although he'd been cleared of wrongdoing, the fallout had stalled her career.

Hernandez led him away from the uniforms to the black-and-white on the curb in front of Checks Cashed. In the backseat, a middle-aged man with a box-shaped head, shaved almost bald, stared at the crowd with a sour expression.

Hernandez turned toward Saul and combed back her shock of white. "Look. I don't care if you take a long lunch, just let me know where you're at, okay? We're partners. We're supposed to trust each other."

Her eyes caught the sunlight like honey. Saul tried to memorize every detail. He could gaze into them for hours. "I went to the Castle. If you want to come next time—"

"Hollywood is too far for lunch."

Was she suggesting somewhere else? A real sit-down meal instead of their usual takeout? Or maybe dinner? The Castle would be ideal for dinner.

Before he could ask, she slapped the roof of the squad car. "We've got the bastard dead to rights, and get this: he can't move his legs."

"He's a paraplegic?"

"Exactly. His wheelchair's in the trunk."

Saul peered through the back window of the car. The man inside had a potbelly. His arms were cuffed behind his back. He looked up at Saul, his face blank and his eyes, shadowed by a massive brow, just dark hollows.

Saul shuddered.

"Sheesh. Is he talking?"

"Not really. He's demanding the right to clean himself, but I'm thinking, you bash someone's head in, you wear the blood-splatter, am I right?"

Saul shrugged. The streaks of dried blood on the man's cheek were of little concern to him.

Hernandez held out her phone. "Check this out. Some woman actually filmed the whole thing."

As he took the phone, his knees trembled under his weight. He looked around for somewhere to sit. But they were pinned into the stretch of sun-bleached sidewalk between the crime scene and the makeshift barricade holding back the crowd.

Pushing his way through the crowd was Chu, the assistant chief coroner, who tended to assign the high publicity cases to himself. Having Chu on the case meant an autopsy with no delay, so Saul was fine with the showboating. He motioned for the uniforms to move the barricade.

As Chu approached, Hernandez asked, "How's my favorite coroner?"

"Good, good. Who's the vic?"

"Luis Luna," she said, "Latino, age forty-seven."

Chu glared at Hernandez.

"I only took out his wallet. Didn't touch anything else, I swear."

Chu snapped on a pair of latex gloves and motioned his crime-scene photographer, who had just arrived with all his gear, through the barricade.

They approached the yellow tape surrounding the blood splatters on the sidewalk and Luna's body, a white sheet was draped over him.

Chu frowned at the sheet. "Who covered the body?"

"One of the unis," Hernandez said. "He's new."

"I can see that. I'll need his shoes. Yours too, Hernandez."

"I wore booties," she said.

Chu frowned again. He activated a digital recorder and kneeled by the body. He peeled the sheet back, revealing Luna's face. The whole right side was beaten beyond recognition. His left eye glazed over. Chu parted Luna's lips. His mouth was full of blood. His teeth broken.

Chu spoke into the recorder. "Severe blunt-force trauma to the right side of the head. Victim's air passage is blocked."

He paused the recording. "So Parker, when are you going to get me in at the Magic Castle?"

"Anytime," Saul said. "Just let me know."

"Next time you're on stage."

"That could be a while." Saul hadn't performed in over a year. For him, it wasn't about performing. He enjoyed watching other magicians, watching the impossible occur right before his eyes. Riding the thrill for a few seconds before mentally deconstructing exactly how the trick was performed. Knowing the method behind the magic gave him a certain assurance.

"You've got to look at the video," Hernandez said again.

Saul had almost forgotten he was holding her phone. He moved beside her and held it up so they could both watch. It began with Luna already lying face down. Near his head, a toppled Starbucks oozed brown liquid onto the pavement.

The wheelchair was on its side. The perp pulled his torso and potbelly up onto the chair, his legs trailed limply behind him.

Luna managed to turn over. To raise his arms in defense. But it was useless. The man reared up on his wheelchair and slammed a baseball bat into Luna's skull. He repeated the beating. Luna's hands fell limp by his side. Finally, two Latinos ran into the frame, snatched away the bat, and wrestled the crazed paraplegic down on the pavement. He screamed in a language Saul didn't recognize.

Saul lowered the phone and stared through the back window at the perp. They had the right guy, yet he seemed different somehow. His shoulders sagged. His head lolled on his neck. He stared up at Saul with eyes that seemed to have nothing inside them. Like he was a spent shell, a remnant of the man in the video.

"I made the woman delete it from her phone," Hernandez said, "but I bet you dinner she tweeted it."

Dinner. Saul felt his face redden. "You're on." Regardless of who paid for the meal, dinner was a win for him.

"So what's the motive?" he asked.

"Who cares? We've got him on video."

"It'll make a difference in court. The DA will insist on something."

"How about: he's a psycho."

Saul mopped his brow for the third time. "Even psychos think they have a reason."

Chu concluded his preliminary examination and motioned for a pair of EMTs to place Luna's body on a stretcher. Saul wished he'd close the lifeless eye, but Luna was no longer a man to Chu. He was a thing to be studied. And a vehicle to rocket Chu into the headlines.

"You don't look so good," Chu said. "You should take

off that coat."

"It's my knee," Saul lied. "I strained it chasing a perp."
No way he was removing his coat with all the bystanders
behind the barricade pointing phones in their direction. His
shirt was soaked through and clung to his belly. Couldn't be
more wet if it rained. Although, he would certainly be
cooler. He shielded his eyes to sun and gazed upwards.
Endless blue sky. Could be hours before marine layer rolled
in.

Saul turned to check the other direction. Same deal. The
crowd extended a full block north, up to Rose. Beyond it
was a gas station, and beyond that a restaurant named
Casablanca beckoned like an oasis. Air conditioning. Food.
No windows.

A place where he and Hernandez could escape all this. A
place they could talk.

He was cooking inside the coat—he had to take it off.
Chu was right about that. But now a van from Fox News
was rolling up beside the black and-white, not even
bothering to park, hardly even slowing before unleashing its
crew, including two cameramen, recorders on their
shoulders already rolling.

As senior detective, Saul was expected to handle the
reporters, make the standard neutral-non-statement. But at
this stage, even saying they had a suspect in custody could
backfire.

He faced the window of Checks Cashed and frowned at
his reflection. "We need media relations. I'll call the L-T."

"Already spoke to her," Hernandez said. "She wants us to
punt."

Saul searched her face. She looked away. Earlier, she'd
acted like her conversation with Levy was perfunctory,
more of an oversight that Levy had called her with the new
assignment instead of him. But now it was clear. Levy had
cut him out of the loop, and she lacked the balls to inform
him.

"Then I guess you should do it," he said, which was fine
with him. He had no desire to appear in the news looking
like an eggplant in a trench coat. Hernandez would look

amazing on camera. Even if all she said was *no comment*, it would come across more positive from her than from him.

"We could just leave." She said it like he had a choice, like maybe this time it wasn't an order, but next time, who knew? "Let's take the perp downtown. Maybe he'll talk in the box."

Fine. Saul was glad to get out of the sun. "I'll follow you."

Gray's Lie

At the intersection of Rose and Lincoln, Gray was stuck in his car, almost choking on exhaust, and basically, it was Claire's fault. He'd suggested coming to the beach how many times? She never said no, not exactly; she just had this way of procrastinating to some unknown date in the future.

He rolled up the windows. If he'd just paid the twenty-two dollars for beach parking, he could be walking on the sand right now. But instead, here he was, stuck—at a green light—with no one moving and not even a chance of street parking. Across Lincoln, a mass of people crowded around an ambulance and three police cars.

Finally, the T-bird in front of him moved. He turned right onto Lincoln, hoping for a better view of whatever was going on the left side of the street. Dumb. You couldn't see anything from the road. He made it maybe ten feet and then had to slam the breaks.

Time to get out of here. He nudged his Camry into the bike lane and turned down an alley. Also jammed. But there was parking: a single open space behind the Fringe Salon marked with "*Customers Only.*"

Screw it. He could use a cut. Anything was better sitting in his car stuck in the gridlock.

He parked and entered the salon through the back. It was a narrow room with three barber chairs and a sink. At the front was a reception desk with a large fern and a shelf of products. Gray was the only customer.

A stylist, a black man with neon-yellow hair, introduced himself as Devan. He led Gray to a barber chair, faced him toward a mirror, and stood behind him. "So, what can I do for you?" He spoke with a lisp.

Gray's dull-brown hair was unkempt, as usual, but thinner than he remembered. "Something different," he said. "What do you think?"

Devan ran his fingers through Gray's hair from different angles. His brows furrowed. He smacked his lips. "Who cut it last time?"

Gray shrugged. "Supercuts, I think."

Devan shuddered.

While washing Gray's hair, Devan recounted what he'd learned from Twitter about the police presence outside, "Some lunatic bashed a guy's skull in with a hammer."

Gray shuddered. "Oh man."

"I know." Devan smacked his lips. "Someone shared a video, but the link was dead by the time I clicked it."

"I thought it was safe over here."

"I don't know if it's safe anywhere. The guy who got killed was in a wheelchair, can you believe that? What kind of psycho kills a disabled person?"

Gray grimaced. A guy in a wheelchair. Anyone could die, anytime. There was no guaranteed tomorrow. Next time it could be him. His pulse started racing as he thought of all the time he'd wasted. He had to do something with his life. Now or never.

Devan wrapped a towel around Gray's neck and ushered him back to the chair. He checked his phone. "OMG. Ashley York might costar in a One Direction biopic!"

"Great." Gray hated Ashley York. If she hadn't been born rich, no one would care what she was up to, and she wouldn't be costarring in anything.

Devan opened a drawer and chose a pair of scissors. "You don't follow her?"

Gray groaned. "No, but my wife does. You'd think her life depended on it."

"Ooh. What does she think of August Grant?"

"Who's that?"

Devan smacked his lips. "He's Quantum-Man, silly. Although, if you ask me, he's too hot to wear a mask. Anyway, Ashley's dating him. Wouldn't surprise me at all if they're the next Kunis and Kutcher."

In the mirror, Gray noticed how much grayer the stubble on his chin had become. And his eyes were more than a little bloodshot, probably from all the late nights, trying to make time for himself before he had to get up and do it all over again. The cycle of dread. How did he get here?

His whole life he'd always been drawing. In college, he'd started painting without much thought about what he wanted to do with his life, aside from the fact that he knew he'd spend it with Laura. And then, after they broke up, it was Claire. When he almost lost Claire, all he could think about was how to build a life with her. He wanted a family, and in order to provide for them, he need some kind of job. The tech industry was paying well, so he'd changed his major to comp sci. He and Claire moved in together, and the years clicked by in a blur.

He'd sort of forgotten how much he enjoyed painting. Until last year. Mindy got into coloring books, and one night, while drawing with her, it all came back. He sketched her sleeping in her little bed. He drew portrait of Claire, who was eight months pregnant with Tyler at the time, holding her belly.

He then bought some acrylics and an easel, and now he was begging Claire just for a few hours alone in the garage. They had agreed on Saturday mornings as his designated time to paint, but there was always something else going on. And Saturdays weren't enough. He needed to paint full time.

Quitting his job would be easy—he looked forward to that—but he dreaded telling Claire. Quitting his job, their only source of income, was a bad decision, a terrible decision, and yet the only option he had. His dreams would not be denied any longer.

But how to tell her? The whole reason he'd driven down to Venice Beach was to find a place to think, to come up with a plan. He needed a way to pay the bills.

What he needed was a drink.

"What do you think?" In the mirror, Devan presented Gray's hair with his palms. The sides were buzzed flat, and the top was coiffed up with product. It looked thicker than ever.

"I look like a new man." Gray smiled. Things were going to work out, somehow. They had to.

—

There were plenty of bars around, but Gray had to move his car from behind the salon, and anyway, it would be a bad idea to have alcohol breath when he explained to Claire how he was quitting.

From the alley, he saw Fox News and NBC vans adding to the to the jam-up on Lincoln, so he tacked through a neighborhood down to Venice Boulevard and turned east, toward home. The sun sunk into the clouds behind him as he waited through one light after another.

A block past Helms, the Library Bar practically beckoned him into its lot. If he stopped for a while, traffic might thin out and he'd get home at the same time anyway. It would be a good idea to at least spend a few minutes thinking through what he was going to say.

Inside, the lighting was dim, and the air thick with the smell of beer and the distinct aroma of old paper from the hardbacks that lined the walls. The bar was polished wood and at the far end, a shaggy-haired man in a plaid shirt was arguing with the bartender.

Gray grabbed the nearest stool. The bartender approached. He had a lantern jaw, and it was set with a look that said Gray had to order fast, and it better be something besides water. So Gray ordered a Corona, because he hated beer and would be less tempted to drink it.

The bartender popped open a longneck. Placed a napkin in front of Gray, centered the bottle in the square, and returned to his argument with the shaggy guy at the other end of the bar.

Gray's phone rang. He pulled it out. In the photo on the screen, Claire was smiling. It was from before the kids, maybe eight years ago, but she looked fifteen years younger and much happier.

He answered, and she opened with, "Where are you? I thought you were leaving an hour ago."

In the condensation on the bottle, he sketched a zigzag. "There's a game at Dodger Stadium. Traffic is jammed."

She sighed. "Just get here."

Gray promised he would and ended the call.

More and more, he'd found himself living in borrowed moments like this. It had started one night after the 10 crawled to a dead stop. He'd pulled off into a neighborhood to wait it out, and yet it seemed like he got home around the same time, so he started doing it every night. Just for a while, at first, and after getting away with it, he snuck an easel into his trunk. He stopped at a park a few times and setup his easel, but he couldn't really focus on a painting. He felt too guilty stealing time when he should be helping Claire with the kids. So, to take the edge off the guilt, he began stopping at bars. For a quick drink, at first, which soon became two. And now, more often than not, he couldn't say how long he'd been sitting there or for how many drinks before Claire had texted. He'd done it so many times that his lies about working late were wearing thin.

But it was an adventure. A new bar each night. He was anonymous. Didn't matter if it was a pub or a cantina, if it was packed or empty, if the bartender had tattoos or a suit. No one cared how long he stayed. Bars were more than just rooms full of booze; they created a kind of slowness. An easy space where he could sit in silence. Like now.

Behind the shaggy-haired man, a door swung inwards to a brightly lit office. A man with glasses and spiky hair emerged and perused the shelves of hardbacks lining the back wall of the bar. Moving toward Gray, he ran his finger along the spines and settled on a novel with bold letters on the dust jacket, "*Tim O'Brien.*" He nodded toward the bartender and returned to his office, where he eased onto a leather couch.

An idea dawned on Gray. This was exactly what he needed: a bar with a back room. He could convert it into a studio, a space where he could paint. He would hire some hip bartender to handle the day drinkers, and then at night Gray would emerge from the studio and sling drinks himself. He could hang his best works out in the bar. Kind of like a gallery. Maybe even sell a few.

Maybe, once he had his own bar, he would stop drinking. He was sick of the headaches anyway and had been intending to cut back for years, but then something always went wrong between him and Claire, and he just needed to take the edge off.

Above the bar was a flatscreen. The bartender powered it on without consulting Gray, even though he represented fifty percent of the customer base. The Dodgers were playing the Giants, the announcers shouting. The manager kicked the door shut to his office.

Gray just needed ten minutes of silence, but instead he got a commercial for a Ford F-150 with a frenetic beat even louder than the game.

He stood up, and the bartender ignored him. Shaggy was jabbering, yelling above the TV volume about who should pitch the second inning while stuffing peanuts into his mouth.

Gray slapped a ten down on beside the napkin, now soaked with condensation from his full longneck.

At the exit, he stalled, pretending to examine the books near the door, but his mind was locked on the Corona, the bubbles rising into the neck…

He turned back. Snatched the bottle from the bar, and tilted it back. He took a long pull. Gulped so hard he almost choked.

Now, the bartender took notice. He paused midsentence to watch Gray slam the half-empty beer back on the bar, then turned back to Shaggy. "Look, all I'm saying is the Dodgers don't have to win, so long as the Giants lose…"

The muscles in Gray's shoulders loosened. All the tension eased out of him. But the glide of the alcohol brought with it the guilt. Which would fade, if he drank more. *Who cares if I finish my beer?* He wanted to drink the whole damn bar. But it wouldn't be enough.

That was the problem with drinking: it was never enough.

—

Outside, a solid mass of low cloud had swept over the city. People liked the marine layer because it cooled LA down, but to Gray the gloom was oppressive. He stood there. The drone of traffic surrounding him. He should just go home, but what to tell Claire? If it not for the kids, he would just quit regardless of what she thought.

Gray got in his car and sat in the parking lot watching the mist grow denser around the streetlights. The road blurred out of focus, fading away. He checked the rear-view mirror. Nothing but fog.

Nothing to be afraid of, he told himself. *It's perfectly safe here.* But his heart was beating faster. He was spooking himself out again. Claire would laugh if she had any idea how easily he was frightened.

He'd always been like this, ever since the *Trollenberg Terror*, which he had watched way too young. The second half of the movie, after the one-eyed alien came out, was no problem (it had looked cheesy even when he was a kid), but the beginning, before he even realized it was a horror flick, when the rock-climber fell out of the fog…decapitated. The scene still sent a chill down his spine, even now.

Near the front of his car, something scuffed the pavement. A boot?

He flicked on the high beams… Beyond the hood, the fog was solid white.

He started the engine, dimmed the headlights, and rolled out of the lot.

—

The traffic had gotten worse. The 10 was jammed. The surface streets, jammed. It took a mind-numbing hour of grid lock just to travel the ten miles to Silver Lake, and, of course, Claire's car was in the driveway. He had to park two blocks from their house. He ran through the fog, and as he reached the front door, he felt a rush like he was digging himself out after being buried alive.

He opened the door.

From the living room, the TV was blasting, a commercial for Sit N' Sleep. "I'm home. Claire?"

She was on the couch with Tyler in her lap, chewing on his rattle. She wore the same sweatpants as she had this morning. Her raven hair was tangled and oily, her skin so pale it almost shone, except for the bruise-like shadows around her eyes. Her eyes had many colors. When he met her, they were blue like the Pacific in the summer sun. Tonight, they were slate-gray. They flicked up toward Gray then back to her phone.

She said nothing.

"Mind if I turn this down?" Gray moved the towels off the coffee table and began rifling through the magazines for the remote.

"What's with the haircut?" she asked.

"My barber quit." Gray glanced at her. "Like it?"

"It's your hair."

The commercial break ended, and the news came on. They showed clips of Lincoln Boulevard. Gray froze. If they showed his car, Claire would recognize it. They cut to a carwash cordoned off with yellow police tape, the crowd pressing in around it. According to the anchor woman, a guy in a wheelchair, a man by the name of Edward Saroyan, had done the killing, and with a baseball bat not a hammer. But it was hard to imagine how a guy in a wheelchair had managed to bludgeon a man who could run away. To Gray, Devan's version sounded closer to the truth than what the NBC was saying.

He found the remote and turned it off.

"I was watching that," Claire said.

Gray sat beside her on the couch and tried to look cheerful. *Start positive.* "How was your day?"

"What do you mean, *my* day?" She plopped Tyler on his lap.

"I just…" Bad question. He knew how her day was, just like she knew about his, and it had been so long since either of them had asked the other that now it seemed weird to ask.

33

A stench curled Gray's lip. Tyler's diaper needed changing, and it couldn't wait. Gray carried him to the nursery and unfastened his diaper. "Oh man, little man."

Tyler started crying.

No big deal. All he had to do was get through tonight. Telling Claire was going to be hard, no doubt about it, but he *would* get through it. Then tomorrow was Saturday, his day to paint.

Lifting Tyler's ankles, Gray gingerly wiped the goo from his butt. Clearly too much for just one wipe. He went to the box for more wipes.

"Don't just dab at him," Claire said from the doorway. "You've got to get in there." She snatched a wipe, pushed Gray aside, and scooped the poo out from between Tyler's legs.

"You got some on your hand." Gray pointed.

"It's just poo."

"Exactly, excrement." His least favorite thing about babies.

Claire wiped her hands and left.

Gray secured Tyler in a fresh diaper. Then made rocket noises while lifting him above his head. Tyler laughed and pumped his arms. It was so easy to make them laugh, sometimes. Gray's favorite thing about babies.

Mindy edged into the doorway, the pink princess dress she got for her fifth birthday still a size too big. Locks of cocoa hair curtained her face as she leaned against the door frame, hugging a doll to her chest.

"Are you ready to go trick-or-treating?"

She looked down. "I guess."

Her level of enthusiasm would go way up once she learned about the candy. Gray couldn't wait to see her face when she learned that all she had to do was knock on a neighbor's door and they'd give her sweets.

"Well, you need to wear a costume."

"I am."

He smiled. Any day of the week he could come home and find her dressed like a princess. "Oh, I thought those were your normal clothes."

"No. I wear girl clothes when I'm a girl."

"So you're not a girl, tonight?"

"I'm a princess fairy-girl." She laughed and spun.

"Well, alright, then." He ushered her forward.

Tyler started to sob.

Gray tried the rocket ship again, but this time Tyler only wailed.

Claire appeared from the other end of the hallway. "Give him to me." She took Tyler in her arms and swayed him with a practiced tenderness. "Who's my baby boy? My bubble-baby-boy."

He stared up into her placid face and seemed to relax.

She carried him into the living room and said over her shoulder, "We don't have anything to make for dinner."

Gray glanced at the door. He didn't feel like to going back out in the traffic but this could be the opportunity he needed to talk to Claire. He followed her to the couch. "I'll call Belinda," he said. "We can go out, just the two of us. She can make macaroni for the kids."

Claire shook her head. "I can't deal with her anymore."

Gray glanced at Mindy, who had no doubt picked up on her mother's animosity toward the one decent sitter they had. Sure, Belinda was a little nosy, but it wasn't that big of a deal.

"I'll deal with her. You can just wait in the car when she comes."

"Won't work," Claire said. "She'll want to talk to me."

Claire was right, of course. Gray shrugged. "I'll make up an excuse."

"No, you won't. She'll ask you something you don't know the answer to, and I'll have to get involved."

"So, what do you want to do? I promised to take Mindy trick-or-treating."

"Elmo's, Elmo's, Elmo's," Mindy chanted. She loved Elmo's because of the chocolate-chunk pancakes they let her order for dinner, which she smothered syrup.

Claire sighed. "Too much effort to get ready."

"Delivery?" There wouldn't be dishes, and after they'd put Mindy and Tyler to bed, they could sit down, just the two of them, and he could finally explain to her why he had to quit his job.

"No." Claire sighed. "I'll just go to Elmo's."

"Great, I'll call Belinda."

"I don't want macaroni," Mindy said.

Claire shook her head. "We're all going."

Mindy clapped. "Elmo's!"

That decided it. Elmo's would be crowded, too crowded to talk, but maybe while the kids were distracted, he could at least lay down some groundwork so it wouldn't be a complete shock later on when he dropped the bomb.

"I have to take a shower," she said.

Gray reached to take Tyler, cupping his fuzzy little head. Amazing that something this small would grow into a man.

Claire pulled him away. "You'll wake him. I'll go put him in the crib. You get the car packed. There's no time to go trick-or-treating."

As she carried Tyler to the nursery, Gray kneeled down beside Mindy.

"Can I get the chocolate chip pancakes with maple syrup?" she asked.

Claire calling off the trick-or-treating had hardly even registered. But next year Mindy started kindergarten, where she would for sure learn that people gave out candy on Halloween. Claire didn't get it. He had to take her tonight. He just had to.

—

In the driveway, Gray took Mindy by the hand and stepped out from the porch light into the fog. Tyler, strapped to Gray's chest in a Bjorn, woke up and dreamily looked around.

Mindy halted at the curb. "Elmo's."

"We're just going while Mom's in the shower. Don't you want to show off your princess outfit?"

"I'm a fairy-princess!" Mindy jerked her hand free, launched into the road, and spun around.

The street appeared empty, at least from what he could see in the thick fog. "Mindy, you have to look first." He grabbed her hand and led her across.

Lining the walkway up to the neighbors' were rows of jack-o'-lanterns with carved expressions alternating from ecstasy to fear and fury, all lit up with orange lights meant to look like candles. Shadows flickered on the pavement.

In the center of the yard a trio of stuffed witches perched on a haystack, held their brooms out like weapons. On the hedge, a black cat arched its back, its tail sticking straight up. On the roof, an orange light silhouetted a group of crow cut-outs.

One squawked. Gray jumped, and Tyler laughed at the sudden movement.

The ebony bird abandoned its wooden brethren and flew off into the night.

"It's just a bird," Mindy said, "and those witches are fake."

Gray pretended to laugh. He glanced back toward their house. It had faded into a shadow behind the fog and the haloed porch light.

On the neighbors' front stoop was a chalk outline of a body, which they had to stand on to ring the doorbell. Gray worried that maybe this house was too scary for Mindy, but then again, she seemed less scared than him. He pressed the button.

Organ music bellowed.

Gray racked his brain for the names of the couple who lived here. They had hardly spoken since he and Claire moved into the neighborhood four years ago.

The organ reached a crescendo. The door creaked open. An elderly man in a brown suit peered out at them. The suit hung limply off his stooped shoulders.

Mindy hid behind Gray's legs.

"And who do we have here?" The old man grimaced, or maybe he was trying to smile, but the way the wrinkles twisted on his face made the expression look painful. As he bent down, his body shook.

Gray gently prodded Mindy out from behind his legs. "We have a very shy fairy."

"A princess fairy," she said, almost too quietly for them to hear.

Gray smiled. "So, what do you say, Mindy?"

"Trick-or-treat."

The old man produced a bowl heaped with packets of Skittles and M&M's. Mindy's eyes went wide. More candy than she had ever seen.

Gray handed her the bag he'd brought for her, which she took as if in a trance, her eyes on the candy as the old man dumped it in.

Gray reached out to stop him. "That's plenty."

"I've got more in the kitchen," he said.

Gray laughed. "No, I mean, that's more sugar than she eats in a year."

"Well, I'll be here all night if you change your mind." He reached for the door.

"Wait." Gray introduced himself and they shook hands. But the old man didn't mention his name.

Gray assumed he must be the father, possibly the grandfather, of either the man or the woman who lived here. "So where is the rest of the family?"

The man's eyes narrowed. "Out of town."

Gray motioned toward the yard. "They set this up and missed the big night?"

The old man's eyes flashed. "You think I'm too old to celebrate Halloween?"

"Of course not, I just—"

"These are my decorations," the old man shouted.

"Wow," Gray said. "Amazing."

The man tilted his head toward the ground. "Yeah."

"Have you had a lot of trick-or-treaters?"

The old man swallowed. "You're the first."

If he was disappointed, Gray could understand. "This isn't a popular neighborhood for Halloween, and most people don't go out when it's foggy."

"The fog ain't nothing," the man said. "It's the crazies. People don't feel safe."

"The crazies?"

"You see the news?" The man's voice went hoarse. "LA is falling apart."

"We don't get much time for news." Gray patted Mindy

on the head, signaling for him to keep the conversation age-appropriate.

"The air makes people's brains go haywire. The wheelchair-crazy is just the beginning."

The murder on Lincoln was definitely not something Gray wanted Mindy to hear about. "We should get back." He turned toward the road.

The fog was closing in. The row of jack-o-lanterns faded off into the whiteness.

"Elmo's!" Mindy took Gray's hand and pulled ahead of him.

"Be careful," the man called after them.

As they crossed the street, Mindy tried to pull her hand free, so she could dig into her candy, but Gray held on. "Wait until we get inside."

"Are you afraid of the crazies?" she asked.

"No, that guy was just talking about people who like to party a lot, in places like Hollywood. We're safe here," he said, but he was afraid, afraid that if he let go of her little hand, she might vanish in the fog.

As they reached the driveway, the outline of their Craftsman house came into focus.

"When we get inside, I want you to put your candy away until tomorrow. Okay? Let's keep this trick-or-treating our secret for now." He knew Claire would eventually find out, but better to keep it from souring the night.

Inside, Mindy ran ahead toward the living room, clutching the bag to her chest.

"Let's put it in the kitchen," Gray said. But it was too late. Claire was on the couch with her phone, her damp hair pulled back. She looked from Mindy to Gray and clenched her jaw.

"Mindy," he said, "show your mother what you got from just one house."

"But, you said—"

"Never mind. Let's just show her."

Claire's eyes were a dangerous blue. Electricity swirled inside them. Mindy held the bag out, but Claire remained focused on Gray. "I can't believe you did that," she said. "I told you I'd be ready quick."

Mindy veered off to a corner, dumped her candy, and began sorting it.

Gray swallowed. He kneeled down and pretended to tie his shoe. "The car is packed if you're ready." He glanced up at her.

"I still have to dry my hair." She sighed, and then threw off the blanket and heaved herself up from the couch. "Screw it. Let's just go."

Ashley

The tires squealed as Ashley turned her Mercedes into the driveway. She gunned the engine and slammed the brakes, skidding to a stop just short of the gate. While waiting for Sammy to open it, she tapped the wheel with her thumbs. She felt his eyes on her, but if she turned toward the guard booth, if she so much as glanced in his direction, he'd smile that big friendly smile of his and yell her name like she was so awesome, and then she would break down.

She did not get the part. During lunch, the dickwad director had been texting the whole time while the producer droned on about how he'd clawed his way up from nothing into a Hollywood bigshot. She had gone in confident, heather-blue culottes and a satin crop top, but when she asked about the film, the producer suddenly noticed his food and the director looked up from his phone and began drilling her with random questions like, "What's your favorite childhood memory", to which she'd answered honestly: playing Marco Polo with her dad. But was that the wrong thing to say? Don hadn't told her what to say. She must have said something wrong, or maybe they had decided already, because after the check came, the producer said, "You don't want this role."

And the director, while sipping his espresso, basically left the conversation and went back into his phone.

The producer began to go on and on about what a great big favor they were doing her by casting someone else. She should have walked out right then, but for some reason she sat there like a little girl being lectured. He had another part in mind for her, of course. Still too early to talk about, of course. And when the time was right, his people would talk to her people. Of course.

But they both knew that call would never happen.

And now she had to shield her eyes, like her shades weren't enough to block the sun. The tears were coming. No stopping them now. The gate finally opened.

"Thank you, Sammy," she choked.

—

In her parlor, she collapsed on the couch and screamed into the pillow.

After a good long cry, she rolled onto her back. Haze-filtered light poured through the wall of windows. She called her dad.

It rang and rang. Finally, his personal assistant answered.

"Where's Dad?" Ashley asked.

"He said not to disturb him," his PA said in a terse whisper.

"Seriously? What's going on?"

"I was going to ask you. He skipped the interview this morning. And now everyone's panicked something's wrong with the new drug."

Weird. It wasn't like him. He wouldn't have scheduled an interview he didn't want to do. And yesterday, he had promised to call her back but didn't, and he always kept promises, at least up until now.

"Put him on."

"But—"

"Just put him on, okay. It's urgent."

Through the phone speaker came a timid knock and a muffled conversation. Then her dad picked up. "Ashley?"

Weird. He *always* called her "baby-love." Had he finally realized she was a grown woman?

"I didn't get the part." Her voice wavered. It echoed almost shrilly in the big, open room, and she wanted to cry all over again. But she was done with crying.

"Sorry to hear that. Is there something I can do?" He sounded a little off. Not the tone of his voice but the way he was speaking. Slower, and maybe... what happened to his self-confidence?

Maybe because this time there was nothing he could do? She wasn't about to let him executive produce again. Last time, all he kicked in was as couple mil for *Butcher Shop*, which was a waste because the script was so shitty, and then the reviews blamed her acting and accused her of sucking so bad that her dad had to buy the role for her, which was worse than not getting cast at all.

"So what happened with the artifact?"

"What artifact?"

"Are you kidding me?" Yesterday, he'd been all excited about finally getting his hands on some artifact he'd learned about from a cave painting in Mexico. He'd thought it would do something spectacular and had sworn her to secrecy without even explaining what the secret was.

"Ha ha. Yeah, the artifact. Guess I told you about yesterday?"

"Are you feeling okay?"

"Yeah. Uh... No, actually I think I'm coming down with something."

"Well did it work?"

"What? The artifact? No, it doesn't do anything."

"Bummer. I guess you're too busy for dinner?"

"Yeah." He sounded almost relieved. "I am really busy here."

"So what happened? Today was the big launch for Endo —what was it again?"

"Right. They told me it launched this morning."

"Then why skip the *Good Morning Show*?"

"I had to take care of something."

Why was he being so vague? He must have realized that it was hard for her to care about InGenetic with so much tragedy in her own life. It was great that he was so passionate about his business and all, but... "So, I'm not your baby-love anymore?"

"What do you mean?"

"You called me Ashley. You never call me by my name."

"Oh. You'll always be my *baby,* love." He didn't sound too convinced. "But I should go."

They said goodbye, and he disconnected.

"Love you too, Dad," she said to the silence on the end of the line.

On the glass coffee table, Andrea had stacked the issues of *Vanity Fair* in some random order again. Ashley went ahead and ordered them chronologically. Then fanned them out in an arc so at least her cover issue from six months ago was still partially visible.

Then she called August, put her phone on speaker, and centered it in the arc of magazines on the table.

As it rang, she curled up on the couch.

"What's up, babe?" he said.

"Want to come over? I'll have Andrea cook us a special dinner."

"Can't do it. What time does she leave?"

"Seven. But I could ask her to stay if that's too early."

"Let's just get together later on tonight."

Ever since they had hooked up, last week, August had been avoiding her. She was almost positive it had something to do with the sex, which she hadn't really been ready for, but what choice did she have? Every heterosexual female in the world wanted August Grant, so why wouldn't she?

Now they were dating, apparently, at least according to the tabloids, where the buzz on August had gone high-key ever since the announcement that he would star in the nine-figure *Quantum-Man.* Dating August, real or fake, certainly boosted her popularity on social media, which helped her career. And she did kind of enjoy making women jealous.

"Want to talk dirty?" he asked. He asked every time, but she had no idea how to talk *dirty.* Raquel would know, of course, but that 'friend' was the last person she wanted to ask.

"Not right now."

Ashley agreed to meet him at the Standard later, which meant he would be there with his entourage, and she couldn't stand hanging around his entourage with all their in-jokes that she didn't care to get in on. So, she would have to bring Raquel. Better to bring her along than to deal with her badditude if she found out Ashley went without her anyway. And she'd find out pretty quickly. Ashley couldn't go anywhere without someone tweeting her location.

She changed into a bikini and stopped in the kitchen on the way to the pool. Andrea was cleaning the counter. From her ponytail, a strand of hair fell across her cheek. She looked up and tucked the strand behind her ear. "Going to soak rays?"

Obvious question. Ashley spread her arms and held them up. And why did Andrea always have to sound so cheerful? Probably because she was thin as a toothpick.

"Can you make me a juice?" Ashley asked.

"Yes, I will do."

"Something with carrots. And bring my robe out."

Ashley opened a drawer in the counter and pulled out one of many vapes. She stepped out into the garden and inhaled a long drag. Exhaling as she walked to the pool, feeling lighter with each step.

She lay in a lounger facing the sun and closed her eyes. She couldn't keep running to dad every time something went wrong, like a kid. He might love her—she *knew* he loved her—but his work came first, always had. Instead of attention, he had provided her with this high-end lifestyle, which he must know was no substitute because almost every time they talked, he gave her more money.

What she needed was someone she could talk to. *Really* talk to. Someone who was there for her no matter what. But her wealth—technically, her dad's wealth—isolated her like a giant golden wall built between her and the real world. Not that she was alone, not physically. When you're Ashley York, everyone's your friend. *Friends*—more like leeches. Especially Raquel, but at least Raquel she could count on to be there.

Ashley texted her.

Ashley:
What's up bitch?

Raquel:
Yo bitch, how did it go?

Ashley never should have told Raquel about the lunch, but last night Raquel needled it out of her. She basically guessed that Ashley has something big the next day when she didn't want to party. No other reason not to party. If Raquel ever managed to attach herself to someone more famous, she would go public every private detail that Ashley had ever revealed about herself. She had no doubt that Raquel would gladly shit all over her if it would raise her own celebrity status, which wouldn't exist at all without Ashley.

What Ashley needed was some dirt on Raquel, some kind of a bomb to hold over her. Pity that the only way to end their friendship was with blackmail.

Ashley:
Director was a dick.

Raquel:
Yeah, they're all 🥒🥒🥒

Raquel thought she was an expert because, as a kid, she was on Disney TV, but she hadn't landed anything since then, whereas just last month Ashley was in a music video, which of course, according to Raquel, didn't count because the video was only online.

Raquel:
What's happening tonight?

Ashley:
The Standard

She looked around for the vape pen. It was on the little table beside the lounger. She took another drag.

Raquel:
August going?

Ashley:
Later

Raquel:
TD. Warm up drinks at my place. 7?

There was the sound of sniffing, and then something licked Ashley's face. She sat up and screamed.

A black, furry thing lunged toward her crotch.

She dropped her phone and stood on the chair. A brawny, black dog of some kind slobbered all over her foot.

"So sorry, Ashley," Sammy shouted as he sprinted down the lawn toward the pool.

"Where did it come from?" Ashley yelled back. It didn't have a collar or anything.

Sammy jogged through the half-open gate. "I don't know." He made his way around the pool and grabbed the dog by the scruff and pulled it back from Ashley. "She sure likes you though."

As if in agreement, the dog wagged its tail, staring up at her with its big wet eyes.

"Well, I'm all covered with fur now. Get it out of here."

"Sure thing." His eyes flicked from the vape to her body and scanned up and down, which she would have been fine with if it wasn't for the dog fur on her leg. She brushed it off, but there was still the slobber on her face. She needed to wash.

"So, did you get the part?" Sammy asked.

Damn it, who hadn't she told? Tears welled up in her eyes again. She blinked them away but there would be no holding them back if she told him how they didn't even give her a chance. "Don't know yet."

"My fingers are crossed for you, Ashley." He held up the

hand not holding the dog to show that indeed his fingers were crossed. "You deserve it."

On the chair, Ashley's phone buzzed. She grabbed it and glanced at the screen. Another text from Raquel. This one demanding she commit to the pre-drinks at seven.

Ashley:
I was just nearly mauled by a dog.

Raquel:
OMG!!! Seriously?

Ashley:
I was laying out by the pool and it got in somehow. Thank god for Sammy.

Raquel:
When you going to bone him?

As Sammy ushered the dog through the gate, his arm muscles bulged beneath the tight shirt of his security uniform. The white fabric looked good against his dark skin, and she liked the way he hadn't told her that the dog was no big deal. If there was anyone genuine in her life besides her dad, it was Sammy. And, if she was honest with herself, she would love to bone him. But...

Ashley.
I'm with August now, biatch.

Raquel:
As if that's exclusive.

Ashley:
What are you talking about?

Raquel:
Are you two seriously dating?

Ashley:
You jealous?

Raquel:
True dat!

But what if Raquel actually knew something? She did have other sources of gossip besides Ashley. If it came out that August was seeing someone on the side while publicly dating Ashley, it would look bad for her image, which could set her back years from being cast in a serious role. So now she had to go to Raquel's for the stupid "pre-drinks" she didn't want to make sure Raquel didn't really know anything about August.

—

Streaks of white light. And red. So many lights. And Ashley can't focus on any of them. Hollywood Boulevard slides past in a blur. They're in the backseat, and Raquel is leaning forward, saying something about Beyonce and Jay Z to her driver, Raul.

"I'm too wasted," Ashley says.

But Raquel can't seem to hear her.

How many cosmos had she had? Too many. She'd said it was too many, but Raquel kept pushing for more. And there were the hash cookies, which Raquel insisted they try even though Ashley was already blasted when she got to Raquel's, and, of course, it had turned out that Raquel didn't really know anything about August. Just the same the pop-news gossip Ashley has already heard. Trash news. That's what it is. No reason to believe what they say about August given all the shit they make up about her. And why does she care if he's seeing other women? Are they even dating? Dating August Grant might be great for her image and all, but she doesn't really like the way she feels around him.

Right now, what she wants—what she *needs*—is to go home and sleep. She leans her head against the window. The car comes to a stop, but the street keeps on moving. They're at the front entrance of the Standard. Cameras swarm toward the car.

"God, they're like flies!" Raquel opens her door to the barrage of flashes. She lasciviously extends her legs from the car and rolls her shoulders back.

"You called them," Ashley says.

"I would never." Raquel glances back toward Ashley with an expression of hurt that, even in Ashley's delirious state, looks like bad acting. The corner of Raquel's lip twists upward. She would and, in fact, had, and this wasn't the first time she'd broadcast their whereabouts to the paparazzi.

Raquel is out of the car now, and Raul holds the door for Ashley. As she slides across the seat, the car sways beneath her like a boat in a storm-tossed sea. She catches herself on the headrest.

Outside, Raquel is on the sidewalk, basking in the dizzying array of flashes, adjusting her posture, obviously getting off on the attention.

Ashley tries to focus, tries to find an anchor in the cacophony of light, but even Raul's face is a blur. She swings her leg out toward the curb. Raul extends a hand to her. "Oh my god," someone screams. Gasps. "Ashley!" Her name is repeated again and again. They're all coming at her —the cameras and the phones—and in that instant she remembers her sexy Catgirl costume that she never changed into because Raquel insisted she looked amazing in the sweater dress, and how, after all the cosmos, Ashley hadn't felt like changing anyway so she'd just taken off her underwear, because the dress showed panty lines—the dress that was now up to her waist with her legs spread for all of Hollywood Boulevard, and nothing on underneath.

The flashes accelerate into a frenzy as the cameras close in like predators to a fresh kill. Ashley just wants to curl up in a ball and disappear.

Raul shouts and body-blocks paparazzi, shoving them back.

Raquel takes Ashley's hand, smiling as if it's a performance. That's really all it is, Ashley decides: a performance.

She swings her other leg out of the car, pulls down the

dress, bats her eyes and smiles her best coy smile.

Using Raquel's arm for support, Ashley attempts to strut, but she can feel how awkward it looks. Vodka and sling backs—bad combination. At least Raquel is also walking stiffly with her leather fuck-me boots zipped up over her knees. Between the top of the boots and a nearly nonexistent skirt, an indecent expanse of thigh jiggles with each step— practically modest though, compared to what Ashley just exposed.

As they reach the bouncer dressed in black, who holds aside the velvet rope, the shouts of Ashley's name grow desperate. They want to see her face, to photograph her shame for all the world to see, and if she doesn't turn, they'll just show her from behind. So, she stops. She puts on a smile. Aping Lady Gaga at the Grammys, she turns her more photogenic left side toward the cameras and waves.

In the lobby, another bouncer ushers them past the long line of people in costumes waiting to get in. There's a Shrek and a group of *Star Wars* geeks, but mostly it's the Avengers, whose names Ashley can't remember.

The bouncer uses the card on his lanyard to open the VIP elevator and helps them inside. Ashley doesn't stop smiling until the metal doors close and it's just her and Raquel. She leans against the back wall and lets her eyes close.

"Crazy biatch!" Raquel says. "You should have told me you were free-balling it!"

"I—" Ashley hoists her lids back up so she can stare at Raquel, who kept pushing the cosmos. *Just one more*, she kept saying, when she knew Ashley was well past her limit. Such that now the elevator seems to be spinning off its axis as it whirls up to the club. She just wants to go home and pretend it never happened. *But no*. No point in telling Raquel it was an accident. No point in saying anything when it takes so much effort just to stand here and not be sick.

Raquel, admiring her reflection in the doors, drapes her hair back over her bare shoulders. She pulls a strand around her cheek, carefully arranging it so it dangles from her collarbone to her cleavage. She pushes her breasts together.

"They better show my picture too."

Claire Wilson

If Claire had known Elmo's would be this crowded, she would have insisted on somewhere else. Or they would have just stayed home and ordered take out, like Gray suggested. She's too tired to be sitting here jostled by the ocean of people on their way to the bathroom. If not for that and the pots clattering in the open kitchen, she could fall asleep right here in her chair.

Claire stifles a yawn, but her eyes stay closed, the darkness tugging her down.

How? How is it possible she can feel so sleepy here yet never in her bedroom?

But truth is, she can't sleep anywhere. She knows that. It's the insomnia—this feeling that sleep always feels just a moment away and yet remains always out of reach.

Every night she collapses into bed, sleep crashing over her like a wave, and then it recedes, leaving her lying there in the darkness, waiting just a little longer before checking the time, just a little longer. Useless.

She has tried it all. Melatonin and magnesium, yoga and meditation. Six months ago, she'd tried pills, only to end up addicted with dizziness and dry-mouth, and still...terrible sleep.

Life feels far away, like nothing can touch her and she can touch nothing. Each day more tiring than the last.

"You okay?" Gray asks.

Claire opens her eyes. But he's not looking at her; he's watching the bar.

If she had slept, she might enjoy the costumes, the people out to see and be seen. Her family are the only ones in the restaurant not dressed for Halloween. Probably why the hostess stuffed them back here near the bathrooms where Gray, of course, said the table was fine. And she is too tired to care.

The bathroom door swings open. A heavy man in a Superman t-shirt two sizes too small bursts through. The door is going to hit Tyler, so obliviously content in his booster seat it's almost cute. Claire stands to block the door...too late.

The door catches two inches from Tyler and retracts. Heavyset Superman trod off without noticing, trailing a stench of industrial soap.

Gray slumps, as if embarrassed by Claire's reaction rather than concerned. His eyes dart to the adjacent table. The couple pretends not to notice, but of course they did. The tables are practically touching.

If Claire wasn't so tired, maybe she'd have seen the door was no danger.

"Daddy, look." Mindy shows Gray the scribble she made on the paper tablecloth.

"That's great," he says. "A horse."

"No, silly. It's a unicorn."

Tyler snivels. Not bad yet, but he'll be wailing soon if someone doesn't hold him.

Gray grabs a purple crayon. "Want me to draw him some friends?"

"Draw Piglet." Mindy assigns him a small circle to draw in.

Claire, left to deal with Tyler, unstraps him from the booster seat. He coughs and starts to cry.

How did I get here? She bounces him in her lap.

She loves him, of course she does, and Mindy too, but

when she was working, she slept so much better. She actually *slept*. The need for constant attention drains her, like she knew it would, and yet still she had let Gray persuade her to have kids. His relentless intensity, which had attracted her at first, now exhausts her. Once he latches onto an idea, she might as well just agree to it instead of fighting and fighting, only to end up agreeing anyway.

When they met in college, she'd no idea what she wanted, and Gray had a head full of dreams. He possessed this passion for life that seemed to be missing in her, and the way he tried so hard to reach through all the barriers she constructed, the way he relentlessly pursued her, made her feel...it made her *feel*. Like him, believing she was more than she was made her a better person, bigger somehow, more alive.

She should have dated other boys. Margo, her roommate, drew them in one after another with the way she let them talk about themselves. She was outgoing, easy to be around. Why had Claire judged her so harshly for just trying to discover what she wanted?

Until Gray came along, no one had showed interest in Claire, so how was she supposed to know how far away he was from what she wanted? Or if she even wanted to be with anyone at all? But now Gray is all she has. It was just too much effort to keep in touch with Margo and everyone else and their perfect lives on Facebook. Maybe if she wasn't so exhausted all the time she could post some cute photos of Tyler and Mindy.

A waitress dressed like Princess Leia plops jars of water on the table. "What can I get for you?"

"We haven't had time to look at the menu," Claire says.

"Dewar's. Neat," Gray says with the usual longing in his eyes. And already Claire can hear the whiskey in his voice.

Every time the waitress returns, he'll order another, until it's finally time to go, and then Claire will have to drive. Doesn't matter that she's too tired. He just assumes she'll drive without asking, like he always does. Tossing them back, while his mood inflates beyond all reason, until talking to him is like staring straight into the sun. And the more he drinks, the more his intense energy focuses her, the more he tries to pry something out from a place inside her where there's nothing, only exhaustion.

Tyler's getting fussy again and he'll start bawling soon if she doesn't do something.

"So," Gray says with that look in his eyes, his volcano of thoughts about to spew.

Can he not hear Tyler?

"Not now, Gray." She digs around in the bag of baby supplies, finds the bottle and gives it to Tyler. As he suckles the rubber nipple, gazing up into her face, his sobbing subsides. Bad idea to feed him this late past his bedtime. He'll be cranky tomorrow.

Claire checks her phone. Forgetting again that the battery had died. She opens the menu. Still the same as last time she looked. Is she even hungry? Insomnia makes her feel disconnected from her own body, like she's puppeteering it from some great distance away, disconnected. Unable to think. And with Gray watching her every move, obviously not going to leave her alone about whatever is on his mind.

"What?"

Gray runs his fingers through his hair. "I just...I wanted..." He glances toward the waitress who still hasn't brought him his booze.

"Just spit it out already."

He plants his hands on the table, inhales, and glances at the menu. "How about we split the bisque?"

Really? That's it? She hates bisque. He knows she hates bisque. She picks up the menu and holds it in front of his gaze. She's not even hungry. But it doesn't matter; she still has to sit here, take care of Tyler, and watch Gray drink.

Gray's Dream

After they came home from dinner, Gray tucked Mindy into bed and read her the story of her choosing, *Where the Wild Things Are*. After he finished, she insisted he read it again. Halfway through, her eyes were closed, so he tested if she was awake by changing the story. "And Prince Spinach parachuted down, and the wild things played twelve string guitars in homage to their new king—"

"Daddy, you're reading it wrong."

He squinted at the page as if in disbelief, and tried not to smile but couldn't help himself.

"And the wild things roared their terrible roars!" she said.

By the third read, her breathing was soft and regular with the intervals of sleep. He closed the book. He turned out the light and stood in the doorway and watched her sleeping beneath the moons and stars projected onto the ceiling from her nightlight. In her little bed, she looked bigger than she was, and he felt wistful, wishing her childhood could go on forever.

He checked the nursery and found Tyler in his crib, sound asleep, beneath his spinning mobile of smiley flowers.

The sound of the TV seeping down the hallway meant

Claire was on the couch. He went into the kitchen and closed the door.

He was still stuffed from Elmo's yet craved something more. Something with flavor. He opened the pantry and stared at the cans, the jars, and the bags of chips. He opened a bag of BBQ chips and stuffed three into his mouth and chewed them into a tasteless sludge. Not food.

What he wanted was an escape. A drink. And why not? The two drinks at dinner were nothing. The second one he hadn't enjoyed at all, what with Claire glowering, ratcheting up the intensity with his every sip, and if he'd tried to explain how the trendy thick glasses made the stingy pours look like more than they were, she would have said he was an alcoholic.

His temple throbbed. It would be a full-on migraine if he didn't have a nightcap, just a few swallows to wash him into the sweet release of sleep.

He ducked into the garage for a quick round of the Dewar's he kept on the workbench by his easel. For the most part, the garage was unusable space thanks to all the junk he and Claire were too lazy to get rid of. Bins and boxes filled the shelves along the walls as well as the parking area, where among the boxes stood a foosball table and a pair of bikes that hadn't been ridden since college. A narrow path, which tonight was blocked with a laundry basket, led from the kitchen door to the workbench by the outer door. Beside the workbench, Gray had hollowed out a cubby for Tyler's playpen and his easel.

The easel was covered with a white cloth, which he considered removing. But the half-finished landscape would fall so short of his expectations for the image that he yearned to paint—that tomorrow he *would* paint—but tonight was too depressing to consider. At least if he left it covered, he could pretend the painting looked like he imagined. Because there was still time.

He didn't want to drink. Not really. Alcohol never gave him the release that he yearned for—that he got from painting, each stroke of color on canvas. That feeling of flow, the current of inspiration.

The feeling that never lasted. It left sometimes as quickly as it came. And when it wouldn't come back, he drank.

But being drunk was no better than being sober. In truth, it was worse. If he could drink successfully then his meaningless job wouldn't matter. He could endure another year, and if he could do another year then he could do five. He could make it until Mindy and Tyler went to college, and then what difference would it make?

He took a long pull of the Dewar's.

He swallowed until his throat burned, until he felt like he would choke or vomit or both. He slammed the bottle down on the workbench and tightened the lid. On the way to the kitchen, he stumbled over the laundry basket, caught himself on the door. He glanced back over his shoulder at the half-finished painting on the easel he was afraid to uncover and then turned out the light.

Charlie Streeter

Earlier that night, at Charlie's daughter's house, after eating four bags of the disgusting skittles, he brushes his teeth in the dark. Outside the bathroom window, the street is completely devoid of trick-or-treaters. Not a sign of life. A porch light illuminates the empty drive across the street. That dolt with the cute little princess packed her up in the minivan along with his wife and their baby, and they all went out somewhere, when anyone who knows anything knows better than to go out on Halloween.

Back in Charlie's neighborhood in Fullerton, they close down the street for Halloween because the hordes of trick-or-treaters, who drive in from who-knows-where, can't be bothered to walk in an orderly manner along the side of the road. The twenty pounds of candy he bought for tonight would have gone in an hour in Fullerton. *What am I going to do with it all now?* Seems like Lynda could have at least mentioned that Silver Lake doesn't give a damn about Halloween before she and her husband left him watching their house for three months.

He stands on the front stoop looking down the hill. No one else is coming. He bends down carefully—the last thing he needs is to lock up his back again—and unplugs the strings of orange lights on the house and the hedge. The jack-o-lanterns, he decides, can just burn themselves out. Not worth his bending over to turn them off one by one. He's not even sure he can. Why had he wasted his money paying the landscaper to put up decorations? Who was he trying to impress? Not the slouchy dolt from across the street. His daughter was cute enough, but she saw only the candy.

Charlie shuts the door and stands in the foyer. The emptiness of the house rings in his ears. He needs to get out, go somewhere, but he can't drive, not with his back hurting worse than ever. How did he end up like this? In Vietnam, he'd humped the heaviest pack in the squad. In addition to all his own gear, including a canteen and spare boots made from alligator skin, he carried an M79, extra grenades, and the praise of his men. They called him Hulk, Hulk, Hulk.

He needs one more Oxycontin. Then he'll quit. But how can he quit if his back won't stop aching?

———

He drives slowly toward the 101 freeway. Headlights appear behind him, and he pulls over to let the vehicle pass. Normally he spends his afternoons people watching in Grand Park, but today he'd wasted time getting ready for the trick-or-treaters who didn't come, and now he feels off. What good are routines if you don't stick to them?

Of course, anyone who knows anything knows better than to drive downtown on Halloween, where it's overrun with crazies, but someone has to keep an eye out. Keep the crazies in check. In addition to the typical homeless crazies who talk to their imaginations, tonight there will be all kinds of young crazies who only come out on Halloween, using it an excuse to prance around in next to nothing, all drunk or high or who knows what.

He should go to Santa Monica Boulevard, the height of debauchery, where—if he believes the *LA Weekly*—the most outlandish crazies parade the street. But there won't be parking. Anyone with a lick of sense would know that. Better to stick with Grand Park, stick to the familiar, on a night like tonight.

There goes his exit. Too late to take it.

Lynda had tried to get him a smartphone, but he wouldn't fall for it. He is not about to become another moron who can't even take a crap if his phone doesn't say so. "If you won't get a smartphone, at least get a navigator," she had said.

But he wouldn't be nervous at all if it wasn't dark out. He's not used to driving at night.

He takes the next exit and, right away, finds himself among the crazies. The homeless ones camped under the overpass and all along the sidewalk. They stare at him funny. And he stares back. As he rolls up to a dimly lit T intersection, one of the more deranged crazies yells at his car.

Charlie scans from right to left, unsure which way to turn. At the bottom of the hill is a building with slits for windows: a jail.

Movement.

In front of the jail, a derelict warehouse casts a shadow on the street, and within that shadow the figure is almost hidden.

It's a crazy alright, and he's striding up the hill...toward Charlie's car. Did he escape from the jail? The bums huddled on the sidewalk go still in their blankets as if petrified.

Past the warehouse, he emerges into the dim beam of a streetlight. Tan shirt. Olive pants. The star of a sheriff. Charlie almost laughs with relief. He'll ask this officer for directions the old-fashioned way. Not like the millennials who would rather look at their phones than talk to anyone.

Still, he waits in his car.

Ten yards away from him, a bum hunched in blankets climbs out of the shadows toward the officer. Charlie lowers his window. The bum murmurs garbled nonsense at the officer, probably his deranged way of begging for money. The officer makes a wide arc around him, but the bum lunges toward him, trying to get his attention.

The officer jerks back as if stung. He snarls, unholsters his weapon, and swings it with demented determination.

With the butt of the gun, he clubs the bum in the head.

He drops to the ground. Drops his blankets. Raises his arms in defense. The crazy officer speaks to the bum, too softly for Charlie to hear. The bum struggles to his feet and hobbles into the road in front of Charlie's car.

Through the window, Charlie locks eyes with the crazy officer. He strolls toward Charlie's car as if nothing happened at all, as if he is a perfectly safe, upstanding officer of the law, smiling, like Charlie could be his new best friend. Mucus runs from his nose into his mustache. His eyes are opened wide, wide open. Charlie has never in his whole life seen anyone crazier than this officer, who is holding his gun not quite pointed at Charlie. But a threat, no doubt about that.

Not much more than a step away, he reaches for the door, which is, of course, locked, but the window is down. The officer raises his gun.

Charlie slams the gas and spins the wheel right, turning uphill and away from the crazy officer.

Thump.

Charlie rips his gaze from the officer just in time to see the bum collapse on his front fender and slide down out of view. Why was he still in the road?

Charlie should stop, should call 911, but the mirror shows the officer is still approaching, undaunted.

He slams into reverse. In front of his car, the bum lies in the street, in a heap just like Private Birdsong back in 'Nam, when Charlie kicked the tripwire which he should have seen —*would* have seen, if he wasn't adjusting his fucking pack.

The rear window shatters. The clap of gunpowder rattles his chest—mortar-fire from the brush—and he shoves the car into drive.

His tires squeal. He clenches his teeth so hard they almost shatter. The bum, lying on the blacktop, flails an arm. As the tires gain traction, Charlie fish tails around him.

He speeds up the hill. The sound of gunfire ricochets all around him.

He speeds toward the skyscrapers looming behind the warehouses. Silver Lake is north—everyone knows that—

but which way is north? If not for the crazy officer shooting at him, he might have some idea where he was.

He stops at an intersection. Beside him, an LAPD cruiser eases to a stop at the light. Charlie looks straight ahead. *Just an old man in a Taurus. No need to look any closer. No need to notice the shot out rear window or the dented front fender. Look ahead. Look at the crazy costumes in the crosswalk, crazy kids hardly wearing anything aside from makeup and spandex.*

Was that crazy who shot at him a rogue officer? They're probably all in cahoots. Regardless, no one will believe Charlie. Of course, if he had one of those damn smart phones people are always gazing into and missing the world around them, he could have filmed the crazy officer bludgeoning the bum. But who could he show it to? They're all crazies. They're all in on it. And now, they're probably all after him.

When the light turns green, he turns right, away from the copper beside him. He turns and turns again, until he sees a sign for the freeway.

As he speeds up the on-ramp, cold air blasts through the shattered rear window. What if that officer got his license plate? There was plenty enough time for a good look—if officer had half a brain in his crazy head.

Fortunately, Charlie's car is still registered to his old address in Fullerton. Good luck finding him there. But still, with a busted window and dented fender, he might as well paint a target on his car.

Charlie only hopes that the crazy has forgotten his face, with the way his eyes were gaping open like they weren't seeing Charlie at all, and that mucus running into his mustache, which he did not wipe away.

Worse was the bum, who Charlie had left in a heap on the black top. His arm flailing uselessly. Helpless and injured, with the crazy, and his gun.

But what else could Charlie have done?

He'll have to hide his car. He'll park it in the garage when he gets back, which means he'll have to move Lynda's car to the curb. Hopefully, the neighbors won't ask why her car is parked on the street instead of his. The mom won't even notice. She's always staring into her phone while pushing the stroller when she should be watching for traffic. But what about the slouchy dolt—he might think it's suspicious. And his little girl: she might point it out. She's a smart one, that little girl.

To switch out Lynda's car, Charlie will have to find the keys. After managing three weeks alone in the house without snooping, the thought of searching their bedroom turns his stomach in a knot. But what choice does he have?

He'll just poke around until he finds the car keys and that will be it.

But then what if he can't stop himself? What if once he starts looking, with nothing but time on his hands and nowhere to go until the heat dies down, he ends up going through everything? Lynda and her husband seem ordinary enough, but everyone has something to hide. Charlie does. Charlie has lots to hide. His Oxycontin, for one thing. His habit out of control, and now... Now, Charlie had hit a man and left him to die in the road.

Saul Versus the Armenian

Earlier, when Saul had checked his watch at 5:53 PM, Saroyan was still sitting placidly behind the two-way mirror in the box. This was interview suite three, which had the broken chair that usually made perps squirm, but not Saroyan. He just sat there. His gray hair was disheveled. He had sallow skin, jowls that sagged down a double chin. A broad shelf of brow over pure black eyes too small for his head.

Saul jacked up the heat to ninety-five.

Behind the glass, Saroyan's lips curled. He hadn't requested a lawyer. Not even a phone call. His one and only demand had been to have the blood wiped from his face. Saul had obliged, if only to lighten things up with Hernandez, which had basically worked. He'd produced a handkerchief with a wave of his hand and a snap, and she half-snorted, half-laughed.

But Saroyan had said nothing more, and he was still just sitting there, staring straight ahead.

Saul's stomach twisted. Something worse than hunger.

Hernandez entered the observation room and stood beside him. "Think he's ready?"

"Hard to say." Saul tilted his head. Saroyan hadn't even

asked for water.

She started the video camera. "Let's give it a shot."

Guess it's her call, he thought, since it seemed like Lieutenant Levy had decided to make her the lead investigator without telling him. Probably hadn't told Hernandez yet, either. She would have said something by now.

"In a hurry to get home?" He regretted the question even as he asked it, the bitterness that leached into his voice. But it was a double standard. How could Hernandez give him a hard time for a long lunch at the Castle when four days out of five she left early?

"It's Halloween," she said.

Saul looked away. He should apologize. After all, she had a son to go home to. The Castle was all about him.

He nodded toward the break room next door. "Coffee?"

"That's more like sludge than coffee," she said. "I'll meet you in there."

She wasn't kidding about the coffee. It was a no-name variety, too low-end to be sold in stores, that the city bought on the cheap. It tended to burn in the pot and was almost undrinkable. But it contained caffeine and it did sort of smell like coffee, which was sometimes enough to tempt a perp.

In the break room, Saul triple-stacked wax paper cups. Poured in the black sludge. Carried it to the box.

The heat hit him like a punch in the gut. He gulped at the stale air and wedged himself between the table and the wall across from Saroyan. Saul sat and sipped the coffee. Bitter. But he pretended to enjoy it.

Saroyan stared blankly. The cans in the ceiling cast harsh light on his face. He did not blink.

Hernandez came in. Took the seat beside Saul and crossed her arms.

"Mr. Saroyan," Saul said. "Mind if I call you Edward?"

"I am called Wayob," Saroyan said. His face remained stolid.

"Way-ob. Is that spelled w-a-y-o-b?" Saul wrote it down.

"In your language, I suppose."

"Okay, Wayob, I'm Detective Parker and this is my partner, Detective Hernandez."

Wayob pressed his lips together, as though he was trying to frown but the corners of his mouth twisted toward a smirk.

"You don't need us to tell you," Saul continued, "you're in a lot of trouble here, Wayob, but maybe we can help. What happened, from your point of view?"

"You will not believe me."

"We've got an eyewitnesses, and we've got the whole thing on video," Hernandez said, "so you'd better give us something if you want to see daylight again."

Wayob leaned back in his chair and stretched his mouth far too wide for a genuine smile, like a child impersonating a cartoon.

Saul would have laughed if not for the obvious hatred—and pain—welling in his dark eyes. "We know there's more to it," Saul said. "There are always two sides."

"There can be only one truth," Wayob said, and he was right about that. If they could lock him into a confession, it would make the case even tighter.

"I agree," Saul said. "If he provoked you, if he was bullying you, that's a form of abuse you know. You can prove it with a lie-detector test. It will help your case."

Wayob's attempted smile vanished, his face hollowed. "You cannot help me. I know of your primitive technology." He enunciated the last part with an air of disgust.

The statement surprised Saul. "You're aware of something better?"

"The Ancient Mayans had a magnet, which, held next to your head, would tell for sure if you were lying."

"Sounds like magic." *Or mindless babble*, he thought, *but at least he's talking.*

"No. It was real," Wayob said bitterly, almost shouting. "Those abominable priests isolated the engineers so they could claim to have the power of gods."

"How do you know?"

Wayob slumped. The energy drained from his voice. "I was there."

"I thought you were Armenian," Saul said.

"I am not the man you see before you."

"Okay…, so who are you?"

"I am Wayob. This I told you."

"Right."

They were wasting time. Nothing that Saroyan, Wayob, or whoever he thought he was said made any sense, unless this was an act for an insanity-plea-defense. Regardless of what the justice system said, Wayob was responsible for his actions. He would not get off with insanity, not if Saul could help it.

"Let me guess," Hernandez said. "You were jealous Luna could walk, so you decided to whack him."

Wayob laughed bitterly. "You understand nothing."

"You won't be laughing in prison," Hernandez said. "Doesn't matter you're in a wheelchair, just makes you easier to rape."

Wayob looked from Hernandez to Saul. "You cannot keep me here."

"Oh no?" Hernandez asked. She had this way of pouncing in interviews then shrugging it off as if it were nothing. "Want call a lawyer? Go ahead. I'll get you a phone."

"You are wasting my time."

"Oh," she said. "So, you've got somewhere else to be?"

He slammed the cuffs on the lacquered mahogany and turned his palms up. "Release me now or I shall take my revenge."

Since good cop, bad cop seemed to have had no effect so far, Saul changed tactics. He slid the two extra cups off his coffee. Turned them upside down on the table. He fished a quarter from his pocket. Showed it to Wayob. Set it on the table between the cups.

"Wayob, I'll make it easy. Guess which cup the quarter is under, and you're free to go. Hell, I'll even drive you anywhere you want to go."

"*Barker!*" Hernandez said.

If he believes he can roll out of here, then he really is crazy, Saul thought, hoping Hernandez was more playing bad cop than angry.

Saul placed a cup over the quarter and began sliding them on the table in slow circular motions, moving one in front of the other. Hernandez shook her head.

Saul stopped and presented the cups to Wayob.

"I know it is there." Wayob pointed to the cup on Saul's left.

Saul nodded. "So where do you want to go?"

"East." He glowered at Saul. "I shall go on my own."

"Oh?" Saul lifted the cup.... It was empty.

Wayob lunged his cuffed hands toward the other cup, but it was out of his reach. He leaned back in the broken chair and tried to straighten his back. "A cheap trick."

"Perhaps." Saul restacked the cups under his coffee.

The two men stared at each other. Saul let the silence hang there like a void that must be filled.

"Release my hands," Wayob said. "I shall show you what I can do."

"I think we've seen enough." The thought of Luna's pulverized face made his stomach tighten.

The heat was unbearable, perspiration had wicked through the pits of Saul's shirt, and yet Wayob's skin was dry, his face ashen in the can lights.

"You have not seen anything yet."

Saul barely registered the threat. He was used to them. "Why?"

"Why what?" Wayob asked.

"Why kill Luis Luna?"

Wayob's brows furrowed and his eyes squeezed shut. His mask had slipped away, and behind it was sadness and fear. Maybe even regret. It looked genuine.

"I had no choice." His chin trembled. "I had to kill him or suffer a fate worse than death."

Saul hoped the video was still recording. *Keep him talking.* "He threatened you?"

Wayob studied his hands as if they were new to him. He looked up and straightened in the chair. "He set me free."

"Sounds terrible," Hernandez said.

Saul glanced at her. *Let him do the talking.*

She got it. They waited for Wayob to fill the silence.

His bleak eyes showed no emotion.

"Come closer." He attempted a smug grin. "I shall give you a taste."

"From where I sit," Hernandez said, "looks like you're the one who gets a *taste*, and a whole lot more, once you're in prison."

Wayob scowled. "You cannot contain me."

"How did you know Luna?" Saul interrupted, hoping to catch him off balance.

"I can become anyone, even you, Detective Parker, or your pretty assistant."

Hernandez crossed her arms and set her jaw. The comment seemed to bother her but he had heard her called worse.

"Don't piss us off," Saul said. "We don't have time for games."

"And here I thought you were the sort of man who enjoys tricks."

"Murder is no trick."

"No," Wayob growled. "It is not. I do not do tricks."

Saul stood and placed his hands on the table, exposing his sweat-soaked pits as he leaned toward Wayob, who still gave no indication he'd noticed the excessive heat.

Saul stared into those beady eyes that seemed to possess an energy all of their own. His massive brows were slack, his face empty, no longer any trace of the emotion that had flickered across it when Saul mentioned murder. As if Wayob felt nothing now and never would.

Hernandez scraped her chair back and went to the door. "Let him cook, Parker. He's useless."

Wayob shrugged, as though he could snap his fingers and disappear into the night.

Hernandez was right. No sense in humoring him. They should investigate Luna. A connection between him and Wayob could prove premeditation, making an insanity defense all but impossible.

"You cannot keep me here." Wayob stared at Saul with no tells, no sign of lying. Could he be so delusional?

Saul squeezed past Hernandez out the door.

"You shall see, Parker. You shall see," Wayob shouted.

Hernandez pulled the door shut behind him, and he turned to face her. She rolled her eyes. "We've got a psychopath who beat someone to death—from a wheelchair, no less, and of course, you entertain him with magic."

"At least I got something."

"You got a lot of bullshit. That's what you got."

"Maybe."

Her shock of white fell across her eye. She shoved it back. "What if he'd guessed the right cup?"

Not possible. But he didn't say it. Already he regretted getting defensive; this was Hernandez. "We should do the death notification." It was the last thing he wanted to do, but talking to Luna's next of kin was their best hope of finding a connection.

"His license is an old address," she said. "He left no forwarding."

"We'll find him. He had to live somewhere."

Hernandez turned abruptly toward the elevators. Was it really the coin trick? He knew she liked magic, which he found even more attractive than her physical appearance. And on top of that, she had brains. She had the whole package. And his gut fluttered every time he saw her.

He entered the observation room to check the recording.

Wayob Versus Bruce

The guards had issued Wayob a wheelchair, if one could call it that. Looks more like a lawn chair fused onto a shopping cart. He cannot reach the tiny wheels. Does not matter. He shall not be here long. Not like this. Fucking Parker. Thinks he can lock Wayob in a prison, but he shall see. He shall see. They roll Wayob like a sheep to slaughter into a dormitory cell with endless rows of sagging bunks.

Wayob can work with this. These men in ragged orange scrubs he can understand. They are like animals, malicious eyes like lions ready to pounce.

"How about a hand?" Wayob shouts.

They stay back. *Perfect.* Let an alpha make his move. Just one brave, foolish alpha is what Wayob needs. But first, he needs leverage.

He reaches for the nearest bunk. Leaning forward, almost falling out of the chair, he manages to reach the chipped-green iron frame.

"That's Bruce's bunk," says a shirtless man with ribs protruding from his tattooed chest.

"Not anymore," Wayob says. He heaves himself out of the chair, trying uselessly to kick his immobile legs.

The shirtless man scurries away, down the corridor of

beds.

Wayob's arms are strong at least, strong enough to lift his potbelly from the chair to the bottom bunk. But as he leans forward and pulls himself from the chair, it rolls out from under him. He must flounder himself onto the bed.

Exhausted, he lays face down to catch his breath.

"De-tec-tive Par-ker," he laughs. Wayob shall show him a trick, a real trick. Once he gets out of here. Once he finds Abuela Luna.

His blood boils at the thought of the old woman who somehow resisted setting him free for so many decades. So much agonizing time spent focusing his mind on her mind and yet he was unable to tempt her. He screams with rage.

The other inmates gather to watch, closing in on him. They should be afraid, and soon they shall be. Soon Wayob shall have his hands around Abuela's wrinkled weak neck. He shall look into her eyes as her life drains away, and she shall know it is her own weakness that has killed her, killed her whole family.

Wayob sits up and locks his arm around the metal bar of the bed frame to anchor himself against whoever approaches first—probably this 'Bruce' who the shirtless, skeletal man went to inform of Wayob's trespass. All that matters is to overcome Bruce before this crippled body Wayob is controlling becomes damaged beyond all usefulness. He must win. Time is running out. Luna's weakness will not last.

Wayob must free himself from this prison, and this time he shall have a good pair of legs, a strong vessel.

"Hey, pal, that's my bunk." A bull-chested man, also shirtless, marches toward him. His scalp is shaved. SIN tattooed across his forehead in bold black letters.

"You must be Bruce." All that matters is the next ten seconds. Wayob shall fight and fight to win.

"Only friends call me Bruce."

"So what shall I call you then? Shit-face?" *Come closer.*

Bruce takes a step forward. "Kiss my feet and maybe I'll pretend you didn't say that."

"This is not your bunk anymore, Brucie-Bruce-Bruce-shitty-Bruce. You sleep on the floor now."

Closer.

"Over my dead body, motherfucker."

"Not dead, just unconscious," Wayob says from his perch on the bottom bunk.

Bruce rushes forward, leaning down to punch him, and Wayob turns his head to absorb the blow. Anchoring himself with an elbow around the bed frame, he reaches down and scoops Bruce's legs out from under him.

Bruce falls backward onto the concrete and lands with his hands behind his back. Wayob launches down onto him and locks an arm around his thick, filthy neck. He slams his head into the man's nose.

Bruce presses a hand to his nose, blood gushing between his fingers. "Motherfucker!" He punches Wayob in the ribs. Then head butts, his skull hard as a boulder.

Wayob ignores the pain and Bruce's mucky blood. He does not listen to ringing in his ears. He must fight through the blackness narrowing his peripheral vision. He forces his eyes to focus on the bloody mess of Bruce's face. Must stay conscious.

The other prisoners around them climb up on the beds, shouting, "Fight, fight, fight."

Bruce shoves Wayob off toward the bed and tries to get up.

All or nothing. Wayob grabs onto his awful head. Wayob forces his torso up. Then, with all the weight of his upper body, he shoves Bruce's head into a steel bar of the bed frame.

With no way to catch himself, Wayob face plants into the concrete floor beside Bruce, who has fallen limp, unconscious or dead. *Please not dead. Not again.*

He uses his last remaining strength pull himself partially onto Bruce. Enough to feel the blood pulsing through his thick neck. Bruce will regain consciousness soon. A good vessel for Wayob.

The other men shout for Bruce to get up, shout for more blood. And Wayob laughs. He is still laughing as he presses his forehead to Bruce's tattooed temple. As his body goes limp.

Magic

Homicide Special had cleared out except for Saul. As a peace offering, and because it was Friday night and Halloween, he had volunteered to finish the paperwork on Saroyan so Hernandez could go home to her son. Of course, she wasn't going to fawn all over Saul because of some paperwork. But he could hope. Plus, the Castle would be filled past capacity and Saul couldn't get into the spirit.

With the video of Saroyan committing the murder, not much detective work was required. They had gone back to using his real name after finding no mention of Wayob in his background. The case had been assigned to Homicide Special because of its high-profile nature. The media was out for blood, the public demanding justice. Once Saul buttoned down the paperwork it would be up to the DA to make sure Saroyan wasn't released on some technicality. Almost certainly, he would plead insanity and vie for a stay at a mental health facility until he could convince the doctors he was no longer a threat. Cases like Saroyan's often had an unsatisfying outcome, if not an outrageous one.

Homicide Special was a windowless room containing four rows of desks. Saul and Hernandez occupied two desks side by side near Levy's office. The room was divided by an invisible wall of rivalry between the detectives who reported to Lieutenant Delrawn and those who reported to Levy.

Lieutenant Levy's team, Saul and Hernandez in particular, tended to draw the media headaches like Saroyan, even though Levy had a decade more experience than Delrawn. Captain Malone, who oversaw the Robbery Homicide Division including Homicide Special, was punishing Levy for backing Saul on the Brown fiasco. Though, of course, he never said so. Nor did Levy. Nor did Hernandez or anyone else. But Saul knew. They all knew.

Three years ago, Saul shot and killed Felix Brown. Saul had tried to keep Levy out of it by saying he'd acted alone, but she'd had to back him or risk losing respect from the other detectives under her supervision. A lieutenant without respect was ineffective, and ineffective lieutenants didn't last, not in Homicide Special.

The media made Brown's case about another Black man shot by a white officer, with little mention of Brown's own actions or the gun he'd drawn. After the Police Commission reluctantly ruled that Saul had followed procedure, a group of protesters blocked traffic on the 110, which didn't bother Saul because they didn't know what he knew. They hadn't been there. What bothered him was that the LAPD settled the lawsuit from Brown's family without a trial. It was like admitting to a wrongful death.

As a distraction from the paperwork, he went to YouTube to watch videos on magic. Bullet Catch, Quarter-Through-the-Cup, Asrah Levitation, trick after trick. He knew them all. It was comforting. And also depressing. He kept on watching though. Some were good, like David Copperfield flying inside a glass box, but Saul knew how the invisible wires fit through the lid. What he was looking for, he realized, was a trick he didn't know—which at this point would have to be real magic. *Real magic.* He laughed.

It was almost midnight when his desk phone rang. The caller ID said, "*Blocked number*." Strange.

He answered. "Parker here."

"Ah, Detective Parker," a man said in a gruff and vaguely familiar voice. "I hoped to catch you."

"Who is this?"

"It is me, Wayob. Strange, is it not, how such a warm day becomes a cold night?"

"Where are you?" Saul asked. He didn't sound like Saroyan, and yet he sort of did.

"You see? This is why I have called, Parker. This is my warning. Do not concern yourself with my whereabouts. Do not interfere."

"Did Hernandez put you up to this?"

"I believe tricks are your forte."

Hair bristled on the back of Saul's neck. Saroyan must have found an inmate with a phone to whom he was feeding lines.

"You'd better tell me who this is if you don't want to get busted."

"Busted? What do you mean?"

"Let me guess. You're in the cell next to Saroyan?"

"Okay. Go ahead and 'bust' me. I am looking forward to this."

"If you think you can hide the phone up your ass, don't bother. They'll find it."

"Disgusting. I would never. In fact, I shall stay on the line."

"Your funeral."

Saul muted his audio on the desk phone and used his cell to dial the night captain at the Metropolitan Detention Center.

"This is Banks."

"It's Detective Parker with the LAPD."

"What can I do for you, Detective?" Banks said with a certain amount of sarcasm. There was a long-standing rivalry between the Sheriff's Department, who ran the MDC, and the LAPD.

"You've got an inmate with a cellphone."

"That's a negative. We run a tight ship here."

"I've got him on the other line. Go check the cells near Saroyan. He's telling this jerk what to say."

"Hold on," Banks said. "Sierra Alpha Romeo Oscar Yankee Alpha November?"

"Right. Detective Hernandez booked him this evening."

"He's in the ICU."

Saul almost shouted. "What?"

"Ten bucks says he doesn't wake up," Banks said.

"How could this happen?" Saul said.

"According to the snitches," Banks said, "Saroyan started the fight."

Saul rubbed his temple. "Why wasn't he in solitary? He's a violent offender. We were still questioning him."

"What do you think we are? The Hilton? We're way overbooked, and Saroyan is no worse than half our population. But feel free to take it up with the county supervisors. I'd consider it a favor."

"Maybe I'll take it up with the warden."

"Good luck with that."

"Look, I get it," Saul said. Banks was right. Despite having the world's largest jails, California lacked the budget to properly house the swelling population of inmates. "Just tell me what happened, okay? Saroyan can't walk. Why did he pick a fight?"

"He had a death wish, I guess." Banks still sounded annoyed, but words quickened with eagerness. "He took down an Aryan Brother, mean bastard too. He knocked out one of my guards."

"Saroyan?"

"Bruce Dunn, the badass Saroyan jumped. We had him handcuffed to the stretcher, but he dislocated his own arm in order to attack Aleman and kicked him into a pipe."

"Sheesh."

"Dunn says he didn't do it, but the prison doc saw the whole thing. Aleman, too, but we can't get in touch with him."

"What do you mean?"

"After he came to, he walked off the job."

Victor Aleman had booked dozens, maybe a hundred, criminals that Saul had delivered to the MDC. He was a squat, mean little man. The sort who struck back. Walking away was out of character.

"Was he hurt bad?"

"We don't know," Banks said. "He didn't even take his car. Probably plans to sue over working conditions."

Saul couldn't help feeling that somehow this was related, that maybe it was more than just the cadence of the gruff monotone on the other phone that sounded familiar. "What's his mobile?"

"I can't give out personal information. You know that."

"I just want to make sure he's okay."

"He's not answering."

"Maybe he'll answer my call," Saul said. "I've known him longer than you."

"If you're such best buds, then why don't *you* have his number?"

"You know how guys are," Saul said, but truth was he didn't care much for Aleman, and he doubted Aleman liked him either.

"You mean he's not into *magic*?"

Saul rubbed his forehead. How did everyone know about the Castle? He'd told Hernandez because she was interested in magic, but she knew better than to spread it around. Guys like Banks, once they find out how you're different, love to lord it over you.

"I can get you into the Castle," Saul said, "if you want?"

"Yeah, thanks but no thanks."

"Look," Saul said. "I just want you to listen to this guy on the other line. You tell me you think."

"Why should I listen? He could be anywhere."

"If you don't listen, then it's your ass when someone gets killed."

Saul put Banks on speaker, set his cell phone down next to the desk phone and unmuted the audio. "Wayob, you still there?"

"So, do you believe me now? I can be anyone. You cannot stop me."

"So who are you now?"

"Leave me alone Parker, or more shall die. I regret the life I must take, but I deserve a *life* in the world."

Saul stopped the audio.

"Aleman doesn't talk like that," Banks said. "But I'll

give you his number just to cover my ass. I've actually got real work to do."

He was right: it was almost impossible to imagine Aleman speaking like that. Could Saroyan have dictated what he should say?

But then, why would Aleman comply?

Banks ended the call and texted Aleman's number. Saul called the mobile. But it rang through to voicemail.

Maybe Saroyan wasn't as unconscious as Banks thought. Saul decided to go to the hospital and see for himself.

His gut tightened. He should call Hernandez and give her the update, but why wake her? What did he really have here? If Saroyan was awake, Saul would make him explain. And then it would be nothing.

—

Saul sat at Saroyan's bedside in the ICU shuffling a deck of cards to the beat of the heart monitor. He'd spent the night in the worn polyester chair, shifting his weight around on the deflated cushions, waiting for Saroyan to wake up. Saroyan had a skull fracture, four broken ribs, and one broken arm and the other one was handcuffed to the bed. He wasn't going anywhere, but Saul couldn't give up and go home—not after the phone call. How the hell had Saroyan pulled it off?

He pulled his phone. Tried calling Aleman again. And again. Still no answer. Saul texted that it was Detective Parker and to call him back immediately.

Whoever had called Saul had threatened to kill someone. And to Saul, the threat was credible. Maybe not enough for a warrant or even a BOLO but Saul had a feeling—Aleman must have seen something, he must know something.

And so did Saroyan. A lot more, probably, than what he'd said in the interview and now he was lying there. Probably more asleep than unconscious. Saul reached for his shoulder. Perhaps he could shake him awake?

The back of Saul's neck prickled. A signal from the amygdala—someone was behind him. He glanced over his shoulder.

Hernandez stood in the doorway. His pulse quickened.

"Why didn't you call me?" she asked.

He felt the blood rush into his cheeks as he lowered his hand, hoping she hadn't seen that he was about to shake Saroyan's shoulder. "Didn't want to wake you."

She glanced at her phone. "It's nine-thirty."

"It was three when I got here."

She nodded toward Saroyan. "I hear he got a taste of his own medicine."

Saul felt bad for sitting in the one chair but if he stood now, with Hernandez right beside him, it would call attention to his belly. He began spreading the cards face down on the bedside table.

"What are you doing?" she asked.

"Pick a card."

The heart monitor beeped.

She combed back her shock of white bangs. "We don't have time for this."

"My feeling exactly. But all we can do now is wait."

"We can go to Luna's last known address. We need to locate his next of kin."

"According to the building manager, he moved out years ago" Plus, right now, Saul was more worried about the phone call than Luna's family. "Let's give Saroyan a little longer to come out of it."

"Last night, you were hot to trot on the death notification. What changed?"

"He called me from a coma."

"What?" She glanced at Saroyan.

He pointed toward the foot of the bed, where a clipboard was attached with Saroyan's information. "Apparently, he was comatose an hour before I got the call. It was someone pretending to be him."

"So now you're conducting the investigation alone?"

"Not at all. This was at midnight. I was going to call you this morning…" How did it get to be nine-thirty? Must have dozed off in the chair after all. "I didn't realize how late it was. Anyway, it was only threats. Nothing to act on."

She frowned. "A prank?"

"I wish. Whoever it was knew details about our interview

with Saroyan and spoke just like him. Maybe his voice was deeper, but remember the arrogance? It was the same. At first, I thought Saroyan had bribed an inmate somehow, or maybe a custody assistant—Aleman walked off his shift last night—but it was like speaking to Saroyan and yet... it wasn't him."

"You get the number?"

"Blocked. I've got someone on it though." He'd have to change the subject if she asked who or how. He had gone a little out of bounds by calling Mark Chen, a systems engineer at Verizon, who owed him a favor. Tracing a number didn't require a warrant, technically, but Verizon would have insisted on one if Saul had asked through official channels.

Hernandez furrowed her brows, as though deciding not to ask. "So, why call you?"

Saul shrugged and turned up his palms. "He claimed to be warning me. I'd better not interfere with his plan to kill someone or else…"

Hernandez snorted. She chose a card from the middle and cupped it in her hand.

He slid the cards into a stack, split it, and shuffled. With a flourish of his hands, he presented the deck. "Put the card back anywhere you like. Don't let me see it."

She slid it in near the top. He shuffled again, then put the cards in his front pocket. "You chose the ace of spades."

"How the hell?"

Saul waved his finger. "A magician never reveals his secret."

"Of course."

He reached for the cards. "You know what? This time, I'll show you."

"Actually, I prefer the mystery."

The notion caught him by surprise. They were detectives. Eliminating mystery was what they did. "Cool," he said. Maybe not knowing made the simple trick seem, to her, like real magic?

Saroyan coughed. They stood over him as the beeping of the heart monitor accelerated. He opened his eyes.

Attempted to lift his head and grimaced. His eyes darting around the room. "Where...am I?"

"You're in the ICU at Good Samaritan," Saul said.

Saroyan groaned and tried to sit up. The handcuffs clinked against the bedrail. "What happened? Why am I restrained?"

"You started a fight, which, apparently, you lost."

"Impossible." His eyes went wide. He jerked the cuffs, testing their hold.

Hernandez turned toward the door. "I'll get the nurse."

"You killed a man," Saul said. "We have to take precautions."

"No. I would never." Saroyan's brows furrowed. He squeezed his eyes closed.

"Last night you admitted it. You don't remember?"

His eyes flicked open. "Last night..." His eyes widened. "No. I didn't." He began breathing heavily.

"Perhaps your head injury has affected your memory, Wayob."

"Who is Wayob?" Saroyan sounded more Armenian now. He blinked at Saul with disbelief as if seeing him through a fog.

"You are."

"No. My name is Edward Saroyan. What is going on?" He rattled the cuffs again.

"Okay, so it's Edward now. Good. What is the last thing you remember, Edward?"

"I remember..." Saroyan's gaze went off into the distance. "I was at my carwash. At the register. It was slow day. Maybe I fall asleep. And then—I don't know, something happened—and I woke up here."

"You don't recall killing Luis Luna?"

"No, I—" His brows twitched. His breathing accelerated, short raspy breaths. What was he hiding?

"You bludgeoned him with a bat," Saul said.

"No!" Saroyan moaned.

A pulsating alarm sounded on the bio monitor. It grew more intense, and Saroyan flung his head from side to side, as if trying to ward away his memories.

"Edward?" Saul said. "Please, help us help you. Help us make sense of this."

But he'd withdrawn inside himself. He twisted and flopped in the bed. No way he was acting. He was recalling the murder, Saul was almost positive, and it was as if he were rejecting the memory with every cell in his body.

Saul placed a hand on his chest, ignoring for a moment that he was a murderer and not just a human being in pain.

A nurse in his mid-twenties, wearing blue scrubs, rushed in followed by Hernandez. Saul got to his feet and stepped back. The chair cushions slowly reinflated. The nurse reset the alarm and checked Saroyan's vitals.

"I'll get the doctor," he pulled his phone and swiped the screen.

Saul leaned toward Hernandez. "He prefers his own name all of a sudden."

The doctor was thin with mousy hair. She looked over the equipment and injected something into Saroyan's IV. "Mr. Saroyan isn't ready for visitors," she said.

"We just need to ask a few more questions."

"I'm afraid he's not in any condition to answer." Saroyan's pulse slowed.

Saul flashed his badge. "Lives could be at stake."

"Our responsibility is to the patient."

"We get it," Hernandez said. "You've got to do your job, but we've got to do ours too."

"I remember," Saroyan said weakly.

Saul exchanged a look with Hernandez.

"You've got two minutes," the doctor said, "after that he'll be out. At least until tomorrow."

Saul thanked her, took out his phone, and began recording. Given Saroyan's condition, whatever he said now might not be admissible in court, but still—it could be useful.

The doctor turned to the nurse. "I'll check back in twenty minutes." She hurried out.

The nurse scribbled a note on the clipboard.

With heavy lids, Saroyan gazed up through his drug-induced haze, pupils dilated, eyes out of focus.

Saul leaned in close. "What do you remember?"

"It seems like a dream. It had to be, but then…how do you really know?" He trailed off.

"He'll be asleep soon," the nurse said. "We gave him a heavy sedative."

Saul wanted to shake Saroyan to keep him awake.

But Saroyan was fighting the tiredness on his own, shaking his head from side to side. "It's strange," he said. "Dreams make no sense after waking up. But when you dream…it's real. Usually, I don't remember my dreams. Only the feeling…

"It was terrible." His eyes blinked fast and wouldn't open all the way. He slid the cuffs down the rail and clutched Saul's arm. "I don't want to sleep, please…"

The nurse squeezed between Saul and Hernandez and tried to elbow them back. "He's suffering from blunt-force trauma. He needs to rest until he stabilizes."

Hernandez moved back a step but Saul wasn't budging. He weighed twice as much as the nurse and he needed information. "Tell us what happened," he said to Saroyan.

"It was like you said. I hit him with a bat. But…it wasn't me."

The nurse glanced at Saul, his eyes wide. He lowered his arms and took a step back himself.

Saul stood there in silence, hoping Saroyan would continue speaking before the drugs overtook him.

"It was like my arms and hands were someone else. I would never…I tried to stop myself, but I couldn't…. It was not—I was like a prisoner. Watching… my hands…. I felt the wood as it struck—that part is clear. Nightmare—" His eyes closed. "Please…make it go…. I don't want to remember…"

"Mr. Saroyan?" Saul asked.

The interval of the heart monitor slowed.

Saul gave Saroyan's arm a tentative shake. The nurse touched Saul's arm, not forcefully, but enough to make it clear that he should stop. When he glanced back at Hernandez to see if she would back him up—they had to know more—she shook her head. Bad idea.

Saul withdrew.

The beeping of the bio monitor slowed. Saroyan's face relaxed. He was asleep now, deeply asleep.

Hernandez clawed back her shock of white.

The room seemed to be shrinking. Too crowded for him and Hernandez and Saroyan, and what he claimed to have happened. The nurse and all the equipment around the bed. And the one chair, its slumped cushion, leaking yellow foam from a coin-sized tear.

New Direction

Gray woke to the sound of sirens winding through the city. Beside him in the bed, Claire's spot was empty. He pulled the covers over his head. The sirens faded, and the sound that replaced them was a percussive swooshing, which it took him a moment to realize was rain. The first rain of fall.

He closed his eyes and rolled onto his side and let the sound of water wash over him, the patter on the roof. Outside the bedroom window, it was pouring into a puddle, probably a clogged gutter.

So far, the kids were silent, and he hoped it would be a while before they stirred. Hopefully, the rain and the moist in the air would calm the whole morning.

He drifted to a place where he could see the dream he was having, like it was waiting for him. He's a freshman, and he's sitting beside Laura on the lawn in the quad listening to who-cares-what-band, sitting closer and closer, high on hormones, hearts pounding double time to the drums. Where can they go afterwards? Because, in this dream, she wants to stay with him all night.

———

"I can't handle everything by myself." The sound of Claire's voice ripped him awake.

He opened his eyes. She stood over him holding Tyler, her hair disheveled, in the same sweatpants and t-shirt she'd been wearing last night.

"Mindy won't get dressed," she said, "and I need to feed Tyler again."

Above Gray's right eye, the remnants of last-night's Scotch tightened like a vise in his skull. "What time is it?"

"It's after eight. I've been up all night."

Gray sat up. Beside the bed, his clothes from last night lay crumpled on the floor. He dragged over his jeans and pulled them on while Claire complained about his snoring and about how then Tyler had woken up and she'd had to sit with him for the rest of the night because every time she tried to put him down he started crying again.

He rubbed his forehead. "How about I feed him?" He reached for Tyler.

Claire shook her head. "He still needs breast milk. You just get Mindy dressed."

He found Mindy in her room, wearing only pink underwear, arranging dolls on her bed as she sang to herself.

Gray opened her closet. "So many beautiful dresses. How about this yellow one?"

"No! Princesses wear pink."

She led him to the garage and dug her pink dress out of the laundry basket, the only thing she would wear. Gray tossed it in the dryer to fluff out the wrinkles. As they watched it spin, he hugged her and rubbed his throbbing forehead.

Once in her pink dress, she launched into the kitchen. Gray glanced at his easel with the cloth still draped over the landscape, which today he would finish. He swallowed.

In the kitchen, Claire had Tyler in his highchair and was cutting up an avocado for him.

Mindy climbed into the chair beside him and snatched a piece with her fingers.

"I told you not to let her wear dirty clothes," Claire said.

"We, uh…cleaned it." Gray winked at Mindy. "Who wants pancakes?"

Claire groaned.

Mindy raised her hand. "Macaroni, please."

Gray smiled. "That's not on the menu."

Claire spooned a green chunk of avocado into Tyler's mouth, which he gummed around and maybe swallowed some, but mostly it ended up on his chin and bib.

"Guess that's like dessert?" Gray asked Claire.

"He's not hungry. I don't know why." She piled avocado on his tray and took out her phone.

Tyler swept the green chunks off onto the floor and squealed. Gray kissed his head and let the avocado remain on the floor for now. If he was going to cook, he couldn't get caught in an infinite loop of pick-up-the-mess with Tyler.

"Oh my god!" Claire said to her phone.

Gray could hardly hear her over the hammering in skull. Food would help, at least a little. But he knew the monster pounding against his frontal lobe. He knew it well. It would never be sated until he quenched its thirst.

He opened the fridge and looked for the butter. It wasn't on the door where it belonged.

"Did you hear me?" Claire asked.

"What?"

"Ashley York pulled a Paris Hilton!"

"What's that?"

"She flashed her cooch!"

"Amazing," Gray said, but if he never heard Ashley's name again it would be too soon.

Claire retreated toward the living room.

Gray found the eggs, but if there was butter in the fridge, he just couldn't see it. He slammed the door.

He followed her to the doorway. "You remember it's Saturday?"

She collapsed on the couch and swiped her phone. "So?"

"It's my morning to paint."

Claire looked up. "What do you mean?"

But she knew. How many times had they talked about it?

"Remember, last Saturday you went out with friends." *And came home drunk*, he might have added.

"God," she threw her phone down on the cushion.

"You're like my third baby." Once upon a time, she might have said it playfully, and once upon a time, he might have laughed at himself, because maybe he was whining a little. But not now. Now there was nothing but bitterness in her voice. She meant it. She thought he was being a baby.

She heaved herself up from the couch, a storm brewing in her eyes.

He braced himself in the doorway. He had to stand his ground, had to at least finish this one painting so he would have something to show her, something to justify quitting his job. When he opened his mouth to try and explain how much he needed this morning, just a few hours to paint, she turned away from him and marched toward the hallway.

"I'm taking a shower," she said.

—

An hour later, Gray opened the garage door. Outside, the street, washed clean by the rain, was drying in the sun. He drank in the moist air and angled his easel into the sunlight.

Claire had taken Mindy and Tyler, and her icy comments about his painting, to the park. It was like the ground between him and Claire had cracked open, and the crack had gradually widened such that now they were standing on opposite sides of a chasm of unknowable depth, with a cold wind blowing between them.

But when had it started? Years ago, it seemed. Certainly, Mindy's birth had changed things, and more dramatically than they had expected. It had ended the evenings of laughter on the balcony of their old apartment as the lights of Hollywood came alive below them. But the cracks were there, even then. Even before Claire was pregnant, the lazy mornings of lying in bed making love had tapered off, and Gray wondered if it had more to do with him than with her. Maybe she'd sensed the disappointment seeping off him. Maybe once he got out of his job and into painting, things would be better.

It didn't have to be his own art, not all the time. Album covers, even ads would be fine. Anything beat writing code no one cared about.

He lifted the cloth, tossed it on the workbench, and

considered his painting. Beside the Malibu Lagoon, a bush was burning. Fire spread toward the dry hills behind it. Burn down and start anew, start over—like he wished he could do with his life—but the painting on the easel, yet again, fell short of his imagination. The strokes were haphazard, unorganized, as if only by coincidence they had formed an image. If he was kind to himself, the painting was competent—the proportions and colors matched the photograph taped to the easel—but competent wouldn't cut it. Competent was not going to feed Mindy and Tyler.

What he needed was a passive source of income, some kind of insurance in case it took longer than expected to reach to the point where he could earn enough from art to support his family. But right now, he needed to focus on his painting. He needed to wash away all these negative thoughts like the rain had washed the city clean. Music, loud music. And, of course, a nip of Scotch.

As the oaky liquid warmed his belly, he turned on the radio. An old song by the Smashing Pumpkins was playing. He turned it up and let the music course through him. This was the feeling he was trying to capture in his painting. He darkened the sky with charcoal-colored smoke. He loved acrylics, the way they layered—no need to start over. He made the sun a glowing red disk on the horizon. As he transformed the scene from the reference photograph into a whole new image, he wondered if this could be his masterpiece.

If he could make a name for himself, people would come to him. They would buy his art, and the more he could produce, the more he could afford to spend time painting.

All he needed was time—uninterrupted, continuous time. If he was going to make it, if he stood any chance at all, he had to give all he had. He had to open a vein and bleed his life's blood into his art.

A news blurb came on the radio with an update on the murder of Luis Luna. The wheelchair-guy, Saroyan, was the killer after all. Now he'd been hospitalized after starting a fight in prison. Gray shivered. A man had had been bludgeoned to death, and no one knew why, and he had been right there.

As he leaned over the radio to change the station, a hoarse voice behind him almost shouted, "Hi, neighbor."

Startled, Gray shut off the radio and turned.

Standing in the doorway of the garage was the old guy from across the street, his pale skin almost transparent in the sunlight. His charcoal-colored suit hung almost flat from his bony shoulders, as if were still on the hangar. *A truly unique-looking man*, Gray thought. Beautiful yet fragile, like a malnourished pug.

"Sorry to scare you," the old guy said. "Halloween *is* over after all."

"You didn't. I… thought I was alone."

He pointed toward Gray's painting. "That's really pretty, aside from the fire."

Gray swallowed. The fire was the whole point. It was the instrument of change, otherwise it would be, at best, just another pretty landscape, unlikely to grab anyone's attention. But now Gray noticed the scale of flames was out of proportion with the foliage they were consuming. The fire didn't fit.

"You're right," Gray said. "I guess it needs a lot of work."

"I think you're onto something though. Reminds me of the way sunsets looked in seventy-three when I came back from 'Nam."

Gray loved the way art was more than the piece itself. It existed in the mind of the viewer, and each person, from their own point of view, experienced it in their own unique way.

He selected a liner brush from the rack on the workbench and began trying to work some more detail into the flames.

He felt the old man staring over his shoulder. He seemed content to stand there all day in the doorway to the garage, watching him paint, which would be fine if Gray could focus with an audience. He needed to make progress. He put down his brush, and turned back to face the old man and his glassy eyes.

"I'm sort of busy, but thanks for stopping by."

The old man stepped inside the door. "I didn't introduce myself last night. Name's Charlie. Charlie Streeter."

Gray carefully shook his bony hand, afraid it would break. Charlie began a tedious explanation about how was housesitting for his daughter, who was on sabbatical with her husband in El Salvador.

Gray felt trapped by the conversation. He wanted to be alone with his painting, his music, and the Dewer's, which Charlie was staring at as he spoke. "I wanted to explain," he was saying, "why my car is in the garage and Lynda's is on the street."

"O-kay," Gray said. "Thanks." He picked up his brush and squinted at his painting.

"They asked me to drive it while they were gone."

Gray glanced toward the kitchen. *Would he follow me inside? Or just stand here and wait for me to come back out?*

"So the battery wouldn't go dead. So, I'll be driving Lynda's car for a while. Just didn't want you to think anything of it."

If Charlie hadn't called attention to the blue Prius on the curb, Gray wouldn't even have noticed. What was the big deal? Perhaps he was going senile. Probably irresponsible of Lynda to leave Charlie alone in their house.

"Anyway, I just wanted you to know." Charlie glanced over his shoulder toward the Prius.

Gray stepped into his personal space, hoping to herd him out. "Sorry, but I really need some alone time so I can concentrate on my work."

Charlie's eyes widened. He shuffled backward, nearly falling. Gray, feeling like a bully, reached out to help him, but Charlie scuffed his feet back into the sunlight of the driveway, sweat glistening beneath the few hairs combed across his spotted scalp, and pretended as though nothing had happened. "Mindy was a cute little princess fairy. If you ever want me to look after her, just say the word. I've got nothing but time on my hands."

Gray nodded. "We'll keep that in mind." *Never going to happen.* They had their issues with Belinda, but at least she could keep up with Mindy.

Charlie shuffled across the street, each step slower than the last, seeming to shrink under all that dark fabric in the sunlight.

—

Later, Gray stood behind his easel, relishing the energy pulsing through his veins, the flow that only came when he was alone with his music and just the right amount alcohol, an ephemeral inspiration that begged for more—more Scotch—but more would only ruin it. Gray had been here and done this. Many times. It produced sorry work, and it was his fear of the letdown, of all the sloppy-Scotch paintings he'd thrown out, that stalled his hand from lifting the bottle again. He pounded the cork in with the side of his fist and turned off the music.

He streaked more red into the horizon. Like the blood that must have been on the sidewalk. It must take incredible strength to shatter a man's skull with a bat and from a wheelchair.

Focus. He stepped back to consider his work. It was colorful, but color was not enough—color meant nothing without emotion. It was emotion that drew people into an image and captured their imagination. He could stare for hours at Van Gogh's self-portrait. The way the lines, which up close were rough and irregular, seemed to actually move as you stood back, as you focused on the depth of his eyes. Art granted you permission to observe a subject, someone who would never allow such scrutiny in person. Someone so different from ourselves, yet the same underneath. A universal human essence which could only be captured in a portrait. A window into a soul.

That's what Gray needed to paint.

Forget landscapes. He should paint someone with character, personality. Charlie. He should paint Charlie—the way he had stood there. The sunlight streaming in around him—the deep furrows weathered into his face. The lines told a story. A story Gray could capture in a portrait.

Gray leaned the incomplete burning landscape against the workbench to dry, though he might not even keep it. His unfinished paintings were stashed in the crate hidden below the workbench, but it was nearly full.

He placed a fresh canvas on the easel. This was his favorite part of painting. The unblemished canvas held every possibility for the image he might paint, the image as flawless as his imagination. He wanted to just stare at the blank canvas, with maybe just a token nip of Scotch, and bask in his imagination of how good it could be—how good it *would* be. In his mind's eye, Charlie came into focus. Gray had to get started before it faded away. He had to hurry.

He used a charcoal pencil to sketch the underpainting... But the man standing in the doorway didn't quite look like Charlie. His face was a little too narrow, his eyes sunken, and the lines around his mouth were tightened into a cruel smile.

Gray had never been any good at drawing from memory. He should just ask Charlie to pose, maybe not for the whole portrait but at least for a reference photo. He might be happy to. He must have been lonely to come over here with nothing more important to say than whose car was in the garage.

Gray stepped outside and shielded his eyes in the sunlight. Charlie's house, with the witches, the jack-o-lanterns, and all the crow cut-outs, would make an excellent backdrop.

Claire's minivan sped over the hill into their neighborhood. She swerved into the driveway and stopped just short of where he was standing. Her window started down, and then—probably because it was taking too long—she flung open the door and practically leaped from the car.

"I thought you wanted to paint."

"I am." Gray glanced back toward the open bay of the garage, where the sketch he'd started was hardly visible, and unimpressive.

"Mindy threw up on herself."

Gray opened up the back passenger door. Mindy was buckled into her booster seat, eyes cast down. Dried orange chunks of curdled vomit on the front of her dress.

"It's ruined," Mindy said.

"I told her to get off the merry-go-round."

Gray looked back at Claire as she went around the car to get Tyler out from the opposite side.

"It'll be fine," he said to Mindy. She wouldn't look up at him.

He lifted her out of the car, pretending not to smell the vomit. "We'll just put it in the wash after we wash you."

As he turned toward the house, Claire stomped past him with Tyler, heading for the easel. Gray hugged Mindy to his chest, bracing himself for Claire's reaction. But she passed right on by as if there was nothing there at all. Did she see it? She had to have seen it. The sketch was rough, of course, and it hardly looked like Charlie at all, but still... it was the start of Gray's first portrait, and those eyes, those sunken eyes... it had potential. He hoped.

And Claire had deliberately ignored it, which was worse than if she hated it.

———

After he bathed Mindy and fed everyone, it was nap time. Mindy said she wasn't tired but agreed to stay in her room for an hour of quiet time.

Claire wanted to take a shower, so Gray carried Tyler, who was sound asleep, out to the playpen in the garage and covered him with a blanket. The door was closed, and Gray kept it that way. He covered his would-be-masterpiece with a cloth, uncorked the Dewar's, and drank in silence, in the dim bulb mounted to the workbench. More than anything, he wanted to get back to that feeling from this morning, ride the swell of inspiration. He wanted to blast the stereo. And not through headphones, which were inside, and he didn't feel like getting up, so he opted for another drink.

From across the garage, Gray heard the water sluicing through the pipes from the hot water heater squeal to a stop as Claire finished her shower. He slumped forward on the stool, his eyes closing. The Scotch had dropped him.

The kitchen doorknob rattled, and the door slammed open into the counter. Gray had to force his lids up, force himself to look at Claire. She was standing in the doorway, wrapped in a white towel, dragging a comb through her damp hair.

She flicked on the overpowered fluorescents in the unfinished ceiling. "What are you doing in the dark?"

Gray squinted and as he jerked open the top drawer of the workbench and began raking in tubes of paint. "I was just closing up."

"God, you're so weird." She turned back toward the kitchen and threw the door closed behind her, leaving Gray in the harsh light from the four exposed tubes, with Tyler whining as he woke.

He rubbed his aching eyes, got to his feet and shut off the fluorescents, which he'd been meaning to replace with LED mood lighting. He lifted Tyler from the playpen and rubbed his back until he quieted down.

"Am I weird?"

Tyler had nothing to say on the subject. His eyes were closed again.

True, Gray was drinking... alone... in the garage. And Claire probably knew it. But she didn't know why, how much he'd rather be painting, how hard it was to focus with all this weighing on his mind. He'd planned on waiting until Sunday to tell her how he was quitting his job, but why wait?

He found her in the bedroom. She was lying on the bed, still in the towel, with a second one wrapped around her hair. Her eyes were closed, but he knew she wasn't sleeping. He sat down beside her, on the bed.

Her brows tensed. His timing couldn't be more obviously bad, so instead, he layback, holding Tyler against his chest.

She forced out a breath, a heavy burst of air, as if it had broken free from her effort to contain it. She rocked herself up off the bed.

Gray's eyes closed, and this time he found them too heavy to wrench open. The darkness behind his lids pulling him down. Claire's hairdryer whirred. Sleep.

—

Claire launches through the kitchen door to the garage where Gray is working on his portrait of Charlie. He can't let her see it. Not like this. It's not finished yet, and there is nothing worse than a bad first impression. He jerks from the workbench, sending tubes of paint flying across the garage.

But it's too late.

Claire comes to a complete halt. Her mouth falls open. Her eyes widen. Gray follows her gaze to his unfinished painting...which is... not Charlie at all. It's a dark figure, an indistinct man on a sidewalk in the fog, emerging from a shadow between streetlights.

Gray's heart pounds in his throat. He's terrified. The image has nothing to do with the portrait he started. It's a masterpiece. The indistinct face of the man contains all the pain of Munch's Scream coiled into short, perfect strokes. It's like Monet, or Monet's impression of Dali, more beautiful and haunting than anything Gray has ever painted, more than he's ever even hoped to paint.

With no explanation as to how this masterpiece materialized on the easel before him, he turns back to Claire, but she is not Claire—she's his mother. And they're not in the garage anymore; they're in the kitchen he grew up in. He is a boy, and she is standing over him. "Do not want what you cannot have," she says.

"I don't want anything." He chokes at the sound of his nine-year-old voice. "I just want to paint."

"Wake up," his mother says, her face harsh, leaving no room for discussion.

And so he runs—that's all he can do. If he can make it to his room and lock the door behind him, he won't have to listen to her. He can paint if he wants.

As he passes, she grabs his shoulder. He tries to wrench out of her grip, but he cannot free himself.

"Wake up," she says again. Her eyes flicker with such a cold shade of blue that it hurts to look at them.

He blinks. He clenches his eyes closed.

When Gray opened his eyes, he found himself staring into the cans in the ceiling which were dialed up to full brightness, and it was Claire standing over him, shaking his shoulder.

Immediately, his head started pounding. The lights

seemed to amplify the pain in his skull. Still on his back, he felt around for Tyler, who had been on his chest when he fell asleep. "Where's Tyler?"

"You slept all afternoon," Claire said. "What's wrong with you?"

He sat up and groaned. The hangover tightened like a vise on his skull. He closed his eyes and tried to remember the masterpiece from his dream. The dark man. Gray caught a fleeting glimpse before the whole image blurred into darkness itself.

"It's almost five," Claire was saying. "So much for the Day of the Dead thingy."

Gray opened his eyes. According to the clock by the bed, it was 4:18. The Dia De Los Muertos parade didn't start until seven. "We can make it."

Claire wrinkled her nose. "Do you really want to go?"

Last weekend, he'd convinced her to go for Mindy's sake while secretly hoping that Claire would enjoy it too. Occasionally, she had fun when he convinced her to leave the house—though not so much lately.

Now, with the way his head was pounding, he hardly cared about going anymore either. But what else were they going to do? Not like he was going to get any more painting done tonight, and his head would be pounding regardless. At this point, his hangover was the only sure thing in his life. Maybe getting out of the house would clear the air between them, so they could finally talk.

He climbed out of bed. "Let's just go."

He trudged past her, ignoring whatever excuse she shouted after him as he left the room. He needed a shower. If he could just stand under the hot water and not think for fifteen minutes, he would be fine.

In the hallway, Mindy latched onto his leg. He rubbed her head and pretended to smile as he bent down and wiggled his fingers near her armpits. Her head jerked as she giggled —the threat of tickling worse than the act itself. He tried to pry her off, but she clutched on tighter.

"If you don't let go, I'm going to tickle you." He wiggled his fingers some more, then made good on the threat.

Remarkably, her laughter seemed to ease the throbbing chaos in his head. As he started toward the bathroom, she remained latched to his leg.

"Time to let go, Mindy, so I can get ready for the parade."

He dragged her along the carpet. She couldn't stop giggling.

"Don't you want to go? There might be ice cream."

He dragged her into the bathroom and turned on the shower. "You're going to get wet if you don't let go."

She didn't let go, so he bent down and hugged her. She squirmed out of his arms and ducked into the narrow gap between the toilet and the counter, still giggling uncontrollably.

He motioned her out. "That's enough."

She made for the door, then sidestepped and latched onto his leg again, writhing around on the tile, desperate for a tickle. He placed a hand on her head. "Daddy needs to shower, Mindy, okay?"

Her giggling tapered off as she gazed up at him with her doe eyes. She released his leg.

Gray's heart melted. Suddenly, he hardly cared about taking a shower.

Mindy left the bathroom without another word, shutting the door behind her.

Ashley's House

Ashley was up early that morning, hoping for a miracle but knowing her crotch would be all over Instagram... and it was. It was everywhere, trending on Facebook and Twitter. She wanted to tweet back that it was an honest accident, that her dress had slipped up on the leather seat, but in the photos she looked so wasted that any comment from her would only fan the flames of the trolls. God, the names they were calling her.

She turned up the volume, trying to drown shame with reality TV while waiting for the inevitable call from Don, her agent.

She hoped her dad wouldn't find out. He was huge on social media, of course, but he let his PR people handle it for him. The question was, would they tell him? Would they show him the photos of her wasted in the back of Raquel's Escalade, her dress riding up as she tried to get out, her legs spread and crotch exposed for all of Hollywood?

Her phone vibrated with the expected call at the expected time: nine a.m. Cue Don. She muted the TV, stood, tightened her robe, and answered the phone.

"Ashley, darling," Don said. "What were you thinking?"

But Don worked for her. She didn't have to explain

herself to him. "Any publicity is good publicity, right?"

"No. It's like bad advertising. Your public image has a huge impact on the marketability of your films."

"But I'm not in any films, remember?" If she'd gotten the role, which Don had basically guaranteed her, she would never have gotten smashed in the first place.

"Ashley, baby, I'll get you a part. Give me a chance and I'll make you a star. But please, help me do my job here. No one will cast you with a bad reputation."

Ashley rubbed her forehead. "Look, I didn't mean to, okay? Yesterday was kind of a bad day, remember? That jerk-wad producer you sent me to lunch with?"

"I get it. You needed to blow off some steam. Just let us help you next time. That's why we hired Clayton. If he'd driven you to the club, nothing like this would have happened."

But she didn't need a babysitter, what she needed was a role. On the still-muted TV, a reporter stood in front of a jail downtown. Inset in the upper corner was the car wash she'd seen in an earlier blurb, the sidewalk cordoned off where a man had been murdered. "I don't understand why my crotch is going viral," she said, "when people are being beat to death in broad daylight."

"That was yesterday," Don said. "Today is all about you."

She turned off the TV and closed her eyes. She felt boxed in. "What can I do?"

"I hired an internet-cleaning service. They can't get everything, of course, but these guys are the best. They'll get the pictures of your little wardrobe mishap taken down. And once there's nothing to look at, it'll stop trending."

But the damage was done. Even without pictures, people were going to remember. *I'll never live it down.*

And Don, predictably, decided to trot out his catch phrase. She could have said it along with him. "One step at a time."

"Yeah, but I'm walking backward."

"Not for long," he said. "I've got something for you."

"What?" She was almost skeptical.

"The biggest opportunity of your career, that's what."

"Seriously? Why didn't you say that to start with?"

It was a Charlie Kaufman film directed by Sean Penn. She leaped up from the couch and paced below the wall of windows. Outside, West LA stretched out to the blue expanse of Pacific. The morning rain had washed the city clean, and Catalina Island seemed closer than ever.

"You'll costar with Zac Efron," Don was saying, "if you get the role."

"So, what do I have to do?"

"Not much. Just a reading."

"So it's an audition?"

"No, no, of course not. They want you. They just need to check your chemistry with Zac. Without someone like him attached, it will never get funded. You know how it is."

Ashley could hardly hear over the sound of her heart pounding. "I guess."

"They want you in costume. They're going to do a full lighting test. Who knows, they might even use it for publicity."

Ashley's stomach lurched. She wasn't ready.

"No need to thank me," Don said. "Just keep a low profile. I'm begging you. I put my ass way out on the line for this."

"Of course." She wasn't going anywhere. She would practice every minute for the next two days before the screen test.

After hanging up with Don, she called Sammy in the guard booth and made him promise to bring her the screenplay the second it arrived.

With nothing to do but wait, she paced around the house. In the dining room, the glass tabletop had streaks on the glass. Circular arcs of dried cleaning solution distorted her reflection.

"Andrea?"

No answer.

Where was she? Not in the kitchen, unless she was ignoring Ashley.

Ashley returned to the TV. For some reason, she felt

guilty asking Andrea to do her job, despite the fact that Ashley was paying her double the usual rate for a housekeeper. The problem was that Andrea—who was trying to make it as an actress as well—was too damn cheerful. Almost sarcastic, the way she said yes to everything, and it had gotten so bad lately that Ashley was considering hiring another housekeeper to do the actual cleaning and cooking. But then, if she hired someone else, what was she paying Andrea for? She couldn't just let her go.

A text came in from Raquel.

Raquel:
How's my favorite biatch?

Ashley set the phone to the coffee table. She had nothing to say to Raquel, but her screen displayed a new notification.

Raquel:
Lunch at the Ivy

Bring underwear 😉

What Ashley needed was an excuse to keep Raquel off her back while she focused on the screen test, which she certainly couldn't tell Raquel about, because Raquel would blab it all over the place and somehow ruin it. The last thing she needed was for Sean Penn to find out and think she was bragging about it.

Her phone lit up with a notification from Twitter. Raquel had just tweeted, *Lunching with Ashley York at The Ivy.*

Ashley:
WTF! I saw your tweet. I've got yoga.

A white lie. Ashley would feed her one after another, and even if Raquel suspected Ashley was up to something, she'd have to just chill, because after all, Raquel couldn't afford to piss Ashley off. She needed Ashley more than Ashley needed her.

Raquel:
Skip it, girl. You're more famous than Lady Gaga! We've got to smoke this while it's hot.

Ashley could have guessed this whole lunch thing was yet another way for Raquel to use her to bolster her image for the wannabes on her feed.

A call came in from August, his perfect face filling her screen—never a hair out of place. Even in his profile pic, he had his eyes focused and lips tightened in a way that came, she knew, from hours of practicing in front of a mirror. He was calling with FaceTime, so she smoothed her hair and loosened her cashmere robe before answering, "Hey, you."

"What's up, it-girl?"

"It-girl?"

"Yeah, you created a sensation."

Last night, she'd been too embarrassed to admit it was an accident, and now it was too late. "I don't know about that."

"Are you kidding me? You're so lucky you're a girl. If I sunned a crowd, they'd put me in jail."

New subject. "Are you coming over tonight?"

"Probably not until after midnight," he said. "Boys' night."

'Boys' night,' she knew, was basically his entourage plus as many girls as they could round up, which hardly mattered to her because he was coming to see her afterwards.

———

Ashley was in the sunroom when Sammy's deep voice bellowed through the house. "Knock knock."

"In here," she said.

He strode in with the screenplay she'd been waiting for all morning, his stark white smile widening with each step, showing off his always-positive outlook on life. Something surged inside her and she leaped up and hugged him, and only then did she remember how she had loosened her robe as a tease for August, to which he'd hardly reacted.

But now she felt something.

As she pulled out of the hug, her hand raked Sammy's neck, and his gaze slid down her cleavage. Blood rushed through her body, headed south, perhaps because it was such a bad idea in so many ways to even be thinking about Sammy when she had August Grant coming over. Any other woman in the world would think she was crazy.

"You okay?" Sammy asked.

Was he talking about now? Okay with him looking at her? She frowned. If she answered honestly, it would start something—bad idea—but she didn't exactly want to shut it down either, so she told him what she'd been dealing with all morning. "I'm trending."

He scrunched his brows together, mirroring the gravity of her expression. "That's not good?"

"I didn't mean to."

"Didn't mean to what?"

Was it possible? Was Sammy the one person in the world who hadn't seen the photos from last night? He must have seen them. Of course he had. He was being a gentleman to pretend.

"Well, it was an accident. Don't believe what's online."

"I only believe what I see with my own two eyes." And as he said it, his two eyes swept over her boobs again, this time too obvious to ignore.

Bad idea. In so many ways. She pulled her robe closed. She wanted him to know that she hadn't intentionally flashed her crotch last night as some kind of a ploy for attention, which as pathetic as it was, wasn't half as bad as the truth: that she'd let herself get so wasted it had happened by accident.

Sammy glanced away. The room felt cold.

She wanted his eyes back on her. "I wish more people were like you, Sammy."

He flashed his white smile. "You'd be surprised, Ashley. People are getting tired of living in their phones. They want something real."

She nodded, wanting to believe him. Maybe once the pictures were gone, the rumors would be just rumors, which maybe people knew about but didn't really believe all the way, like all the porno sites claiming to have movies of her but they were of other girls—girls who looked nothing like her except maybe they wore an outfit like one she'd worn once, before they undressed and screwed some man whose face remained offscreen.

"So…" Sammy said, "um, about that dog…"

"It's still here?" She didn't mean to snap, but she had specifically told him to get rid of it. This was first time he had ever disobeyed her.

"I can't find the owner. I've got signs up at both gates to the neighborhood, but no one has called."

As if on cue, the dog barked. And it was a deep bark, loud and close.

"Oh my god—is it in the house?"

"No." Sammy glanced toward the door. "She's outside, but I thought you might want to meet her again. She's calmed down a lot since yesterday. I swear."

"Sammy, I can't. I have to get ready." How was she going to focus with some dog barking? She held up the screenplay. "This is Charlie Kaufman. With Sean Penn directing."

"Way to go, Ashley!" Sammy flashed his smile. Did he know how endearing it was? Hard it was to stay mad at that smile.

"They haven't cast me, yet, but I've got a screen test, and I need to nail it."

"I'm sure you will." He stepped toward the door. "I'll leave you to it then. You won't hear a peep out of us. Don't worry."

But she would hear the dog if it barked, even from all the way up at the guard booth. It was that loud. And even if Sammy kept it quiet, just knowing the dog was there was a distraction. She did sort of want to meet it though, and if she did, she'd want to play with it. She'd be thinking about it when right now she needed to focus more than any other time in her life.

"Isn't there some shelter or something you can take it too?"

"Shelters kill dogs. I mean, you wouldn't believe—"

"Just figure something out. I can't have it here."

"Will do." He turned toward the door. "Call if you need anything, anything at all."

He meant it. Ashley knew he did. She could count on him, and it didn't matter that she was paying him; he wanted something more than money. The only one in her life who didn't want something from her was her dad.

Overcome by a sudden bout of weakness, she snatched up her phone. She had to know if he knew.

Ashley:
Hey, Dad. You there?

She stared at her screen and waited. She couldn't straight-up ask him if he'd seen the photos without tempting him to go look, but she had to talk to him. He'd say something if he knew. He would have to say something. And then she could tell him how it had been a horrible accident, maybe without mentioning how messed up she had been at the time. If anyone would understand, it was her dad.

She called him.

His phone rang twice and went to voicemail. She ended the call.

Ashley:
Give me a call, okay?

The little animated dots in the blue bubble appeared, showing that he was typing. She waited.

And waited.

Dad:
…

Eventually, the bubble with the dots disappeared. Now it was just her text at the bottom of the screen. After another minute, she refreshed the app.

Still nothing.

"What the hell?"

Death Notification

At 2:11 p.m., on the 10 east from downtown, an overpacked pickup cut in front of Saul. He hit the brakes. Beside him in the passenger seat, Hernandez rocked forward, her neck tensed against the decrease in speed. Her eyes remained on her phone.

He swallowed back a belch. "I give up," he said. "How did you do it?"

"Do what?"

"With the neighbor. How'd you get her talking like that when she wouldn't even open the door for me?"

Hernandez shrugged. "I speak Spanish."

"Yeah, but you had her feeding us tamales."

"I told her your blood sugar was low."

Saul felt his cheeks flush. He pretended to laugh. "I only ate to be polite." In truth, he'd been starving, and the tamales were so tasty, he'd eaten four in spite of himself. "I'm actually on a diet."

Hernandez chuckled but she looked serious. She combed back her shock of white bangs. "It was just to get us in the door."

Saul nodded. "Much appreciated." The elderly woman knew where the Lunas had moved. And now, thanks to

Hernandez, they were on their way to do what should have been done yesterday: notify Luis Luna's family of his death.

Like all cops, Saul dreaded death notifications. They weren't trained for it. No amount of experience made it any easier. And this time would be particularly bad because unless Luna's family lived in a total news blackout, they had by now seen the horrific images of his death. They'd know how he was murdered, and they'd demand to know why. A death needed to be understood in order to move on. People could not accept murder as some random act that defied explanation, and neither could Saul. There had to be a reason, a story behind it. That was his mission: to make sense of the madness.

In front of them, in the truck bed, a tilted stack of wooden chairs bounced against an inadequate length of cord.

It had been twenty-four hours since the murder, and Saul and Hernandez were even further from a motive than when they'd started. They had the perp, Saroyan, chained to a bed in the ICU, but he had changed. Last night he'd confessed to the murder, but now he denied it.

Saul couldn't help feeling like they'd only glimpsed the tail end of a monster who had shed Saroyan like some insignificant appendage it could regenerate.

Keeping one hand on the wheel, Saul pulled out his phone and hit redial.

"Who you calling?" Hernandez asked.

"Aleman."

"I still don't think it's related," she said.

"I don't believe in coincidences."

"They happen every day. Statistically unlikely, I'll give you that, but odds are Aleman needed a break after what happened."

"Maybe." It *was* hard to imagine that Aleman would want anything to do with Saroyan, but Saul had to find out for sure. "Aleman's not the sort of guy who runs off with his tail between his legs."

"He got knocked out. Maybe he wasn't thinking straight."

"So where did he go? His car's still at the MDC."

"Where does he live?" she asked.

"Highland Park. A ten-mile walk, if there's even a way over the 5."

"Maybe he got a Lyft."

"Possible, but then why not answer his phone?" They had been over this already, and as much as Saul wanted harmony between them, he couldn't let it go.

She shrugged. "Heard of Occam's Razor?"

"Is it any better than Gillette?" he joked, rubbing his bristled chin, hoping to make her smile.

Her lip twitched slightly. "It means stick with the simple explanation."

"Which is what? At this point we have no explanation at all for Aleman's behavior."

"I don't see how it makes a difference. Saroyan killed a man, and we've got it on video. Case closed."

"But he claims to have had no control over his actions." And he claimed it with such conviction that Saul knew he truly believed it.

Hernandez shrugged. "So, he's a psycho."

"You think he has multiple personalities?" He'd never encountered such a case, but even if it were true, Saroyan was still responsible—at least a part of him was—and Luna still deserved justice.

"No," she said, "I think he's a good actor."

"That's what I thought at first, but then why change it up?"

"Yeah." She brushed back her shock of white. "That was weird. I didn't like his new accent any better."

"If he can pull off an act like that while heavily sedated, he should be working in Hollywood. Not at a carwash."

"I'm thinking it's because of the drugs that he dropped the performance from last night. But don't worry, we'll talk to him again when he wakes up. I just don't see a reason to go chasing irrelevant leads."

Ahead, the overfilled truck slowed down. Saul swerved around it and accelerated.

Hernandez went silent, gazing out at the blur of palm trees and warehouses below the freeway.

"Must be a tough commute," Saul said. "I can't believe people live out here."

"Some people can't afford to get closer."

She was right. Even middle-class families had been forced further and further out by the inconceivable sums of money in Hollywood and Silicon Beach. The city of LA had a budget that topped ten billion a year, and the chief of police alone pulled down more than three hundred grand. Although Saul was barely scraping by, he was rich compared the majority of people they dealt with: people like the Lunas, the ones who couldn't afford to live closer.

Saul exited onto Loma Avenue and followed the road as it passed derelict warehouses and veered right, turned again, and then dead-ended into the parking lot for the Lunas' apartment building, almost underneath the freeway. A two-story stucco affair, typical of urban blight apartments built during the 1950s boom. Designed to last maybe thirty years at the most. Now the stucco was discolored and cracked. The roofline sagged, and a blue tarp had been tied down over a corner as a cheap patch for a leaky roof.

"Depressing," Hernandez said.

Saul rolled to a stop in front of a sign with faded red letters: *TENANT PARKING ONLY.* When he opened the door, the hiss of the freeway filled the car. He climbed out. Shattered safety glass sparkled on the asphalt as they approached the rusty, metal stairs attached to the exterior of the building. When they reached 2B, Saul knocked on the faded blue door.

Behind it, a female voice asked, "Quién es?"

"La Policía," Hernandez said.

Saul buttoned his coat and sucked in his belly as the locks clicked and a chain unlatched. The door opened.

Behind it was a girl with sepia-colored skin and furrowed brows. She was short, five feet at the most, with high cheekbones and salon-perfect hair combed down over one shoulder. She turned toward the apartment's interior and shouted, "Abuela!"

"Do you speak English?" Hernandez asked.

"Of course." She stepped back for them to enter.

Inside the door, a series of photographs lined the wall portraying the girl as she grew from a child into nearly a woman now. Whether the background was a church or a beach or a park, she stood between Luis Luna and an older woman, Luis's mother, probably—same chin, same penetrating eyes—who seemed to shrink as the girl grew taller. The one outlier was a black and white of a young man with a striking resemblance to Luna. In the photo, he wore a dark uniform with light trim and lapels. Insignia like a sun. Like Luna, he had prominent cheekbones and shiny, dark hair. Maybe two inches long. Brushed but a little tousled, with a clear tendency to wave. He was Latino, but as much Aztec or Mayan as Spanish. Plenty of Native American in him. That was for sure. All the Lunas had indigenous features.

The old woman from the photographs touched the wall of the inner hallway as she approached the main room of the apartment. Her eyes were glazed white.

As the girl went to help her, Saul looked back at the photos, and this time he saw the change: as the old woman's hair lightened from gray to stark white, her eyes lost their clarity and focus. He had missed it before because in every shot, she still knew where to look, right toward the camera. A proud, knowing expression on her face.

Saul and Hernandez waited by a shelf of ceramic owls near the entrance to the small, overheated room. Bright Mexican blankets draped the couch. Dark fabric curtained the one window. Below it, marigolds were scattered on a small shelf illuminated by flickering prayer candles that flanked a framed photograph of Luis Luna.

Saul introduced himself and Hernandez to the old woman, but she didn't mention her name, and they didn't press for it. She was undocumented and they didn't need to know it.

At the end of the hall, she reached out a trembling hand for the recliner that faced the couch. The girl took the woman's other arm to help but she pulled her arm away. She could sit on her own. She settled back into the recliner and pulled a red and blue blanket across her lap, as if unaware of the heat.

"I know why you're here," she said in a thick Latina accent.

Saul nodded toward Luna's shrine. "Was he your son?"

Her face hardened. She said nothing. Her glazed eyes stared straight at his chest.

The room felt too small for his massive frame. He was towering over her, and already he was sweating. If he weren't so fat, he would take off his coat. He sidestepped around the shelf to the couch.

The dark eyes of the ceramic owls sparkled in the candlelight. As he sat, the cushions sagged from his weight. Hernandez wedged herself between him and the armrest.

The girl pulled a wooden chair out from the dining table turned it toward them. "Abuela doesn't speak English. And you're right, he was my father."

The old woman inhaled deeply, as if gathering her strength. "Rosa, por favor, ir a su dormitorio."

Rosa argued with her in Spanish. Before Saul could interject, Hernandez placed a hand on his knee. They had worked together for more than a year, and this was the first time they had touched. And it felt as natural as if it happened every day.

"Sentimos mucho su pérdida," she said. "We're very sorry for your loss."

The woman pulled out a worn handkerchief from the bag beside her chair. She mopped her eyes and blew her nose. Then, with slow trembling hands, she folded the cloth into a neat square.

With his limited Spanish, Saul couldn't follow what was said next, but there was something more than grief in the lines on the old woman's face. And Hernandez, who was never at a loss for words, seemed taken aback.

"She doesn't think we can help," she said.

"Did you tell her we've got the perp?"

Rosa's eyes darted to the floor, and she straightened, gripping the bottom of her chair.

"No, es imposible," the woman said.

Saul heaved himself up from the couch and showed

Saroyan's DMV photo to Rosa. "Do you recognize this man?"

"No." Her eyes darted from the photo to Saul and back to the floor.

"He must have known your father, somehow. Anything you can tell us would help with the investigation."

Rosa looked at the photo again and described Saroyan to the old woman.

Saul's phone buzzed in his pocket. He was tempted to check who it was, but right now it was crucial to study the woman's reaction.

She shook her head. "No era ese hombre. Es mi culpa que su nieto está muerto."

"She says it's her fault," Hernandez said.

Saul slid the photo into his pocket, rubbed his temple, and returned to the couch. He couldn't follow much of the ensuing conversation between Hernandez and the woman, but he understood she was in a lot of pain—that much was clear from the strain on her face. After every few words she gasped for air—short, raspy breaths.

Hernandez paused, and then asked a question.

The woman's milky eyes glanced down and to her right. A jolt of current surged through Saul's gut. People glanced to their left when recalling a memory. To the right was the imagination center. Right and down was a lie.

The woman looked up at Saul. Her eyes seemed to focus on something inside him. She spoke carefully measured English. "Leave it alone."

Hernandez inhaled. "We should go."

"What else did she say?" Saul asked.

"She says Saroyan is not our guy."

"Then who killed Luna?"

"Era yo," the woman said. "I did. Y mi corazón va a estar en una terrible prisión para siempre."

A wireless handset on the counter rang, startling Rosa. She leaped up from her seat.

The woman abruptly started coughing. It sounded like a lot of fluid in her lungs. She turned sideways, pulled out a handkerchief.

The phone kept ringing.

The woman waved Rosa toward it, and they argued in Spanish.

Rosa answered the phone as the woman climbed out of the recliner.

"One moment." Rosa carried the phone to her Abuela.

The old woman wiped her mouth and guardedly folded the handkerchief. She took the phone and shook it toward Saul. "Es importante." She turned toward the hallway.

Saul glanced at Hernandez, who stood up. "Entendemos," she said to the woman.

The old woman, clutching the phone, touched two fingers to the wall on her way to the back room.

Saul asked Rosa, "Mind if we ask you just a couple more questions?"

She slumped back into the chair. "I don't know why she's acting like that. Normally Abuela is the sweetest woman you ever met."

"She's grieving." Hernandez combed back her shock of white and sat on the armrest beside Saul. "As I'm sure you are too."

Rosa nodded and looked at the floor.

Saul leaned forward. "Do you know what she meant by 'things aren't as they appear'?"

Rosa bit her lip and shook her head. "Something's wrong with her. She won't go to a doctor."

It would be easy to dismiss the old woman as senile, if not for the phone call last night—the man who had claimed to be Wayob, but who had sounded like Saroyan and yet, not like Saroyan at all. The old woman wasn't crazy; she was scared.

Why blame herself? They all knew how Luis Luna had died. Maybe he'd gone to Venice for her. Maybe she'd sent him on some errand, but... it seemed like more than that. Like she knew Saroyan herself. And maybe she knew about Wayob.

She knew more than she'd said. That was for damn sure. Perhaps much more. But she'd said all she was going to say, for now. So the only question left was, what did Rosa

119

know?

"I believe your grandmother," he said. "There's something more going on here."

Rosa's eyes widened, and she looked directly at him. "Like… what?" Like she wanted to know as much as he did.

He heaved himself up of the couch. Went to Luna's shrine. Picked up the silver frame and examined the dark-skinned Latino. Luna's penetrating eyes seemed to be peer out from the photograph, staring at Saul. Had Luna known Saroyan? "That I intend to find out."

He lifted the curtain and squinted into the sunlight. Behind the glass, the window was secured by vertical bars with patchy, white paint surrendering to rust. Beyond them was the freeway. Sunlight glinted on the cars careening past. Their case against Saroyan remained the same. Hard to imagine what could change it. Saul closed the curtain and turned around.

If Rosa knew anything, this was her chance to fill the silence in the room. But she had withdrawn inside herself, smoothing her long hair between her hands, looking down at the floor.

Hernandez was already standing. She tilted her head and Saul agreed. They should leave, let Rosa and her Abuela deal with their grief. Try again later. Hernandez gave Rosa her card. "If there's anything we can do to help, please call."

Wayob

After trudging all through the night and half the day, Wayob is thirsty, so thirsty. So annoyingly, utterly, thirsty. And so sick of this vessel, this body of Victor Aleman and all its petty, physiological needs, which Wayob would shed himself of, except that he is so close, so very close. He can almost hear the hum of old woman's mind, even without entering a state of meditation.

Why is Wayob still free? For if anyone knows how to recall Wayob to the Encanto, the miserable stone which imprisoned him for so many centuries, it is Abuela. *Abuela.* Who held the Encanto for decades and refused to use it, despite all the effort Wayob wasted whispering into her sleep. She kept Wayob imprisoned in the utter darkness, alone and disembodied. She forced Wayob to suffer in the awful torment contrived by the despicable priest, because she blames Wayob for the death of her husband, when it was her husband's own fault. Out of utter desperation, Wayob whispered into her deepest stage of sleep—as if the idea was her own—that if she destroyed the Encanto, Wayob would die along with it. Although, in truth, destroying the Encanto would set him free. He would have one life left to live in the first vessel he finds. Yet, she had failed to act.

Ignorance?

No, she knew. She must have known, like she must now know that Wayob is free. So, unless she has become benevolent in her old age—for Wayob does not deserve such torture—she must be using the Encanto. Finally, after all this time, Abuela is just as greedy as everyone else. And her greed shall be her demise.

Wayob should thank the man, whoever he is, who returned the Encanto to Abuela. For her mind rings out louder than anyone else who has ever held the wretched device. So loud it's almost annoying.

Despite all the agony she inflicted upon Wayob, he still does not wish to kill her. But he must. After all he has suffered, Wayob deserves to be free. But Wayob shall not repeat the mistake of killing the one who holds the Encanto without first finding the wretched device. Abuela must surrender the Encanto before Wayob kills her. This vessel, Aleman, is unacceptable. Wayob must find someone else, and he requires the Encanto to transmigrate, and then he shall destroy it and be free. Abuela would not even have to die, if she could be trusted to let Wayob live the life he deserves, after all he has suffered.

Wayob's feet are so heavy, almost too heavy to lift in the awful boots Aleman wears. Wayob groans and drags his feet along the pavement, across yet another street.

An iron fence blocks his path. His eyes hurt from the sun as he forces his gaze up along the wretched iron fence, which seems to stretch on for miles to the north and just as far to the south, but Wayob must go west. Beyond the fence, Abuela is near.

A block to the south, sun glints on a gate. Wayob trudges toward it. Perhaps this miserable vessel shall prove useful after all, for Wayob learned, decades ago, of the power a man in uniform commands from the chief of the police of Guatemala City, Miguel Arredondo Sosa, who tracked Wayob down when Wayob was finally almost free. Sosa—so like Parker—with his misguided notion that Wayob should suffer for those who died, who had to die. And why should Wayob suffer? What for? Killing Wayob cannot bring them back. So Sosa, the meddling bastard, he had to die too. Ironic that, so many years later, it was Sosa's son, little Luis Luna all-grown-up, who released Wayob from the Encanto. *Karma.*

As Wayob approaches the gate, an electronic trill rings out like a demented songbird, the phone in his pocket again. Wayob contains his impulse to hurl the wretched thing away, to smash it into the sidewalk. The phone might prove useful. He reaches into his pocket and squeezes and presses the wretched device until finally its incessant chirping ceases.

From metal box mounted by the gate, a deep voice bellows out, "State your name and the nature of your business."

Excellent, Wayob thinks, *no wasting time.* "My name is… Victor Aleman. Let me through."

"Where's your car?"

A reasonable question. Wayob should have driven, clearly. Would have, if he'd known how far he must travel. He prefers to let Aleman live, but in order to find his vehicle, Wayob would have had to peer into Aleman's memories, which would have exposed Wayob's own memories to Aleman.

Like with the crippled vessel Saroyan, who Wayob only peered into out of utter desperation to escape Parker's unwarranted treatment—odious Parker—all Wayob found was Saroyan as a child, his mother using her own body as a shield against Saroyan's drunken father, his father hitting her, over and over again, the vein bulging in his temple, his neck red against the white collar of his shirt.

Saroyan's memories proved a colossal waste of time during which Saroyan might have gained some dim knowledge of the Encanto, so now Saroyan must be dealt with, unfortunately. No choice.

"Still there?" the voice barks through the metal box.

Wayob glares at the camera mounted above it on the fence. "Of course I am still here. Let me through. I am an officer of the law." Approaching the camera, he points to the to the badge on the uniform that belongs to Aleman.

"No one here called the cops."

"My business is elsewhere. I need only to pass through your fence."

Laughter bellows through the box. The voice laughs at Wayob. "That's a new one."

Wayob grinds his teeth and forces his face into a smile. Just a peaceful officer in need of a shortcut. For official police business.

A motor engages. The gate rolls open. Behind the fence, a parking area stretches out to a rectangular building composed of metal, concrete, and glass. From the building, a man with a huge upper torso emerges. He has square shoulders, and a uniform of his own. Dark blue. A rectangular device affixed to his belt. A weapon? *We shall have to find out.*

For Wayob can tell by the way this man is marching toward him that he must be dominated, immediately. Wayob has traveled too far to back down.

Wayob steps through the gate. Draws the gun from his pocket.

The man slows down. He reaches toward his belt... then withdraws. Holds his hands out by his sides. "What's this about?"

"I do not wish to harm you," Wayob says, and he means it, "but I shall, if you make me."

When Wayob shot the man in rags, it was a mercy kill. It had been the deranged old man who hit the ragged man with his vehicle. Wayob merely ended his misery. A favor for the ragged man and for Wayob, who simply could not afford witnesses after all the effort he had expended freeing himself from jail and the crippled vessel of Saroyan.

Too bad the old man escaped. He must have reported the encounter, probably blamed Wayob for running over the ragged man. Thanks to the meddling old man, this officer, with his disproportionate upper torso like an upside-down triangle, now takes a step forward. He means to challenge Wayob—live or die.

Clearly, this man holds the same barbaric notion as

Parker and Sosa that Wayob should suffer for those that died, when Wayob never wanted to harm anyone. The priest made him like this. The vile fucking priest.

"It was the priest." Wayob fires into the air. The force kicks his arm back so hard he nearly drops the weapon. As he struggles to remain in control, the gun fires for a second time.

The man falls to the ground.

Then he climbs to his knees, raising his hands. This time high overhead. "Don't shoot. Take whatever you want from the warehouse."

"What is in there?"

"I don't know, man. They don't tell me shit."

Wayob levels the weapon. "How many people inside?"

"No one."

"Do not lie to me."

"It's Saturday, man. No one works weekends."

"Keep your hands up," Wayob says, "Take me to your vehicle."

"Aw man. Not my ride." The man rises, his hands still in the air. "Take one of the trucks. I won't call it in, I swear. It probably won't even be missed until sometime next week."

Cooperation is good. Cooperation is key, since Wayob has little experience with vehicles. He allows this man to lead him around the warehouse to one of the white trucks parked in a row.

Wayob climbs into the driver's seat. "How do I drive this contraption?"

"Are you serious?" the man asks.

Wayob shoves the gun barrel into his ribs.

The man leans into the vehicle and shows Wayob how the gears are on the steering wheel. Just forward and reverse. No clutch. Driving seems easier now than the last time he tried it in Guatemala.

Wayob takes the key from the ignition and climbs out. "Get in and show me."

The man gets into the truck and shows Wayob the controls for a second time, speaking as if Wayob is an idiot.

Wayob withdraws the cuffs from his belt. "Keep your

hands on the wheel." He cuffs the man's wrists to the wheel.

"You can't leave me like this. I thought we had a deal."

Wayob shrugs. "This is the deal."

"Come on," the man begs. "You can't leave me here. I need to use the bathroom."

"Disgusting," Wayob says. "But you have already delayed too much as it is."

Wayob chooses another truck, identical to the one with the man chained to the wheel, and drives out through the gate.

The man's directions prove accurate: just a mile and a right turn, and then Wayob is cruising east on a freeway elevated above the sprawl. He should have obtained a car sooner. He is moving so fast. Too fast. He slows a bit and closes his eyes. Just for a second. Just to get the bearing of Abuela's mind, which he can hear even without slipping into a trance. The sound of her mind grates on his nerves.

Almost right below him.

Wayob opens his eyes. The barrier wall along the side of the road rushes toward him. The highway had veered to the left. How was Wayob supposed to know that? He spins the wheel and slams the brakes—too late.

Wayob sees it happen and then hears it. The crunch of the truck against the wall. Wayob squeezes his eyes shut as he is thrown sideways.

When he opens them, he is facing the opposite way. Cars zooming toward him. Squealing tires. Slamming horns.

His head throbs.

The smacking sound he'd heard, he realizes, was his forehead thrown against the glass. The windshield remains intact, as does Aleman's skull, it would seem. Wayob gingerly traces with his fingers the swelling lump on his skull. The flesh is tender, but the skull served its function. Will Aleman remember how this happened? Unlikely. The sooner Wayob finds a new vessel the better.

Wayob pulls the handle, but the door refuses to open. He shoulders into it. The metal groans. Using both hands, he shoves with all his might.

As if to spite him, the door suddenly swings open,

spilling him out onto the pavement. He lands on his shoulder in a puddle of brown filth.

Pain.

He has never felt pain like this before—inside the Encanto, there is no such thing as pain—but these wounds are not mortal. He struggles to his feet. Muck has soaked through his sleeve. He tears off his outer shirt and uses the dry part to clean his hands and face.

He looks down over the barrier wall. Below the highway is a derelict building, blue plastic on its roof. Inside the building is Abuela. So close. He can almost jump down upon her.

Wayob laughs.

Wayob jogs along the freeway. Wayob laughs and laughs.

Saul and Hernandez

The 10 was jammed. Saul and Hernandez were halfway up the on-ramp when the car in front of them slowed. Saul hit the brakes. Too late to turn back. "Should have checked traffic."

"It's an accident," Hernandez said.

Sure enough, on the opposite side of the divider, a white truck had hit the barrier wall, spun out, and was now facing the wrong way. Its front bumper missing. Grill crunched into the engine. Oncoming traffic had all but stalled. Cars snaked around the truck one or two at a time.

By the truck, looking over the barrier on the opposite side of the freeway, was the driver. He wore a wifebeater and olive pants, both smeared with dark grime, maybe oil. A mechanic, probably, or a landscaper. Something about the stocky man triggered a sense of *deja vu*.

"Should we stop?"

"Not our beat." Hernandez pulled her phone. "I'll notify dispatch."

She was right. They would only end up directing traffic, and he would look ridiculous climbing across the divider.

He eased forward a few feet then had to a stop again, despite there being no obstruction on this side of the freeway, only lookie-loos craning their necks as if they had never seen an accident on the side of the freeway.

The driver remained standing there, looking down over the barrier. His shoulders trembled like he might be crying. Probably shaken from the accident.

"Unis on the way," Hernandez said.

As they passed the accident, traffic accelerated. Sirens wailed in the distance.

Saul's phone buzzed in his pocket and he pulled it out. On the screen was a text from Chen, the engineer at Verizon who owed him a favor. Chen had traced the blocked number which had called Saul last night: Aleman's cell phone.

Saul relayed this to Hernandez. "It doesn't make any sense," she said. "He was really acting like Saroyan?"

"Almost exactly. He claimed he was Wayob. I'm thinking we should stop by his apartment."

"Okay," she said. "I guess it can't hurt."

They exited the 10 onto the 5 north.

"It's sad," she said.

"Aleman?" If he wasn't such a mean little man, Saul might feel sorry for him.

"No, Rosa. She's going to have to drop out of school now. They're undocumented, so it's not like she can get financial aid or anything."

"Terrible..." Saul racked his brain for something more to say, but in truth he had been so concerned about Saroyan and Aleman that he hadn't considered the long-term ramifications of Luis Luna's murder on Rosa and her grandmother.

He took the 210 to Highland Park. Aleman lived in yet another example of cheap 1950s construction, but given the proximity to downtown, his rent was probably three times more than the Lunas'. His building had been renovated. A stone facade built over on the stucco around the entrance. White letters mounted on the stone spelled out "The Avalon," like inside was somewhere better than LA.

The entrance door was unlocked. Saul held it open for Hernandez and immediately regretted it when she had to swerve around his belly. Might as well put a sign on it.

"Front bumper," he said.

She stopped in the entrance and squinted at him.

Not funny. "Never mind," he said.

The interior floor was some kind of faux wood. They took the hallway on the left toward Aleman's. 112. They knocked on his door.

No answer.

Saul glanced at Hernandez. She shrugged. He knocked again. "Police!"

Behind them, a door opened. A man with a bushy beard leaned out into the hallway, mid-twenties, sporting a Dodgers t-shirt with a torn collar, a brown stain on his belly.

Saul asked, "Have you seen Aleman?"

"Who?"

Saul pointed with his thumb at 112. "Victor Aleman."

"That guy." The bearded man shook his head. "He's usually not back until like five on Saturdays."

Saul checked his phone. It was 3:10. He waited for the man to close his door then pulled out his lockpicks.

Hernandez frowned.

"Exigent circumstances," he said. "Aleman has been missing for fifteen hours. We need to make sure he's okay."

She shook her head. "No indication he's in danger. He ditched work, but maybe he's just out on a bender."

"He threatened to kill someone."

"But who, when, and where?"

"That's the problem. All he said was 'Another must die,' but if you'd heard *how* he said it—"

"Doesn't matter. He's got a clean record."

She was right, of course. No judge would sign a warrant based on what Aleman could claim was some general statement about the human condition.

"Let's wait outside," she said. "This isn't worth your career."

Saul's career had stalled, and he didn't really care, but hers he had to consider. If Aleman had passed out or was hiding in there, then no big deal if they waited. At least she would see for herself how he was acting.

They re-parked across from the Avalon, with a clear view

of the entrance and the alleyway to the tenant lot. What if, while they sat here, Aleman was stalking his victim? What if there were clues in his apartment as to whose life he meant to take?

Without a warrant, the evidence might be useless in court, but Saul could worry about that later. He just had to slip in and out unseen. And if he found nothing, he could relax, because he'd know waiting here for Aleman was the best they could do. He could enjoy his time with Hernandez instead of staring out the window, worrying uselessly.

The longer he sat there, the less he cared about Aleman because here he was with the woman of his dreams incarnate. And he was blowing it.

Think, man, think!

"Why don't we use first names?" he asked. "I mean, cops are supposed to be friends, right?"

"We're supposed to think rationally," she said.

"And friendship prevents that?"

She crossed her arms. "Emotion does."

Saul rubbed his chin. "I don't know. Emotion helps me make connections. You can't always follow the evidence."

"That's intuition. Not the same thing."

A Prius pulled out of the alley and turned. The driver, an Asian woman, strained to see over the wheel.

"I wouldn't mind if you called me Saul."

"Okay, *Saul*. You know Aleman might have just pranked you, right?"

"Mind if I call you Rhonda?"

She raised her eyebrows. "Yes," she said, like maybe she was kidding. But she wasn't. That was clear.

"Aleman doesn't strike me as a prankster," he said. "Wish you could have heard his voice."

She flipped back her shock of white. "Maybe Saroyan bribed him somehow to waste our time. I bet he'd get a kick out of that."

There was more to it. Saul was sure. There was more than just a casual connection between Saroyan and Aleman. Hernandez would have to see it for herself. She had come this far.

He changed the subject. "Why do you think the grandmother is blaming herself for the murder?"

Hernandez shrugged. "Maybe she sent him to Venice. Maybe he was doing something for her."

"That makes sense. But seems like she'd still want justice. She told us to leave it alone."

"Yeah. That was weird. If Saroyan murdered my son, I'd want the bastard put down."

Saul recalled the old woman's glazed-over eyes, which rotated down and to the right as she spoke, even though she was blind. A force of habit. She was hiding something.

"How did she hear about the murder?"

"I got the feeling she just knew, you know? Like she felt it."

"You mean… clairvoyance?"

"Not exactly." Hernandez gazed across the street at the row of palms rustling in the wind. A wistful look came into her eyes. "Socrates said the soul is made of energy, separate from matter, and this energy creates a vibration that impacts all living creatures."

Saul was dumbfounded. Here he was suspecting the Luna elder and her son of something nefarious, while Hernandez was suggesting something so far out there it might as well be magic—real magic.

She turned to face him. Her brow furrowed. "You don't think it's possible?"

Realizing he was squinting, Saul smoothed his expression. "It's possible, I think." He wasn't about to disagree with her belief. But magic was real only to those unaware of the trick. And he knew all the tricks.

What he didn't know was science. Science was real. Science he could get behind. "I read that at a sub-atomic level, everything is energy. You think it's all connected some way we can sense?"

"We're capable," she said. "We're probably taking it in, subconsciously, but the logical part of our brain drowns it out. Maybe if we slow down and really concentrate, we *can* feel it." She smiled. "Like *deja vu*. Maybe this energy is what causes *deja vu*. It's all connected across time and space."

Maybe she was right. Who was Saul to say? Maybe it explained the sparks he'd felt earlier, when she placed her hand on his knee. Had she felt them too? If she had, maybe she would fancy a kiss? (Just as an experiment. Just to prove her own theory.)

It should be so easy. All he had to do was lean across the seat and plant one on her. If he did, and *if* she kissed him back...

But if she refused, then it was game over. Forget about a relationship.

He glanced down. His belly lay in his lap like a sack of old clothes that needed to go. What did he expect?

She squinted out the Avalon. Her streak of white fell across her forehead. She pulled out her phone and glanced at the screen. "I need to get home for dinner with Rumi and my mom. Mind dropping me at the PAB?"

"Not at all." Saul started the engine. The Police Administration Building was only ten miles away. In less than an hour, he could be back here searching Aleman's apartment on his own.

As he merged onto the 210, Hernandez's gaze raked over his belly. He tightened his grip on the wheel and pretended to focus on the road.

"You going to the Castle tonight?"

Was she just making conversation or, maybe, fishing for more? "I'll put you on the guest list," he said. "If you want to stop by for dessert or a show, or something."

"Can't tonight."

Saul's chest tightened. He stared out at the Prius to their left, like it suddenly required all his attention.

"It's just...," she continued, "on Saturday nights, my mother and I watch our telenovela, and I've hardly been home all week."

He tried to sound upbeat. "I get it. I'll just put you on the list in case some other night works. Whenever, you know? Anytime."

Hernandez swiped on her phone. "Sure."

Saul merged the 5 south. A bank of low clouds pushed in

from the coast. Darkened out the setting sun.

By the time he reached Elysian Park, the sky was a solid gray mass. Lights were on at Dodger Stadium. On the 110, traffic slowed to a halt. He exited on Broadway. While waiting at the light, he tried calling Aleman again. If Hernandez could just hear for herself...

Five rings. No answer.

When they rolled up to the PAB, it was dusk. The lower floors were lit up. The glass building was shaped like a boat moored among the taller buildings behind it. Officers coming and going. A hive of activity. Light from the lobby spilled down the steps to the sidewalk. Saul parked by the curb.

"See you later." Hernandez smiled slightly and turned to get out. Did her smile have something to do with him? He sure hoped so.

She took her time getting out. As she approached the wide steps to the lobby, her broad hips swayed in her cotton slacks. Saul felt lightheaded.

Later, she'd said. Later when?

He could have asked. He could have at least waved goodbye instead of just sitting like a silent lump of lard.

His phone buzzed, and he checked the screen.

Victor Aleman.

As Saul answered, he flung open the door and heaved himself out.

"De-tec-tive Par-ker." That same mocking cadence.

"Where are you?" Saul asked.

"I am closing in."

Saul scanned the dozen or so pedestrians within sight. The only one with a phone was a guy in a suit, crossing First toward City Hall. Too lanky to be Aleman, too tall.

"Where are you?" Saul asked again, as he bounded onto the sidewalk. He had to keep him on the line. Hernandez had to hear this.

"My concern, Parker, is that you keep calling this device. I told you to leave me alone."

A man in three layers of dirty coats steered his cart of belongings toward Saul. He pointed at the no-parking sign.

"Twenty bucks and I'll watch your car."

Saul swerved around him. No way Hernandez could hear him through the glass. Saul charged up the steps.

"So, who are you this time?"

"Wayob," said the gruff voice on the phone.

Saul shouted, "What happened to Aleman?"

Just as Saul made it to the entrance, on the opposite side of the vast lobby, Hernandez stepped into an elevator. As the doors closed in front of her, she raked back her shock of white.

"Aleman shall be fine," Wayob said. "Many decades ago, I encountered a man just like you, a *policia* who refused to leave me alone. He died, and it was his fault for meddling with my freedom. Do not repeat his mistake."

Hernandez was headed to her car, Saul knew, but there was no cell service in the garage, and no way he could catch up to her now, so he lumbered toward Main, the closer of the two exits to the garage, hoping to flag her down as she left.

"Who died?" Saul asked.

"I do not have time for another of your *interviews*, Parker. Leave me alone or there *shall* be retribution. I shall have no choice." Wayob ended the call.

Saul halted, chest heaving. He leaned forward, hands on his knees, to catch his breath. No point now in racing to catch Hernandez.

Was that Aleman pretending to be Wayob? Or someone else with Aleman's phone?

Saul called Mark Chen.

"You get my text?" Chen asked.

"I'm going to need a little more." Saul doubled back toward his plain wrap. "I need a location on that number."

"Whoa. I can't do that."

"Can't or won't?"

The homeless man held his hand out, wanting payment for watching Saul's car.

Saul stepped into the street to avoid him.

"It would mean my job," Chen said.

Saul stuffed himself behind the wheel of the plain wrap.

"I'm not asking for more than what you guys are already handing over to the NSA."

Chen went silent for a long moment. "I don't know anything about that."

"Look, I get it. But lives are at stake. If someone dies…"

"I'll be covered. I don't mean to sound ungrateful or anything, but I've already gone way out on a limb for you. Verizon has official channels for coordinating with law enforcement."

"Vicky around?"

"Aw, man. Don't go there."

The Chens had promised—Vicky, emphatically—that they would do anything to repay Saul for recovering their stolen artwork.

"I'll go where I have to," Saul said. "Nothing personal. Like I said—"

"Alright, alright. I'll hook you up—this one *last* time. Then we're even."

"Of course," Saul said. As far as he was concerned, they were already even. More than even. There was no quid pro quo for doing his job. He just lacked any other option. Verizon would demand a warrant. A warrant required the signature of a judge. And judges required more than some vague threat from a public servant with a clean record. Hernandez was right about that.

Chen sighed and ended the call.

———

Saul turned from Cesar Chavez onto Main. The Olvera Street Plaza was packed. Some kind of festival. He swung a U-turn and parked beside the plaza, behind the row of cars already lined up along the red curb.

He pulled out his phone and clicked the link from Chen. It opened a map with a red pin indicating the location of Aleman's phone. He was on Olvera, the cobbled street between the plaza and Cesar Chavez.

A dotted line traced backward in time showing the movements of Aleman's phone over the last twenty-four hours. Last night, after leaving the MDC, Aleman had traveled east—on foot evidently, moving at less than four miles an hour. At around three in the afternoon, his speed increased suddenly and his path moved off the surface streets and onto the 10. Where it stopped for a while, almost exactly where Saul and Hernandez saw the accident.

Maybe it was a coincidence?

One coincidence was possible, but then Aleman had circled the Luna's apartment. Two coincidences? Impossible. He must have known, somehow, that Saul would be there. Or maybe his strange trip had something to do with the Lunas. However, he hadn't gone to their apartment; he'd zigzagged to a Metrolink station in El Monte, where he took a train to the nearby Union Station and then walked here.

After traveling all night and day, Aleman must have a reason to attend the street festival, and Saul very much wanted to hear it.

A crowd was gathering around the gazebo in the plaza. As Saul pushed his way through, he called Hernandez on impulse—then cancelled the call. She would ask how he was tracking Aleman, and avoiding telling her would be the same as lying. This much he had learned from his failed marriage, from all those nights he had let his now ex-wife assume he was working late when he was really at the Castle. And then she had blamed her affair on his secret life. She had said magic turned her off, but still. He should have told her.

As Saul swiped back to the map, Hernandez appeared on the screen, her LAPD profile pic, dress blues and classy smile. He had to answer. If he screened her out now, she would know.

"What's up?" she asked.

Saul hesitated. If they were ever going to be more than just partners, he had to trust her—all the way. "I've got a bead on Aleman."

"Where?"

"Olvera Street."

"*El Pueblo?* How did you find him there?"

"Would you believe I just happened to stop by for the Day of the Dead festival?"

"No."

"I'm tracking his phone," he said.

She inhaled. Saul knew, just from the sound, that the corners of her mouth were drawn in.

"I'm just going to hang up," she said. "We'll pretend I never heard this."

The crowd was bunching up. A pair of uniforms were sweeping people back to make to make way for the parade. Holding out his badge, Saul shoved through the human barricade while keeping the phone to his ear. "That's why I changed my mind about calling you."

"Why are you jeopardizing your career? Aleman's not worth it."

"This is bigger than Aleman. I don't even know for sure if he's the one calling me."

"Look," Hernandez said. "Levy's asking if you're pulling your weight. If she finds out—"

"She asked you that directly?" If Levy came out and actually said that, then Saul was in the shit for sure.

"Nah, she beat all around the bush. You know how she is."

"I see."

"I didn't mean like you're fat or anything."

"No, I know." *Freudian slip.* He had been on Levy's shit-list ever since the Brown shooting, and he doubted she would ever let it go. "She's going to make you lead detective, and I want you to know there's no hard feelings. You deserve it."

"Oh, I doubt that."

"Trust me—it's already happened. She just doesn't have the balls to tell us, and by us, I mean me."

The buildings of the historic pueblo flanked Olvera Street. At the entrance was a stone pedestal with a giant cross. Behind it, a row of kiosks divided the street, forcing the crowd into two separate lanes. Saul took the left fork, heading for the location of the red pin—the last ping from Aleman's phone.

"We're off topic," Hernandez said. "My point is, you're going overboard, like you always do, for what might be a prank call."

At least if it was, then no one would be in danger, but finding Aleman, or whoever was pretending to be Wayob, meant more to Saul than his career—what little might be left of it.

"Better to go overboard for nothing than to do nothing if someone's in danger." The way he spoke left little room for doubt.

"True," she said with more than a little hesitation in her voice.

"He called me again. And this time he basically confessed to killing an officer."

"Why didn't you say so?"

"He said it was decades ago and didn't give any other details, but he threatened me again."

"Alright. I'll be there in thirty."

"No, let me find him first. You've got family night." Saul ducked under a low awning.

"Dinner's over. It took Rumi all of two minutes to wolf down his dinner and then he asked to be excused."

"Teenagers," Saul said, like he knew anything about teenagers. He had been one once, thirty-five years ago. "What about your soap opera?"

"You don't want me there?"

If she wanted to come, then he was happy to have her. More than happy. "Oh, I want you," he said. *Too obvious?* "When I find Aleman, or whoever the bastard is, you're going to want to see for yourself."

After she agreed to come, Saul ended the call.

The sight of a kiosk selling churros triggered a vast hollowness in his stomach—*churros*. He forced himself past the almost overwhelming scent. Cinnamon, sugar, fried dough....

In a shop window, Mexican blankets similar to the one on the Lunas' couch were arrayed over a railing. Saul stopped and checked the map on his phone. The blue dot representing his location was almost right on top of the red pin. He scanned the crowd. Mostly Latino. Aleman's pale complexion would stand out. Unless he was one of the dozens of men wearing masks. Plenty were stocky enough but most were too short. Aleman was medium height... the same height as the man in a big sombrero, dressed like a mariachi, facing away from Saul. He plowed toward the man. A woman in a formal red dress clung to his arm.

Saul tapped him on the shoulder.

They both turned at once. The woman's face had been painted like a sugar skull with a colorful pattern around her eyes. The man's upper face was hidden behind a half-skull mask, only his eyes peering out at Saul through sockets of the skull. Below the mask, he frowned.

Too much chin. And his face was too lean. Not Aleman.

Saul backed away. He surveyed the mass of people. There were too many. Aleman was slipping away. And with each ticking second, so was the truth.

Something bumped Saul's leg. A stroller. Behind it, a woman in her mid-thirties tightened her grip on the handle as if preparing to mow him down. "Excuse me." She had mocha hair and steely eyes ringed with dark circles of exhaustion. Her skin was so pale it was almost blue.

Saul stepped back. Behind her, a little girl in a pink dress paused, enthralled by the woman in the red.

"Mindy." The woman with the stroller tugged the girl's arm.

"I'll help you get through," Saul said.

Using his girth, he plowed through the crowd, still scanning the faces for Aleman. The woman trundled her stroller behind him on the uneven bricks, towing her little girl. Saul led them through the tightly packed crowd and emerged into a more free-flowing throng of people milling to and from the plaza. He stepped aside and motioned the woman ahead.

She pushed past him. No eye contact. But her little girl looked up at Saul. He smiled and waved goodbye, and she gave him a big grin. Two missing teeth.

He checked the map on his phone and found that his blue dot had moved a bit but not the red pin. He called Aleman's number. As the ringtone played in his ear, he scanned the crowd. There were phones out all over the place, people taking photos or texting, but no one seemed to notice a call.

Aleman's voicemail picked up. Saul ended the call and swiped back to the map. The red dot jumped. Must be some kind of lag. Aleman must have passed on the opposite side of the street behind the kiosks. Now he was near where Olvera met the plaza.

Saul marched toward the location, watching his phone the whole way. The pin placed Aleman in the restaurant on the corner, La Golondrina.

Saul wedged himself through the crowd. He passed by a table just as a waiter delivered a steaming pan of fajitas. His stomach rumbled. The tables were jammed together, each with a platter of chips and salsa. Margaritas. Guacamole. He swallowed. He tried to focus on the faces. They stared back with glassy eyes.

An arched doorway led to a dimly lit interior. A split-level with terra-cotta tile and exposed brick preserved from the former pueblo. Saul tried to concentrate on the faces, not the food going into them. Chicken mole. Enchiladas. Quesadillas.

A hostess intercepted him. "How many?"

"Two." He gestured toward the back wall.

She seated him at an empty two top next to an elderly couple. The man nodded his fedora at Saul then turned back to his wife who was dressed all in red.

The table hid much of Saul's girth, but a fat man at an empty table looked suspicious, so, just to blend in, he ordered the nachos grande with cheese, sour cream, and carnitas. Not to eat—the last thing he wanted was to be stuffing his face when Hernandez arrived—but she might want some. Maybe they could eat together.

At the bar, a man with his back turned had the same squat torso as Aleman, the same oblong head and thinning hair. Though the plaid shirt, untucked over faded jeans, seemed out of character for Aleman. Saul had only ever seen him uniform.

The nachos arrived. The bottom dropped out of his stomach. He had every intention of waiting for Hernandez. He was on a diet, after all. Yet, the nachos were going in his mouth. Almost involuntarily.

Basically, he had to. He would look suspicious just sitting behind a platter of nachos grande and not eating. He tried to slow down but his body demanded fuel.

The man was doing no harm at the moment, just drinking Tecate and reading his phone. If he was Aleman, then Saul should wait for Hernandez.

But what if he wasn't Aleman? What if, while Saul was sitting here gorging himself on the nachos he already regretted, Aleman was closing in on his victim?

Outside, drums hammered. Tambourines rattled. The sound of the parade moving closer. People rose from their seats.

The man who might be Aleman stood. Aleman's height. He merged into the crowd already shuffling toward the exit. Saul had to catch him before he was lost in the crowd. Time to find out if he was Aleman or not.

Saul plowed past the tables, into the crowd. Once he was in earshot, he shouted: "Hey, Aleman."

The man kept moving, out into the plaza, toward the performance at the gazebo. He seemed in no hurry.

Saul caught up to him, grabbed his shoulder, and spun him around.

"What the hell?" The man was clean shaven with a big nose, expansive forehead, and a receding hairline. Aleman's brow was narrow. And he had a mustache.

"Thought you were someone else," Saul said.

The man grumbled and turned toward the gazebo.

Saul checked his phone. The red pin was still on La Golondrina. He hurried back, and was glad to find his table as he'd left it. Still, a large portion of the nachos grande remaining for him and Hernandez to share. The table beside his had been cleared. Aside from a cellphone. The old couple must have left it.

The nachos Saul had eaten burned in his stomach. He called Aleman's number.

On the neighboring table, the phone buzzed. It chirped.

Saul snatched it up and stared at it, stared at his own number on the screen. The phone continued to vibrate and chirp in his hand.

He flagged over a waitress. "Who left this phone here?"

She reached for it. "I'll take it to the hostess in case they come back."

"I'll do it." Saul marched to the hostess stand.

He showed her his badge and pointed out the table, next to his, where the elderly couple had been sitting. "Do you have their number?"

She swiped the screen of her iPad, and showed Saul the number they had used when they made their reservation.

He dialed. It rang four times.

The woman answered.

"Where's Victor Aleman?"

"Who?"

"Victor Aleman."

"Who is this?"

Saul introduced himself and described Aleman.

"I'm sorry, but we haven't seen him. We don't know anyone like that."

Saul wasn't surprised. He thanked her, ended the call, and returned to his table.

He pocketed Aleman's phone, hunched over the nachos and plowed in.

Gray's Dilemma

Earlier that night, on the way to Dia De Los Muertos, Gray merged into the left lane, just to do something, but all four were equally slow. The alcohol had left his system and taken with it the fluid in his skull, shriveling his frontal lobe. It felt like all the cars on the 101 were plowing over it.

He checked the rear-view. Tyler was strapped in and sound asleep. Beside him, Mindy frowned. She'd complained about going to the celebration, but once she saw it, she would change her mind. They just had to get there.

He glanced over at Claire in the passenger seat. She looked up from her phone. "What?" Her thumb kept right on swiping the screen.

His chance of finishing a painting this weekend—let alone of finishing a good one—were dwindling down to impossible, and with nothing to show, not even one worthy painting to back up his plan, how could he give notice at work? How could he tell Claire? Realistically, it might take months to finish his masterpiece, and months become years. Even if his painting was amazing, even if the world agreed, Claire might not be into it. The way she had breezed right past the portrait he'd started without saying anything, said *a lot*. She might be the last person in the world who would recognize him as an artist.

He had to think from her point of view. Maybe she'd be supportive of his new direction in life, if there was something in it for her. She had griped often enough about how lucky he was to go to work, so maybe she could get a job while he stayed home to paint. He wouldn't mind more time with the kids.

"You ever think about maybe going back to work?" he asked. "You know, maybe after Tyler's old enough for daycare."

"Seriously, Gray?" Her eyes seemed to spark from the headlights in the oncoming lane.

He looked straight ahead. The car in front of him slowed to a stop, and so did he.

"Do you know how tired I am?" she continued. "I can't think about anything but sleep."

Ahead, the 101 stretched out like a serpent of red and white lights tightening around the skyscrapers downtown. He eased forward.

By far, the biggest problem was the mortgage. $4,200 a month was a tough pill to swallow, and on top of that, property tax was $950. Plus insurance premiums, utilities, car payments, and cell phones added up to another $1,500 at least. $6,700 wouldn't be a problem considering he made $12,400 per month, except after all the taxes, plus withholdings for Medicare and Social Security, his actual take-home was more like $7,900. Add then after food and daycare, most months they ended up in the red. Next fall, Mindy started kindergarten at a public school, but then he and Claire had already agreed on daycare for Tyler—$1,200 a month. And they should be saving for college, and retirement.

Even if Gray kept on working, he wasn't making enough, and there was no opportunity for a raise. He'd been passed over for enough promotions to know it would never be him, and no matter how fast he coded, Brad merely compressed the schedule such that Gray was always struggling just to keep up.

And if he quit working, their savings would be gone in

four months. Kids came with responsibilities. He knew that, and he wanted them, of course. He was the one who had to convince Claire, but somehow, in the midst of all his convincing, he'd never considered that having kids might mean sacrificing his dreams. He'd assumed he could have it all.

Gray was barreling forward when the car in front of them stopped. He slammed the brakes.

Claire grabbed his shoulder. "Shit, Gray!"

He stopped just in time. He swallowed and adjusted the rear-view mirror. Mindy's lip quivered.

"You ready to see the parade?" he asked her.

She shook her head.

"Did I mention the chocolate-covered churros?"

Mindy's lips betrayed her with an almost smile before she managed to suppress it with a clown-sized frown.

"I can turn around if you want," Gray said. "I guess we don't have to go."

"Yeah, let's just go home." Claire said. "By the time we get there, the parade will be over."

Gray shot her a look. He knew she hated downtown, but staying at home was like living in a pressure cooker. Why was it always up to him to drag them out? By the time they were driving home, they would be laughing, maybe singing, or at least everyone would be so exhausted that when they got home, he could paint.

"It's up to Mindy," Gray said. "But I should point out we don't have churros at home, and we're all out of chocolate sauce."

Now Claire shot Gray a look. *Touché*. Maybe he was being manipulative, but it was true.

"Keep going, I guess." Mindy straightened her pink dress beneath the seatbelt.

Gray chuckled, raised his eyebrows, and winked at Mindy in the mirror.

Half an hour later, he exited the 101 and rolled into a long line of cars waiting to park at El Pueblo de Los Angeles. Complete standstill.

Claire sighed deeply.

"I'm thinking I should open a bar." He just blurted it out, without even intending to say it but now that he'd said it, a certain looseness sank into his shoulders. He felt almost relieved.

"Seriously?" Claire practically shouted. "Our house *is* a bar... and you need more to drink? Seriously?"

"It's not about that. It's my job... we can't get ahead." And it was true. A bar that doubled as a studio and gallery would not only give him the time and space to paint, it could even turn a decent profit.

Claire crossed her arms. "Bull. Shit."

Gray did not want to argue in front of Mindy. In the mirror, she looked already close to losing it, and if she started crying it would upset Tyler, who was awake now and looking around.

He lowered his brows at Claire and nodded toward the back. "We should tone it down."

She rolled her eyes, like he was the one and only baby in the car. "Right." She leaned back in her seat and shut down.

Gray pulled out his phone, opened Candy Crush, and handed it back for Mindy to play under the condition that she let Tyler watch.

The primary parking lot was full. It took another twenty minutes to inch along to a dimly lit secondary lot. At the entrance to the secondary lot, the attendant, whose shaved eyebrows had been replaced by tattoos of braided barbed wire, wrapped Gray's twenty around a fat wad of bills and peeled off three ones for change.

Gray parked and unstrapped Tyler while Claire set up the stroller. He took Mindy by the hand and they followed the crowd as it wormed around a busker with long, gray hair, his guitar case opened for donations, which so far consisted of about seven dollars and some change.

Adjacent to Olvera Street was a restaurant. A barker shouted from the door, "Tacos, burritos, tamales, es deliciosa! Tacos, burritos, tamales."

Gray salivated. A burrito and basket of chips would cure his hangover, and, although he was a Scotch man, he could stomach a decent tequila. Maybe even a wine or sangria.

Too bad there wasn't time before the parade.

They followed the crowd funneling into Olvera. Mindy tugged his hand and pointed out the bricks. He explained how it had been paved by hand, and how Olvera was the oldest street in LA. He hoisted her up to his shoulders and made his way toward a kiosk selling sugar skulls and fresh baked churros.

"Ice cream!" Mindy pointed toward a window between shops. She could find ice cream in the Sahara.

"You don't want to try a churro?" Gray asked. "They're really good."

"Ice cream!" Mindy said. "They have sprinkles. I can see them from here."

Gray glanced back at Claire, who was a few yards behind with the stroller. "We're getting ice cream."

She groaned. "Of course."

At the window, Mindy ordered chocolate with extra sprinkles. When he attempted to lower her from his shoulders, she clutched his neck. "I can't eat standing up. Please, Daddy."

He laughed. "I wish someone would hold me up above the crowd."

He wrapped the cone in a stack of napkins and handed it up to Mindy.

Ahead, a face-painting booth encroached on the sidewalk, creating a narrow passage through which navigating the stroller would be difficult. Claire had stopped just short of it and parked the stroller outside a store selling Mexican blankets. She watched him approach with an expression of such intense exasperation that Gray might have laughed if it wasn't exactly the wrong thing to do.

"Want to trade?" Gray asked her, pointing at the stroller where Tyler seemed content staring up at the faces in the crowd.

Something landed on his chest and slid down his shirt. Wet, cold. It was Mindy's ice cream.

This time, she was too ashamed to protest as he lowered her to the ground.

He patted her head. "I know you didn't mean to."

He glanced up at Claire. "I'd better go wash this off," he said, already salivating for the drink he would snag on the way, and maybe a quesadilla.

"It's fine," she said. "It's dark. No one's going to notice."

"It'll stain."

She rolled her eyes. "Just hurry."

Gray started off, pumping his arms like he was jogging, though there were so many people he could hardly walk at a fast pace. While scoping out a bar, he noticed a long line for the men's room. *Better join it and see how fast it's moving.* He knew better than to come back with ice cream still on his shirt or Claire would right away know he had had a drink.

The line descended a short flight of stairs and made its way into a stone alleyway with a low, arched ceiling. The air in the alley was cold, and the ice cream on his shirt wasn't helping.

From the restaurant above, a mariachi band trumpeted, like sirens calling him. The margaritas were flowing. Tequilas, sangrias, and cervezas. A full bar, probably. Maybe even Scotch.

"Sounds like fun up there," Gray said to the guy in front of him, who was dressed like a skeleton, all black with white bones, skull mask, and top hat.

He grunted and kept right on scrolling his phone.

The line inched forward. Tucked under the stairs to the restaurant was a fortune booth with a modest sign, "El Fortunas Cinco Dilores." Below the sign was a black curtain through which a thin Latina emerged, dressed all in black. She leaned against the doorframe and looked directly at Gray.

The trumpets blasted.

She was awkwardly beautiful, with gangly arms and a nose just a little too long her face, which made her more interesting as a subject. And she showed no reaction to Gray staring at her, so maybe she was focused more on the line than on him. Hard to tell. Her eyes were shadowed by drapes of black hair. She yawned and rubbed her eyes.

Behind her, through a crack in the curtain, candlelight flickered. Gray had a feeling it was warm back there. And he needed an escape, just for a minute, and since there wasn't time for a drink, a quick fortune couldn't hurt— nothing for Claire to smell, and better for his ego. Fortunetelling was basic psychology, right? She would ask leading questions, predict a change in his future, and then he could finally tell someone that, yes, he planned on becoming an artist, somehow, full time. And, of course, she would *foresee* that he'd find great success (and a generous tip for herself).

If nothing else, it would give him a chance to study her up close. Maybe she'd let him take a photo with his phone, from which he could compose a portrait.

He tapped the skeleton guy on the shoulder.

The guy glanced up from his phone.

"I'll be back in a minute," Gray said. "Mind saving my place?"

He grunted affirmatively, sort of nodded, and went back into his phone.

Gray stepped out of line and had to restrain himself from leaping across the alley. He didn't want to scare the girl, who for sure saw him now. She averted her eyes and lifted the curtain for him to enter.

He stepped inside.

And was met with the smell of burning sage. Its smoke curling up from a ceramic smudge pot, half-encircled by prayer candles, on a small, wooden table in the corner of the narrow rectangle of a room walled in with black cloth. Through a break in the curtains, a narrow split, Gray glimpsed another room, more candlelight.

"Have a seat," the girl said. "Abuela will see you in a sec."

Gray turned to face her. "Abuela?" He felt almost duped. He wanted the girl to tell his fortune.

"My grandmother." She snaked her hands through her hair, glanced up at him and laughed. "You'll be glad when you meet her, trust me."

He swallowed his disappointment. But he was here already, so he might as well.

He paid the girl his five dollars. She parted the curtain to the inner room and slipped through.

———

Gray waited in the narrow room walled in by black cloth. He sat in the chair nearest the curtain through which the girl had disappeared, the girl who hadn't said her name. He leaned his head toward the cloth and listened hard, but the fabric dulled the whispering on the other side. He wasn't sure what he heard, if it was even words.

He inhaled the sage. The candles flickered in a draft.

What was he doing? Quitting his job? A fantasy. Nothing more. That was why he hadn't told Claire, why he couldn't tell anyone. No way to say it out loud without hearing how ridiculous it sounded.

What he had was a hobby. To think it could be something more was a pipe dream with no basis in reality. Who does that? He had not even one finished painting. It was like jumping from a plane with only some rope and nylon, and a vague idea to build a parachute on the way down.

The room felt smaller. Like the walls were drawing in.

What was he doing here? A fortune teller? Please. Like that was going to help.

As he stood to leave, the girl slid through the inner curtain, tripped, and caught herself. "Abuela is ready for you."

He opened his mouth to say he was leaving—Claire would be boiling over by now—but the girl held the curtain aside. Warm light poured in from behind her. It shimmered from hundreds, possibly thousands, of candles. His mouth remained open but no words came out. He was out of the chair. Practically floating toward the light.

Beyond the curtain, there were only fifty candles, maybe a hundred, arrayed on two shelves flanking the room. An ancient woman with hunched shoulders sat at a small, wooden table in the center. The room wasn't much bigger than the waiting area but somehow it seemed more spacious, the walls of black cloth even darker, as if they were empty space. The woman sat over a white, bowl-shaped candle, a pool of wax around its wick. The flickering light cast deep shadows between the wrinkles etched into her face. A wattle of loose skin sagged from her chin to her neck, and her eyes were milky white.

Gray had to paint her. This was more than want, more than desire... this was a need. He felt it in his heart. Would she pose for him? She was obviously blind, so he could snap her photo and she would never know.

He glanced over his shoulder. The girl had vanished behind the curtain, leaving him alone with her abuela.

"Sit, sit," she said, her voice raspy and wet. Her body was shrouded in a colorful shawl. From beneath it emerged two meaty arms sleeved in black. She reached across the table toward him, palms extended on either side of the candle.

He pulled out the chair across from her. It was low to the ground, as was the table. When he sat, he bumped his knees on the table.

As she cackled, the lines around her mouth and her eyes stretched up in pure joy. He felt warm inside, and then he started laughing, too. All he'd done was bump his knees on the table, but now it was more than that. Something had passed between them. They had shared a moment.

Her cackle sputtered into a cough. She tried to contain it as she snatched a white cloth from her shawl and covered her mouth. The cough spasmed up from deep in her chest. She shook. She had blotches on her the skin on the back of her hand.

She coughed and coughed all while her eyes seemed to probe into him. He could almost feel her gazing in. He looked away.

On the shelf to the left, marigolds had been strewn among the candles around a photograph... which at first Gray doubted. The Latino smiling out from the silver frame bathed in flickering light—it couldn't be—but there was no mistaking that cleft chin.... It must be him. It had to be him, the man whose brutal death he'd almost witnessed on Lincoln Boulevard: Luis Luna. Here, in the black-curtained back room of a fortune booth, surrounded by candles and flowers.

Gray gulped for air. The fortune teller and her milky

eyes... Somehow, she had known he would come here. She had placed this photo on the shelf for him to see, as if this were his future. A cruel fortune for five dollars.

But this was impossible. There must be some other explanation. Maybe she knew Luis Luna. Maybe he'd been a member of the community who took part in this celebration of Dia De Los Muertos. Maybe, if Gray looked around, he'd find the same photo displayed in other shrines on Olvera tonight.

After her coughing jag ended, she stuffed the handkerchief back in her shawl.

Gray asked, "Did you know him?"

She said nothing. The deep grooves in her face were like weathered rock, thousands of years old, maybe older. Why did the girl have to leave them alone?

He smelled incense. When he looked around for the source, he noticed the photo seemed to have changed. Luis Luna was still sort of smiling but now his eyes were sad, and the all the color had drained from the marigolds, like an overcast sky at dusk.

"Su nombre." The fortune teller had produced a scrap of paper and a pen. She pushed it toward him on the table.

Was this a joke? He squinted at her.

Her milky eyes seemed to gaze right through him. Maybe she would show his name to the girl, who would look him up online and find something real to put in his fortune.

He scribbled his name, sort of curious what the trick was.

Her brows furrowed. She pressed her lips tight, and a powerful emotion crossed her face, whether it was remorse, pity or a deep sadness, Gray wasn't quite sure. "I'd love to paint you," he said.

She snatched his hand and held it palm up.

"I'll do it for free," he continued. "What's the best way to contact you?"

She said nothing. With her fingertip, a hard bloodless thing of leather and bone, she traced his palm.

The silence was intense. He felt the need to say something. He swallowed, preparing to ask if he could take her picture, for reference for his portrait of her, when finally, she spoke.

"Tienes…" She seemed to struggle. "You have… eye."

Like an eye for painting? She was following the clue he'd given her. Gray chuckled, awkwardly, despite the dead serious look on her face.

"Tienes un buen corazón."

"I don't understand Spanish," he said. "No comprendo."

"Todos se aprovechan de un hombre con un buen corazón, y lo siento, pero ahora yo también debo hacerlo." She reached inside her shawl and produced a round, white, porous stone the size of an orange, flattened on top where a black was mounted, carved from obsidian. Rows of jagged ridges chiseled into its back looked like feathers. A pair of fangs protruded from its wide-open mouth.

She placed the stone in Gray's palm. It felt cool and somehow right, like it belonged there in his palm. She folded his fingers around the stone and twisted the snake a half-turn counter-clockwise. Its fangs pointed at him.

A tingling sensation nettled his palm as though his hand was falling asleep.

She spoke in soft Spanish, her voice catching on the wetness in her throat, the wattle below her chin trembling.

He nodded, not understanding a word. Her hands were cold and leathery, like mitts pressed around his hand that held the stone.

She began singing in an unfamiliar language. Her eyes closed. Beyond the candlelight, a deep blackness seemed to open up, as if the room were floating in space.

The stone warmed in his palm. The tingling sensation slid up his arm, along the back of his neck. The candles faded away.

He drifts on a cloud. Below him is LA…

He sees a garden, a grassy hill warmed by the setting sun, overlooking the city and the sea. And now he's standing at an easel. His easel. His painting of the dark figure is nearly complete. The figure comes into focus: a short man with brown skin, not much older than a boy, standing in the shadow of an immense stone temple. His expression is placid, but his eyes… his eyes are solid black, deeper than night. Not eyes at all—they're holes.

Behind Gray, a door closes. He spins toward the sound. Above the garden, stands a modern looking house with a wall of dark windows and a turret. The old woman descends the steps from the patio and approaches him with a glass of deep-red wine. She hands it to him. Her expression is somber in the waning light, which seems to smooth the wrinkles on her face, and her eyes are now dark pools. They take him in, all that he is, as he drinks the blood-red wine.

It tastes of nothing. He gulps and his mouth remains dry. He holds up the glass. Instead of wine, it contains a milk-like vapor that swirls like fog in the glass.

She extends her wrinkled hand and takes the glass from him. She drinks.

Gray opened his eyes. He was seated again before the fortune teller, back among the black curtains and the candles. She had stopped singing. Her pupils were frosted again. Seeing nothing.

The marigolds were bright orange and red, but as he watched, they faded. Incense burned his eyes. He blinked. "I must have drifted off…"

She had withdrawn her hands from his fist. The stone felt cold in his palm. The snake had been mounted such that it could rotate like a dial, and he had a vague notion that if he did so, the stone would somehow pull him back into the dream. *Was it a dream?* It had felt like one, yet he'd been wide awake. He wanted another look at the painting—his painting. If he could recreate what he'd seen and maybe give the man some eyes, it could be his masterpiece.

Gray traced his finger along the snake, along the ridges of the feathers chiseled in the obsidian. He nudged the head, which gave only a token resistance and then started to turn.

"No!" The fortune teller's hands pounced on his, gripping his hands with surprising strength. Her milky eyes remained fixed, unfocused. How had she known he was twisting it?

It was a foolish notion anyway to think this thing could help him see what he'd obviously dreamed. She pried his fingers from the snake, although there was no need. He was going to give it back to her. But when he tried to, she jerked away.

"Lo siento, lo siento," she said. "Destroy! Nada vale la pena abrir las puertas de Xibalba. Lo sé, créeme. Lo siento." Tears streamed down her weathered cheeks. She balled her fist and brought it down like a hammer above the charm, which was still in his palm. She repeated the motion, then mimed twisting the snake-dial and fiercely shook her head.

"No entiendo," he said. "I don't understand. No hablo."

"Abuela! No se puede dar!" the girl said.

Gray turned in his chair. The girl had emerged through the curtain.

"Hice!" the fortune teller said.

"What is it?" he asked.

The girl shrank away from him. "She should not have given it to you. You must destroy it."

If they were so afraid of this thing, why keep it around? "Do you have a hammer?"

The fortune teller shouted hoarsely in Spanish.

"It is yours now," the girl translated. "You must do this yourself."

"Uh…" Gray looked down at the stone charm in his palm. Didn't he have enough to deal with already?

"Time for you to go." The girl held open the curtain.

She was right about that. How long had he been here?

He considered just leaving the charm on the table. It looked like it was worth more than the five dollars he'd paid for the fortune he hadn't received.

The fortune teller set her jaw, and the girl avoided his eyes. He had the feeling they would freak out if he tried leaving without it.

As he stepped out through the curtain, the fortune teller shouted after him, "No te utilizarlo!"

Outside the booth, he was assaulted by the sounds of the parade, which somehow the curtains had muffled. His hangover, which he'd almost forgotten about, returned with a vengeance. The drums pounded in his skull, making him dizzy. He leaned against the cobbled wall.

Was that all a performance? The fortune teller had

seemed for real. Her tears had been real. If that was acting, she should get an agent—she and her granddaughter.

Gray clutched the porous stone and hefted it in his hand. It was surprisingly light.

The line for the bathroom was just as long as before. No sign of the skeleton guy who was supposed to hold his place. He'd have to tell Claire that he waited but the line just wasn't moving.

He pushed off the wall and turned toward the street, colliding with a stocky man whose head hit Gray's chin.

They both stepped back. The man had wild eyes and dried mucus in his mustache. He was dressed as an officer, his uniform disheveled and untucked. He apologized and asked for the time.

Gray checked his phone. Texts from Claire filled the screen:

In the plaza near gazebo.

Ready to go.

Where are you?

"It's 7:30," Gray said.

"Where are we?" The officer looked around like he'd just dropped out of the sky. His badge featured the California golden bear encircled with the words "*Sheriff Los Angeles County.*" It looked too real for a costume.

"Are you okay?" Gray asked.

"Yeah, I'm fine. I just..." He wiped sweat off his forehead into his thinning hair. "I was... in an accident."

"I'll call an ambulance."

"No no. If you could just show me where I am?"

"You're lost?"

"I don't know. I was walking, and... I don't know. I spaced out, I guess."

Gray showed him the map on his phone. "You're basically downtown."

"That's what I thought. It's the parade. You know? I got

turned around." He stood there with his mouth half open as if trying to remember what he was about to say.

"I've got to go," Gray said. Claire was already upset. "Sure you don't want me to call anyone?"

"I'm fine," he said, still looking confused.

Gray exited the alley. The main part of the parade had passed, and the crowd was joining up behind it, some carrying tambourines and gourd rattles. Paper mâché skeletons bobbed and swayed to the beat.

Gray drifted into the procession milling toward the plaza. He rubbed his thumb along the porous stone.

It fit in his pocket, but Claire would notice the bulge.

She might not be mad anymore. He could picture them in the plaza: Mindy in awe of the parade, Tyler asleep in his stroller—he could sleep through anything, the louder the better—and Claire on her phone scrolling through the endless feed of Ashley York.

He could spare two minutes to figure out what to do with this thing he didn't want but which felt wrong to just leave in the street. He slipped out of the procession and into a gap between kiosks to study the snake. It must have taken hours to carve, maybe days.

It was a shame to destroy it. And why should he? Why him? If they wanted it smashed so badly, why give it away? Why advise against twisting the snake-dial yet also show him how. The fortune teller had placed it in his palm and turned it herself.

He was he never going to get ahead in life doing what other people told him. If he lacked the nerve to turn a dial, which probably did nothing at all, how was he ever going to quit his job?

With his index finger, he traced the *S* of the snake. A sense of dread welled up inside him. He clenched his jaw. No old woman's hands to stop him now. He had to do this. Or he'd never change. He might as well keep living his life the same old way.

The snake faced him, almost grinning. He poked it in the head. It spun from the six o'clock position to the twelve, where the flattened tear shape on top came to a point.

Inside the stone, something clicked.

Something stabbed Gray's palm.

He flipped the charm over. On the bottom, little holes in the stone traced the pattern of a spiral. He rubbed his palm on his shirt and examined the wound. It looked minor—just a tiny streak of blood near in the meat near his thumb—and yet it burned all out of proportion, as if his whole hand were in flames.

The shutters slammed shut on the kiosk beside him. The person inside it switched off the lights.

Hair prickled on the back of his neck. Across the street, a blackness filled the alley so dark it swallowed all nearby light. He shivered.

He marched toward the crowd amassing at the plaza, with a fear growing inside him that someone was watching, which made no sense, but what if they were? He couldn't just lead them to his family.

He forced himself to stop. To turn his head. To look around.

No one seemed to notice him. They were all absorbed in the festivities, or their family and friends or their phones. The fortune teller had spooked him was all. Nothing to be afraid of.

He shuddered and started to run.

A Different World

Ashley awakens to a pain in her right hand. Like something pricked her palm while she was sleeping. How could that have happened?

She stretches her legs, which feel oddly big, and something blocks her feet. She rolls on her side and feels and unfamiliar fabric on her legs—jeans? Is she wearing jeans? After having sex with August last night, he'd mumbled something about being on set early and left, and she specifically remembers slipping on a pair of black panties. That's all she ever slept in.

She opens her eyes... and is greeted by beige carpet and kids toys strewn all around a coffee table, which is covered with a mishmash of magazines and coloring books, as if deliberately disarranged to get on her nerves. On top is the *Vanity Fair* with Jennifer Lawrence.

She leaps to her feet. Above her, a low ceiling hangs unreasonably close. Her legs are wrong, way, way wrong. Too thick and long, and the jeans are baggy. She doesn't *own* baggy jeans. And it's not just her legs: her whole body feels off. She stumbles back onto the faded gray couch she'd woken up on and has never before seen in her life. *What the hell? What is going on?* Her hands are man's hands. She holds them in front of her face. Dark, unsightly hair on every knuckle, even the pinky. And on her ring finger, a wedding band. Yellow gold. Who wears yellow gold?

She rubs her eyes. Her cheeks feel like sandpaper. Is that stubble? And her nose… it's too wide. Her brow is bony. Her whole face feels unfamiliar, wrong, wrong, wrong-wrong-wrong.

She leaps off the couch again, and it's like these legs, which are definitely not her legs, know what to do. They take a step forward, a wide stride, unsteady. She forces her next step to be shorter, like her normal walk, and stumbles. Catches herself on one knee and rises again. *Just focus on where you're going.* One step, then another. She lets this awfully wrong body lope along in its strange, gangly way, an unnatural stiffness in the right knee.

She reaches a dim and depressingly narrow hallway with an even lower ceiling than the den where she awoke, if she's even awake, which she better not be. *I can't be. No way.*

The door on the right is half-open. It's a minuscule bathroom. She pushes in and flips on the light.

The man in the mirror has thin, brown hair and frantic eyes that widen as she raises her brows. She shakes her head, and he mocks her by mimicking the action—he *is* her.

She falls into the wall and screams. But the pitch of her voice is too low, as if she's screaming with his voice. She pinches her forearm. *Time to wake up….*

She doesn't wake up. Instead, she feels pain. She squeezes the skin between her fingertips. More pain. Real pain. This man—she is this man!

"What the fuck, Gray?" A woman with dark tangled hair shoves in through the door, her hands balled into fists and her eyes electric, practically sparking with blue light, like she's super pissed, like any of this is Ashley's fault. "You woke up Tyler."

Who the hell is Tyler? "Who the hell are you?" Ashley asks with the stubbled face in the mirror and the voice that's not like her voice at all.

The woman crosses her arms over her shapeless blue night shirt. "Why are you acting so weird?"

"Are you kidding me? What the hell is going on?"

"Did you throw up?" the woman asks. "I told you not to eat that burrito."

"No, I—" Ashley raises the pitch of her voice, struggling to make her voice sound normal. "I'm Ashley York." Her voice cracks.

"Are you trying to be funny?"

"No! Who is he?" She points at the man in the mirror. The man points back. *This is not real. It can't be real.* It's a nightmare, that's all. So why can't she wake up?

As Ashley tries to leave the bathroom, the dumbfounded woman stands in her way. Ashley plows past her, willing this man's body in this nightmare to run. It strides into action down the narrow hallway, and she's carried along inside it, feeling the exertion in the legs that aren't hers. They feel heavy. Her whole body feels heavy and slow and out of shape.

She flees through the front door and stumbles around the minivan, which barely fits in the short driveway. The street is unfamiliar. She looks up and down the hill. Where the hell is she going? Where is she?

From the house across the street, an elderly man emerges and cuts across the lawn toward Ashley. "Morning, Gray," he shouts.

"I don't know you," she says. *Gray?* Does everyone see this man's body instead of her?

The old man keeps on coming. He's frail and stooped and wearing a brown suit so old it looks retro.

He steps off the curb. "I should have told you yesterday, but I moved Lynda's car to the street because there was... It was an accident... and this crazy officer, I think he's after me."

Ashley backs away.

The old man creeps toward her. "I didn't mean to. Okay? Alright?"

Ashley runs. From the man, from everything, from this person who everyone seems to see instead of her.

For lack of anywhere else to go, she dashes back into the house she woke up in, through cluttered, claustrophobic rooms condensed into a floor plan smaller than her den, until she finds a bedroom. She locks the door, kicks her way through the wrinkled clothes strewn all over the floor, and plops down on the bed.

I just have to go back to sleep. If she goes to sleep, this nightmare will end. Obviously. Sleep put her here into this body, into this life, this world, that isn't hers, and sleep will get her out again.

But as she climbs under the covers, someone pounds on the door. "Gray?" the woman calls. "Gray, I know you're sick, but I still need help with the kids."

"Go away."

"Why is the door locked? *We don't lock doors.* You're breaking your own rule."

"I need to sleep."

"Take some Ibuprofen. It's too late now."

Ashley ignores her, and her hammering on the door. She imagines herself in her own house—her immaculate house—in her big white bed where she belongs.

A baby screams through the thin walls of the house, and the woman stops pounding on the door. Ashley would scream too if it would do any good. Tears stream down her cheeks. She closes her eyes and focuses on how she should look in the mirror: blonde hair and unblemished skin, the woman she's always been and still is.

She can't relax. The linens on the bed scratch her skin, like they have a thread count of like yarn. She throws them off. The awful underwear she's wearing fits like it's two sizes too small.

The baby stops crying and is replaced by the sound of the woman cooing through the wall. The din of cars on a highway sound like they're right behind the house.

She had made this body run, more or less, but she can't make it sleep—or make herself sleep. She can't even settle on how to think of herself now, just like she can't focus on remembering how she looks, because she's in a man's body now. *What the fuck?*

The woman returns to the door and pounds harder, as hard as the heart that isn't Ashley's is pounding against her ribcage, pumping someone else's blood through her head. Sleep is not an option. Not now. Anyway, who ever heard of going to sleep in a nightmare? She has to face this, somehow. She's got to do something.

Ashley climbs from the bed and jerks open the door.

The woman's eyes flash. "Don't ignore me, Gray." She clutches her phone in her fist like a weapon, like she might actually use it to club Ashley.

Ashley snatches the phone, ducks around the woman, and lunges down the hallway.

"What the hell?" the woman yells after her. She pursues Ashley into the living room. "Who are you calling?"

The Face ID refuses to unlock. The phone demands a passcode.

She holds the phone toward the woman's face, hoping to unlock it. The woman grabs her arm and tries to wrench the phone away. "What's got into you, Gray?"

"I told you. I'm Ashley York. I need to call someone to come get me."

The woman, with surprising strength, pries the phone from Ashley's fingers and steps back. "Are you making fun of me? Yeah, I'm into celebrity gossip, so what? At least I'm not shutting myself in the garage all the time." The baby has started crying again and the woman turns toward the hallway. "Why don't you help instead of acting like a jerk?"

"Oh, so you won't let me make one call and I'm the jerk?" Ashley says, but the woman has already hurried away.

There's got to be another phone here. Ashley looks around the couch where she woke up, or dreamed she woke up, or whatever. On the cluttered coffee table, on top of a coloring book right next to the *Vanity Fair* is an iPhone.

Ashley holds it up to her face that isn't her face. The phone unlocks.

There's only like four contacts: Claire, Dad Wilson, Leonardo, Mom Wilson, and Steve... and, of course, Ashley doesn't know who any of them are. She also doesn't recall the numbers for anyone she knows. Not even her own number, which she just changed because some jerk posted her old one online. She'd always had everything she needed right there, synced across her devices, people she could call would come help her at a moment's notice. But now she's lost access to her life?

What if this is real? It seems like it's going on too long to be a dream. What if she's stranded in this strange body forever?

She collapses on the couch and rubs her face in her hands, then pulls her hands away in shock when she feels the coarse, bristly cheeks. She closes her eyes and tries dialing her dad's personal line on an imaginary keypad. She pretends she's a girl again, calling him at work. She can see her little finger pressing buttons, but she can't visualize the numbers. They're lost in the past. She must have been seven or eight the last time she manual-dialed, before he gave her her first phone, a pink flip-phone with his number programmed as contact number one.

She opens her eyes. Still under the claustrophobically low ceiling—still in this man's body. The question is, what happened to her body? Does it even still exist? What if this Gray dude has it?

She has to find a way home.

She glances at the wrinkled shirt she's wearing. A black t-shirt with a stain of what looks like chocolate down the front. Dream or not, she can't go out like this.

She hurries back to the bedroom. The clothes on the floor are all women's, as are those in the closet, which won't do. Everyone will think she's this Gray dude, won't they?

In the hall closet, she finds a stack of t-shirts, a few button downs on hangers, and three pairs of dark blue men's Levi's—who still wears Levi's? Better than nothing. She grabs a pair and tugs them on over the awful underwear. She chooses one of the least offensive button downs, a brown one, and impulsively checks the tag, which is faded and unreadable, and anyway, who cares?

She yanks off the stained shirt and ducks into the bathroom to line up the buttons in the mirror. Gray—or is it her?—looks pretty good in the shirt. *Him.* She can't start thinking of this body as herself. She needs to get *her* body back—and she's going to do that how?

She opens the door and inhales a deep breath. *One step at a time, Ashley.*

What she needs is a car. She searches around and finds a set of keys on a little table by the front door. As she snatches them up and heads out, the woman storms after her. "Where are you going?"

Better just to play along with her narrative. The last thing Ashley needs is this woman freaking out and trying to follow her or something. "Work."

"It's Sunday."

This situation is so ridiculous that she hasn't even considered the day of the week. She snatches the keys. "Yeah, well, doesn't matter."

She steps outside, ignoring whatever the woman says, and closes the door behind her.

Gray Day

The sound of water splashing. The hum of bugs all around. A pillowy bed perched on the bank of a river. Dark water flowing languidly through a warm afternoon. The long slow notes of a bird. Gray leans his head back in the pillow, scans up the banana tree above the bed, and finds a yellow bird. Its song trails off. Then, from higher up, the song is continued.

He sits up. Beside the bed is a table with a bottle of wine and a papaya sliced in half. Beside that, on an easel, is a painting, which he must have started before drifting off. It's the scene right before him, except standing by the river is Laura, smiling, just like when they'd arrived in Paris for the summer of their sophomore year.

And then he hears her. He actually hears Laura laughing —she's here. She's in the river, splashing with three umber-colored boys. She beckons for Gray to join her.

He pats the bed beside him. *Come up and dry off.*

She laughs.

Gray picks up a papaya half, holds it out, and with his other hand, motions her toward the bed.

She shouts that the water is perfect, dives under, and disappears below the dark water.

Gray wants, no *needs* more than anything, to be with her there in the water when she comes up for air. He runs toward the bank. The boys cheer. He dives in.

The water is cold.

It wakes him up. He blinks in the harsh sunlight.

No wonder you can't sleep. "Why did you open the curtains?" he asks Claire.

He closes his eyes, but even through his lids the light feels too bright. He turns his head away, pulls up the covers, and nestles into the pillow. If he could just go back to sleep, to Laura… but there's too much sunlight on his face.

Yet even with the curtains open, their bedroom doesn't get direct sunlight until late in the morning, almost noon. He bolts upright.

"Claire?"

She's not beside him. And this bed, it's giant. It has a plush white comforter. He's in a vast, airy bedroom. Cream-white curtains frame cathedral-sized windows, six of them. Outside, a green hill rises to a blue horizon. Sunlight fills the sky.

Across the round room is a chaise lounge, also white, and a daybed buried beneath neatly stacked pink pillows.

This cannot be real.

Last night, after they'd put the kids to bed, he'd decided a drink was in order, which was followed by an argument with Claire—about what, he can't remember. If not for the Scotch, they probably wouldn't have argued at all. He has no memory of going to sleep, or leaving the house. Certainly not of coming here. Which is where?

He climbs off the bed, expecting to find his clothes on the floor where he'd normally leave them, but the floor is bare, blond wood, and his feet… they're slender, too tan—not his feet at all!

Dizzy, he breathes fast with seemingly no air reaching his lungs.

Slow down. Breathe slow. He must be hungover, more than ever before. The alcohol leaving his system is making him see things that aren't real, some kind of short-circuit in his synapses. That's what this is. A waking dream.

He rests his hands on his hips—but they're not his hips. They're wide, curving out from a slender waist. *This cannot be! What is happening?*

Heart pounding, he looks down… Protruding from his chest is a pair of breasts—naked breasts. He cups them in his hands. *Must find a mirror.*

As he lifts his right foot, his leg feels unexpectedly limber. His heel hits the wood. His foot pivots, and he bounces—too high—and tries to correct as his left foot lands, sending him stumbling. He starts again. By giving into the movement, although it feels foreign to him, it works —left-foot bounce, right-foot run. It's automatic, controlled by some part of the brain that operates below his level of consciousness.

The bedroom has three doors. He opens the middle one to find a tiled bathroom the size of a spa, blue and white mosaic on the floor.

He approaches the mirror above the sink and sees not his reflection but a brown-eyed blonde, a girl he knows but can't quite place. *Is this a dream? A lucid dream?*

He admires her half-naked figure—flat stomach, bony hips supporting the thin straps of lace panties. He grabs a lock of long, salon-perfect hair and pulls, half-expecting a wig to come off or maybe a mask, maybe a whole suit. It hurts, like pulling his own actual hair—it *is* his hair.

This somewhat familiar girl in the mirror is him, somehow. Although she's not him. Or is he her? Are they her breasts or his?

He pinches a nipple—it stiffens. It hurts. These breasts are definitely a part of his body. He squeezes them, and the sensation of the skin from the touch of his hands is unreal— it's amazing.

Intricate.

Vivid, in every detail.

In dreams, things seem to change every time you look, but this is solid, real. And he feels more awake than ever. He never knew a dream could be like this… but perhaps they all are? Perhaps they only fade upon waking.

He's dreamed of women, of course, but *being* a woman?

Crazy. And then to know he's dreaming while still dreaming —insane!

He leans toward the mirror and gazes into her-his chestnut irises. So clear.

Gray's mouth goes dry. When he tries to swallow, his front teeth are too big. His slides his tongue over them, and they feel too big, too. These are not his teeth. This isn't him.

He leaves the bedroom and follows a hallway to an interior balcony that overlooks an immense living room. Sunlight filters through a wall of windows, across polished wood floors. He descends the curved stairway and passes a loveseat, an ottoman, and a white-linen couch submerged, almost entirely, by pastel-colored pillows.

In front of the couch is a glass coffee table framed with silvery metal, on which dozens of lifestyle magazines are fanned out in a neat arc. This house should be featured in one of them. Hell, it belongs on the cover.

Outside the windows, an expansive lawn stretches out between rows of palms and slops out of sight. A distant ridgeline rolls down into a brownish haze which almost obscures the city below. LA, probably, SoCal for sure, from the looks of the dry scrub on the ridge, but not his neighborhood—not even close.

He crosses the room to the French doors and steps out onto the patio, where he can almost taste the moisture in the air from the lawn sprinklers. All he needs is an easel and this will be like his dream from last night in the fortune booth. Crazy—he's remembering a dream within a dream. But then, doesn't everything seem familiar in dreams? Because you always dream of things you've seen before.

So, where is he?

Claire probably has every one of the magazines on the coffee table. So maybe this place is in one of them? As he turns to go check, the sound of whistling rises above the swish from the sprinklers. A familiar tune.

From around the corner of the house strides a muscular, black man in a security uniform, his head shaved bald. When he notices Gray, he stops abruptly and shields his eyes to the sun. His mouth drops open.

He cuts across the lawn, jogging through a sprinkler to reach the patio. *Mission Impossible*, Gray realizes. The security guard was whistling the theme song to *Mission Impossible*.

"Ashley," he shouts, "is everything okay?"

Ashley York. Gray remembers now: he should have known right away. It was definitely her face in the mirror, Claire's idol, Ashley York. Somehow, he is in her body.

"Ashley?" The guard runs a hand over his scalp, his wet shirt clinging to his torso, and stares—at Gray's chest.

Gray wonders if he should feel embarrassed since it's not actually his body that's practically naked, but still, he crosses his arms over his breasts. "I'm fine," he says, with a voice that's not his.

If this is a dream, he *should* be waking up in a cold sweat right about now.

The guard inhales. Places a tentative hand on Gray's shoulder. "Girl, let's get you inside."

Gray allows himself to be steered back in through the French doors. With each step, he can almost feel the guard's eyes on his butt, the revealing lace panties.

Inside, the guard releases Gray's shoulder, and follows close behind, almost too close. *Where are we going?* Gray stops and turns to face the guard.

The man's eyes dart from Gray to the floor to the kitchen. "Where's Andrea?"

"Andrea?" *Who's Andrea?*

The guard whistles. "Girl, what did you get into last night?"

Last night, Gray got into the Scotch, nothing unusual about that, but, of course, there was also the white stone with the snake mounted on top, its fangs practically sneering. The old fortune teller had begged him to destroy it, but instead of heeding her warning, he'd spun the chiseled snake, expecting nothing to happen. And nothing had happened... at least, not until now.

Had she known he'd awaken in Ashley York's body? And if so, how could this have caused her so much distress? *This is incredible.* It could be an even more amazing experience if not for the guard's eyes probing the lace panties and then crawling up Gray's midriff to hover around the breasts, which are technically Ashley's.

The guard lifts his gaze, and they lock eyes. His brows mash together. "Do you want me to... I don't know?"

Gray swallows, his heart hammering in his ears. "I should get dressed."

The guard's eyes dart to the floor. He starts toward the kitchen. "I'll find Andrea for you."

Gray hurries toward the stairs.

In the bedroom, he grabs the phone by the nightstand and opens Instagram which comes up on the account for Ashley York and now there is no doubt. He is her. In her body. So, if this isn't a dream, what does it mean for him? For his life? His body?

He dials his own number, but who does he expect to answer?

The question staggers him. He's seen enough science fiction to guess it could be another version of himself, like from a parallel universe, or maybe he and the Ashley York swapped bodies. What will he say? What can he say? *Hello, I am the real Gray Wilson. Who the hell are you?*

After five rings, when his voicemail picks up, he releases the breath he's holding and ends the call.

But what if no one answered because there *is no one* to answer? What if his body vanished in the night? Or what if, it's like *It's A Wonderful Life*—to everyone else he never existed at all?

He has to know.

After another full ring, with phone-glued-to-hand Claire still not answering, he begins to worry. What if his whole life doesn't exist?

She answers the call. "Who is this?"

He swallows. He can't speak with his own voice, but he has to know if his life as he knew it still exists. "Is Gray there?"

"Who is this?" she asks again.

What can he say? He can't get side-tracked trying to convince her. He just needs to know. "May I please speak with him?"

"I'm going to hang up if you don't tell me who you are."

"I'm—" He was about to invent a friend from work, but Claire would see through the lie in an instant. "He's there, right?"

"Why would I tell you?" She sounded annoyed and maybe a little suspicious.

If he had disappeared, she'd be freaking out. That meant his body is there, but who is it? Some parallel-universe version of him, or is it Ashley, or maybe it's just on autopilot? It wouldn't take much to slog through a Sunday without raising Claire's suspicion.

"How would you like to earn a thousand dollars for five minutes of your time? I'm conducting a survey—"

"Nope." Claire hangs up.

At least his life is there, but how can he get back to it? The charm. When the fortune teller placed the porous stone in his hand, she'd dialed the obsidian snake a half turn. Maybe that's all he has to do and then everything returns to normal. It would be easy to try, if he had any idea where he put damn thing after the parade.

He could also sneak around the side of their house and spy in, but then what? Claire would freak if she saw Ashley York. And what was that show in which a guy from a parallel universe came in, took over the real guy's life, and murdered him? Is that what the fortune teller was worried about?

Tomorrow, the house should be empty when Claire takes Mindy to daycare, but how can he wait until then?

He glances around the circular bedroom with all the sunlight streaming in through the drapes over the matching white furniture. On the nightstand beside the bed is a pink vape pen with a silver mouthpiece. He reaches for it. Presses the button. The heating element glows electric blue.

He inhales just a little of the steam it produces. It tastes vaguely of peaches... no, definitely peaches but with a musky aftertaste.

He flops back on bed, closes his eyes, and exhales as he nestles into the down comforter. His scalp tingles, like his hair is lifting off his head.

I needed this. A day for himself. For so long, he'd needed a break from his life where Claire hardly cared if he came home or not and couldn't give him ten minutes alone. He never had time to paint. He needs a break from all the wasted hours of working and writing code, which only gets rewritten by someone else anyway.

He takes another drag.

It all seems like a dream, now. How can you ever really know for sure that you're awake? He runs his fingers through his hair. It's long, sleek, and thick, as though transformed by some styling process into golden Taklon.

Is he really a woman? He doesn't actually feel any different.

"Ms. Ashley?" A waif-thin woman, who looks to be in her early twenties, appears in the half-open door to the hallway, her brown hair pulled back tight into a ponytail.

Gray launches to his feet, pulls the comforter from the bed and covers himself. "What's up?"

"What shall I make for breakfast?" The woman, who must be Andrea, asks with an accent that sounds somewhat European.

"Right," Gray says. He could get used to this. "I'll have an omelet."

Her eyes flicker, but her oval face remains blank. "You do not like eggs."

Gray scratches his head. "What do I normally eat?"

She leans forward and squints. "Maca smoothie-bowl."

Since she thinks he's Ashley, it means she works for him, so she'll make whatever he wants, right? But maybe he should try the bowl. Could be better than an omelet for all he knows.

"Sounds good," he says. "Are there any paint supplies here?"

She glances around the room. "You are tired of white?"

"No, I mean acrylics. It's a beautiful day. I want to setup an easel on the lawn."

She squints at him and then at the vape on the bed. She laughs, dryly, as if obligated to laugh.

"No, I'm serious," he says, but then he starts laughing too. He can't help it. It's the expression of pure bewilderment on her face. *She has no idea.*

She laughs for real this time, her face turning beet red, then she regains her composure and backs out through the door. "You need eat before your massage," she says and shuts it behind her.

To resist the temptation of another toke, he opens the nightstand drawer and shoves the vape inside it. While it's open, he notices a remote control. He presses the power button, and a screen descends from the ceiling, lit up with icons for all the various streaming platforms.

He opens Netflix and chooses an episode of *Black Mirror*. When it starts playing, he realizes he's seen it before, but now the idea of a fabricated human, who looks and acts exactly like your deceased loved-one, no longer seems far-fetched—not after he's awakened in the body of Ashley York.

He can't relax. Instead of the show, he keeps picturing the look of distress on the fortune teller's face, and his mind keeps racing. He should try and find her—but what's the point? He's sure he needs the charm, and didn't he already decide to wait until tomorrow to go home? Doesn't he deserve to enjoy himself? Just for a little while?

He goes into the bathroom to splash water on his face. He dries off by the giant tub sunken into the tile. Claire always took baths to relax. If he's ever going to try it, now's the time. He turns on the faucet and adjusts the temperature. He bends over and slides the panties down his legs, and as he does so, the lack of his usual anatomy disorients him, and he almost falls. He plops himself down on a white stool by the sinks.

A thin line of white skin cuts between the deep tan of his stomach and legs. He runs his finger over it, pausing at the trimmed strip of light hair leading down. His pulse throbbing.

He feels guilty. He wouldn't want Ashley toying around with his body. And what if she can see what he's doing? What if she's trapped in the back of her mind with him in control?

He sighs. Just a bath. That's all. Nothing wrong with that. He'll just relax for a few minutes and that's it.

He eases himself into the hot water. Ashley's nipples peek above the water. The controls for the tub are conveniently located by his right hand. He activates the jets. A current gushes between his legs, surprisingly well-aimed. It creates a tingling sensation that almost tickles, but in a good way. He turns up the pressure of the jets.

It feels… amazing.

All over his body.

He slides his fingers down his side, across his hips. The sensation of touching a woman and feeling his touch as a woman is overpowering. He hadn't planned on reaching down—he really was just going to take a bath, but now—now-now-now—now he must. Doesn't matter if Ashley can see this. Probably she's in his body, probably right now fondling his erection, enjoying it as if it's hers.

Ashley's legs are his legs now, and the slipperiness between them—that's his. He slides his fingers into it… and draws upwards. Grazing the nub of flesh, he inhales sharply. Sensitive. And the feeling isn't just there at the surface, it goes deep inside. Is this the way Claire feels when they make love? Do all women feel like this?

The sensation builds and builds throughout his body. Not like the out-of-control-all-at-once male orgasm. He moans, and his moan is her voice—begging for more. With one hand, he increases the pressure of the water jets and with his other, he increases the rhythm.

His fingers keep moving, keep pressing as the pulsing energy builds from deep inside… Waves crash through him from his thighs to his head. He screams, gasps.

Water splashes onto the floor.

His pelvis shakes uncontrollably.

A wave of relaxation washes through him. Every muscle in his body seems to loosen.

His throat burns and then he chokes back a sob. *What am I doing?* Here he is with the time to finally do whatever he wants, and what does he do? Abuse a body that's not even his.

He climbs out of the tub, towels off, and dresses as fast as he can.

Sammy

The dog, which looked to be mostly pitbull, licked Sammy's hand as he scratched under her chin. He slid open the window to the guard booth, popped his second Red Bull for the day, and leaned back in his chair. The dog raised her big, black head and sniffed at the air.

Sammy gulped the fortified soda, but the rush of sugar and caffeine only served to perplex him. He'd fantasized countless scenarios in which Ashley came onto him, yet he'd never in a million years imagined that she might just walk out of her house practically nude.

He would've taken her too, right there on the patio, but she hadn't seemed to know where she was. Of course, he could have pushed the situation, but he didn't want to push. In the long run, he knew that pushing would get him nowhere. He wanted to be pulled into her. She was the boss, and it would have to be on her terms.

So here he was, day after day, telling Greta that he was close to his big break when he wasn't close to anything like that. All he cared about getting close to was Ashley York, with her skin tanned to the color of honey—probably tasted like honey too.

She'd stood there with her breasts out, but the look on her

face had been pure confusion, and when she noticed him running toward her, it became fear. After all the effort he'd put in, always smiling and kind, for her be afraid of him… nothing could be worse. He downed the Red Bull and crushed the can.

His phone rang. *Greta.* He crushed the can, tossed it in the recycle bin, snatched another from the mini-fridge, and answered.

"What are you doing?" Greta asked.

"Working."

"Working on making something of yourself or sitting there staring off into space?"

"Right now, I'm trying to find a home for this dog."

"It's still there? Ashley told you to get rid of it. This is what I'm talking about."

Sammy closed his eyes. "Look, I was thinking, she's a friendly girl—part black lab, I think—we should adopt her."

"Adopt a dog? Are you serious? I'm going to have your baby. And you think I have time for a dog too?"

He rubbed his forehead. "You're not even pregnant."

"Who's fault is that?"

Maybe it was his fault, technically, but she wasn't exactly helping the situation. "We agreed the extra OT was a good thing."

"Yeah, six months ago. It's time Ashley sees you as more than just another Black ass in a uniform."

Greta wouldn't be pushing so hard if she had any clue that the OT was just an excuse to spend all his waking hours at Ashley's. If he could just sleep here—probably, no one would notice if he slept in the guest house, and he could tell Greta it was a promotion—then he wouldn't have drive all the way back to their the shitty duplex in Inglewood, where she was always pushing him to rise above a life he hardly lived.

But she was right: you had to push to make something of yourself—at least, they did—and he wasn't pushing hard enough. That was the problem. He didn't care.

All he cared about was Ashley. He should not be thinking these thoughts, but he couldn't help it. They were consuming him.

"You hearing me, Sammy? Ashley York tells you to get rid of a dog, it's gone. Just drive it off somewhere and let it go. The dog's not your problem. Your problem is getting noticed. If you can't even handle a simple order, Ashley will never hook you up. How are we supposed to support a child on your shitty paycheck? I quit my career for this!"

"I gotta go," he lied.

He was sick of hearing about all Greta's unrealized expectations for him. All the trying so hard, for so long, to get nowhere. Why couldn't things just come easy for him like they did for Ashley? As she had appeared on the patio in those panties, hardly more than a scrap of black lace.

He hung up and crushed the third Red Bull of the day.

Maybe he didn't mean much to Ashley now, but there was a reason why she wanted him on OT and not Franco. And maybe he could ride that good vibe. Maybe she *would* hook him up with some kind of big-league gig where he wore a suit and had his own people who answered to him… and then she'd see him differently.

A Camry turned into the driveway. Unannounced guests were rare, and Sammy doubted that anyone Ashley knew would drive a Camry.

As it slowed toward the guard booth, the dog leaped up on the windowsill and started barking. The guy behind the wheel lowered his window. His hair was tousled, and he looked stressed. Ashley's fans who found their way here were usually women from somewhere in the Midwest, thinking they could hang with Ashley just because they were friends on social media or whatever.

Sammy stood and patted the dog's head. "Good girl," he said softly. "I'm thinking Ashley will change her mind once she sees you're a guard dog."

The guy in the car frowned. "Why is that dog still here?"

Sammy furrowed his brows and pulled the dog back from the window. *How does he know?* Ashley must have posted something, obviously. She shared everything on social media.

"Are you just here to check on the dog?"

The guy leaned out the window and raised his brows. "*It's me*," he said emphatically, and pointed at his face. "I'm Ashley."

Sammy had encountered his share of stalkers, but this was a first. "And here I thought I was having a crazy day, but you just took it to a whole new level."

"I know it sounds crazy," he said, "but I am Ashley. How else would I know about the dog?"

"You've got a phone, don't you? How many times did she post about it?"

"None. And how would I know your name is Sammy Johnson? You've worked here for three years."

"Uh huh. I already know who I am. Thanks for telling me, though. You seem to be the one who's challenged in the identity department."

"But I am Ashley." The guy rubbed his hands over his face, through his thin brown hair. He glowered at Sammy. "I'll prove it if you let me in, please."

"I'm sorry," Sammy said. "You need to back out, all the way to the crazy house." He decided against extending the usual courtesy of opening the gate so he could circle forward and around the booth.

The guy clenched his jaw. He tried to get out of his car, but Sammy leaned out of the booth and held his door closed. "Sir, this is your last warning."

"You can't keep me out of my own house!"

"You're from those tabloids, aren't you?" Sammy was sick of the way they tried to make Ashley look bad. "I'm calling the police. You don't want a harassment beef on your ass, trust me." Ashley had a strict policy of not talking to the press, and he had probably said too much already.

He shut the window to the booth and held up the phone.

The guy who claimed to be Ashley screamed.

Sammy made a slow performance of dialing.

The guy slammed his Camry in reverse. On his back way up the drive, he clipped a palm.

Sammy sat back in the chair and shook his head. The dog sat on the floor and stared up at him.

"What a loony-bird," he said. "I should have let you bite

his ass."

The dog glanced at the window.

"What's you're name, anyway? Alice?... Ariel?... Shera?"

She perked her ears and tilted her head.

"Shera. Your name is Shera."

She nuzzled her head between Sammy's legs and wiggled her butt. He laughed. His heart swelled. "You're not going anywhere are you, Shera? No, you're not. I'm thinking we keep you in the guest house."

Hostage Exchange

"What do you want?" Aleman sounded more annoyed than surprised, when Saul finally caught up to him in the cinderblock hallway of the MDC. His forehead was bruised and swollen above his terribly narrow brow, which made his whole face look too small. His mustache was frayed and underlined by chapped lips.

"You hung up before we finished talking last night." Saul said.

"I don't know what you're talking about." Aleman's gruff monotone lacked the cadence from last night, but the pitch was the same.

"You don't remember calling me?"

Aleman ratcheted his brows down and glanced to the right. "I never called you."

"The call came from your phone."

On the second call, Aleman had forgotten to block the caller ID, so now Saul could confront him without admitting to the trace.

"Yeah, well—" Aleman glanced over Saul's shoulder, down the hallway. "I lost my phone. So, whoever called you, it wasn't me." He shouldered past Saul and continued walking.

Denial or amnesia? Saul could have predicted his reaction. It was just like Saroyan.

"Hold up." Saul started after him. "I might know who has your phone."

"This had better be quick," Aleman said without looking back. "Only ten minutes left on my break."

He led Saul to a windowless break room that was almost an insult. Five foot by ten, most of which was consumed by vending machines and a two-seater table. Aleman slouched into the chair by the machines.

Saul bought him a Coke then squeezed into the narrow gap across from him, between the table and the wall. He tried to sit without bumping his belly on the table. And failed. The table's metal legs groaned as they skidded a few inches on the polished linoleum.

Aleman snorted and pushed back on the table.

Saul pretended not to notice. "I went by your apartment yesterday."

Aleman looked down and said nothing. In the harsh fluorescents, his skin looked sallow, highlighting the bruise.

"Where were you?" Saul asked.

Aleman blinked rapidly. "What's it matter to you?"

"We're friends, right?" He didn't care much for Aleman, but it was worth a try.

"I don't know about that."

"I get it," Saul said, hoping Aleman's ill will was more due the rivalry between Sheriff's Department and the LAPD. "I'm a Montague and you're a Capulet."

"What are you talking about?"

"I was worried about you. I heard you left your car here."

Aleman clamped a meaty hand on the Coke can and frowned. "Guess I needed some air." Seemed he had no intention of mentioning his trek out to El Monte.

"Totally understandable," Saul said. "So, what happened with Saroyan?"

"Who's that?" Aleman said guardedly.

Did he really not know? "The one who took down the bastard who attacked you."

"Dunno," Aleman said. "Wasn't my fault."

"Saroyan's a paraplegic," Saul said. "So, help me understand how he took down Dunn."

Aleman wiped the perspiration from the unopened Coke. "Must've had help."

Another dead end. Saul changed direction again, hoping to catch Aleman off guard. "How did you get that bruise?"

Aleman gingerly touched the swollen knot on his forehead. "Dunn kicked me into the wall, remember?"

"According to the doc," Saul said, "it was the back of your head that hit the pipe."

"Yeah? Well." He pointed at the bruise. "What's the evidence say?" He stood. "I've got to get back."

Time to lay down some cards. "Hold on." Saul reached into his coat, pulled out Aleman's phone and slid it across the table.

It skidded to a stop in front of Aleman, whose eyes went wide. He grabbed it, pressed his thumb to the screen and unlocked it. Now there was no denying it was his phone.

"Who else has access to the phone?" Saul asked.

Aleman swiped the screen. His brows furrowed.

Saul waited a few seconds. "Do anyone else's fingerprints unlock it?"

Aleman didn't look up. "No…"

"Check your call log." Saul recited his number.

Aleman's eyes darted from the phone to Saul and back. His mouth fell open. "Impossible."

Saul shrugged. "You were identified."

Aleman reached out and steadied himself on the chair. "Where?"

"Ever been to La Golondrina?"

"What's that?"

"The restaurant on Olvera where you left your phone."

Splotches of pink appeared on Aleman's throat. He tore open the Coke. Swallowed hard.

"The hostess identified you from a photo," Saul said.

"Guess I didn't notice the name. Something happen… after I left or something?"

"Like what?" Saul asked as casually as he could.

Aleman blinked. Then his face hardened. He started

toward the door.

Saul heaved himself up after him, his belly bump the table back again. He lunged into Aleman's path. "What happened last night?"

"I don't know what you're talking about."

He tried to shoulder past, but Saul shoved him into the wall and stared down into his terribly narrow eyes. "What happened? Tell me."

"This is bullshit." Aleman's brow wrinkled around the bruise. He looked more confused than defiant. "Nothing happened."

Bullshit alright. Saul was sure now: it was Aleman who had called him.

"You saw me there, didn't you? Did you think I was tracking your phone?"

If he had left his phone on the table to throw Saul off course, then why report to work as if nothing had happened?

As Aleman glanced down, Saul could almost see the wheels turning in his head. Aleman was a mean little man, and mean little men, when cornered, always went for the groin. Saul caught Aleman's knee as it came up for the blow. He should have stopped there, but he had to retaliate. Violence was the language of men like Aleman, so he shoved Aleman's knee away and rocked forward with his huge upper torso, swinging his head like a bowling ball. It could have been a knockout blow, except Saul needed Aleman awake and submissive, so at the last instant he pulled back and merely knocked foreheads, smacking the swollen flesh of Aleman's bruise.

The back of Aleman's head thumped the wall. He slid sideways and caught himself on the snack machine. He cradled his forehead in one hand and shoved his phone into his pocket with the other. As he withdrew his hand, his elbow stiff, his next move was equally obvious, which left Saul no choice—Aleman was dumb enough to tase him, no doubt about that. As Aleman reached for the taser on his belt, Saul slipped a hand into his coat, freed his Glock 22 from the shoulder holster, and swung it out, aiming at Aleman's center of mass.

The taser shook in Aleman's hand. "You're not going to shoot me," he shouted.

"Only if you make me." Saul held the gun steady. "Muscles contract when a four volt electrical stimulus is applied. A taser delivers fifty thousand. Guaranteed contraction of all muscles in the body. In the case of joints rigged with opposing muscles, such as my trigger finger, the stronger side, would be the curling motion, wins. So go ahead, tase me. You'll be shooting yourself."

Aleman clenched his jaw. He lowered the taser. "Now what?"

"I'm arresting you for murder."

Aleman's eyes went wide. "What are you talking about?"

"You confessed to killing a cop yesterday."

He shook his head slowly. "Who?"

"I'm giving you a chance to tell me. If someone put you up to it, maybe I can help."

Aleman snatched the Coke from the table. He gulped the soda and coughed.

"Don't you think I would remember?" His eyes found Saul's and then he looked away, down and to the right.

Maybe he'd experienced something like what Saroyan had described—some dreamlike memory of losing control. He certainly remembered *something*. Something bad. And whatever was going on seemed bigger than just Saroyan and Aleman, two of the most unlikely men to work together. Yet they had both had spoken with the same cadence, both claimed to be Wayob.

Saul holstered his Glock. "Tell me what you remember. I'm trying to help you here."

Aleman chuckled dryly. "I don't need your help." He slammed the can on the table and crushed it with his palm. "I'm going back to work now. Do what you've got to do."

Saul dug through his overstuffed wallet. Handed Aleman a business card.

"What this for?"

Saul tapped the pocket where he kept his phone. "That's my personal number. For when you're ready to talk."

Aleman crumpled the card and dropped it on the floor.

"Just tell me who Wayob is," Saul said.

Aleman stepped on the card, shouldered past Saul and out the door.

Saul flattened a five-dollar bill and fed it to the snack machine. He punched in the number for BBQ chips. The steel coil jerked into action and took five full seconds to release the bag. As Saul squatted to retrieve it from the slot at the bottom of the machine, he groaned from the strain.

He sat at the table and opened the chips. If Aleman wasn't talking, what could he do? His only other possible lead was the Lunas, and they weren't home. He'd spent the night in his car outside their apartment, listening to the din of the cars careening up the 10 freeway, wondering where Rosa and her blind, sickly grandmother could have gone.

Fifteen minutes later, Saul was still sitting there in the break room when his phone buzzed. He pulled it out and glanced at the screen. Lieutenant Levy.

"What's up, L-T?"

"Parker." She enunciated the second syllable harshly. "We need you at the Beverly Hills Library, now."

On a Sunday? He held the phone to his shoulder as he opened his second bag of chips. "I'm kind of in the middle of something." The chips rattled in spite of his effort to keep them quiet.

Levy snickered. "I can hear that," she said. He pictured her sarcastic half-smile, the closest she ever came to laughing. "A gunman has taken Bob Jaggar hostage, and we've got media up the ass."

The name sounded vaguely familiar. "Should I know who that is?"

"He was in a couple eighties sitcoms," Levy said. "Remember *Houseboat*, the *Full House* spinoff?"

"What's this got to do with Homicide Special?" The unit investigated only serial and high-profile homicides. Saul had no experience with kidnappings.

"Nothing," she said. "Except the shooter is requesting you by name."

A chill shot through Saul's gut. "Who is it?"

"Robert Rydell."

The name drew a complete blank. "How does he claim to know me?"

"He said you were following him last night."

Saul's stomach churned. He snatched up the bag of chips and started down the hallway. "I've never heard of Rydell. Last night I was looking for Victor Aleman, a custody assistant at the MDC. There's a connection between him and Saroyan."

"Saroyan?" Levy said. "I closed that case. It's with the DA now."

"We don't have a motive."

"We've got video of the murder. Move on."

"So who's Rydell?" Saul asked.

"He's a rich guy in his mid-sixties, white, with no prior record, and now he's killed a man. You really don't know anything?"

"No." Saul held the phone away from his mouth so she wouldn't hear him panting as he jogged down the hall.

"Well, he's holed up in the library. If you can't break the stalemate, we're going to have to send someone in."

Saul hit the button for the elevator, which from the fifth floor should be faster than the stairs. "I'll call Hernandez."

"She's already on the way."

He restrained his chuckle and tried to sound surprised. "You called her first?"

Levy hesitated. "High brass is up my ass to put a good face on this. The media is all over it, and now some asshole is live-streaming outside the library."

The elevator arrived and Saul stepped inside. He understood. The image of the LAPD mattered more to Levy and the high brass than the fact that the shooter, with one confirmed kill and a hostage, was requesting Saul by name. He was the status quo. A fat, white male. A statement from him would sound like bullshit. Especially after the Brown shooting, which the media would dredge up all over again if they discovered he was assigned to the case. And Hernandez was a Chicana who spoke with authority and intelligence. And she was slender.

But Saul was glad for Hernandez. The exposure would be

great for her career.

Meanwhile, the bag of chips in his hand was going stale. Better go ahead and eat them, better now than while driving. He held the phone away from his mouth while he chewed.

"So," he said, "what you're saying is that Hernandez is in charge now?"

"Well, you're still the senior detective, of course. I just can't make you lead on this."

Saul released a strained laugh. "You weren't going to tell me, were you?"

"It's out of my hands. Anyway, Rydell knows you, somehow. You can't lead a case you're involved in."

Chicken shit. He crunched hard into the phone. Not enjoying the chips at all.

The elevator doors parted. He marched out into the parking deck toward his plain wrap, glancing at his phone to make sure he still had reception.

"Rydell picked up the landline," Levy said. "I'll transfer you."

There was a click. A hiss came on the line. He climbed into the car and transferred the call to the car's audio system. "This is Parker." He started the engine.

A nasally, male voice blared through the speakers, "Parker." That voice—not the tone but the enunciation—was familiar.

Saul checked the mirror and hit reverse.

"Who is this?" he asked.

"Why it is Robert Rydell."

Hair prickled on the back of Saul's neck. "Do I know you?"

"No, but I know you, Parker. Yes, I do."

There it was. That cadence, unmistakable, and he pronounced Saul's name with an air of disgust. Rydell pretending to be Wayob, Saul assumed. He wanted Rydell to admit it, wanted Levy and whoever else was listening to hear it for themselves. If Rydell implicated Aleman and Saroyan, they would have to grant Saul some leeway for his investigation.

Saul turned out of the garage toward the 101. "So it's

Rydell… not Wayob?"

"Ah, very clever, Parker. Clever, clever."

"So which is it?"

"I don't have time for games. Tell these imbeciles to release me."

"Funny. I'm supposed to tell you to surrender."

"Don't waste my time, Parker. Release me, or people shall needlessly die."

"And why is that?"

"They say I am surrounded and they will shoot if I do not surrender, but as you know, for me, death is a mere inconvenience, whereas those that I slay shall cease to exist. Same with Rydell, if they shoot me. Does no one care about his fate? No one has to die here. I would prefer not to harm anyone, of course, but I am running out of time."

Saul accelerated up the ramp toward the 101. The freeway was jammed. As Saul tried to edge between a Range Rover and a white Audi, the Audi sped up and blocked him. He had to swerve onto the shoulder.

The Audi driver flipped him off with both hands. Her blonde hair flapping in the wind.

"Are you listening to me?" Rydell almost screamed.

"How do you know Edward Saroyan?" Saul asked.

"Are you toying with me, Parker."

"No, I just— I don't get it. Friday night, Saroyan said *he* was Wayob. How do you explain that?"

"That was me, you dullard."

There it was. Rydell had just implicated himself with Saroyan. The connection was not surprising to Saul, but it baffled him. Why claim to be Wayob?

"Believe me or not," Rydell continued, "it makes no difference to me. Just tell them to let me to leave in peace, or Bob Jagger's death shall be your fault."

Saul engaged the blue strobes in his grill. "I don't see why you need to kill Bob Jagger. You're immortal, right?"

"I can find a new vessel, and I shall if they shoot me. Wait and see, Parker. I am done wasting my breath. Either they let me walk out of here with Bob Jagger or he shall die."

"We can't let you leave with a hostage," Saul said. "Take me instead."

"Are you outside?"

"I'm almost there," Saul lied.

"I am done with waiting."

The car in front of Saul moved aside. He gunned up behind the white Audi. The driver noticed the strobes and slowed down. Saul bleeped the siren. "I know who you're looking for." Yesterday, Aleman had walked practically all the way to the Lunas' apartment, so Saul assumed Rydell shared Aleman's interest, just like they had shared the same act.

Silence on the line.

"I'll take you to them," Saul said, although in truth he had no intention of allowing Rydell anywhere near the Lunas.

"How can you know?" Rydell asked, suspiciously. "Where is he?"

He? Rosa and her grandmother were on their own now that Saroyan had murdered Luis Luna. So who was this he?

Aleman's words from last night echoed in Saul's mind. *Another must die.*

Saul exited on Beverly. "Once Jaggar is safe, I'll show you."

"I do not need you, Parker. I shall find him on my own."

"But how long will it take you? I know exactly where he is."

Rydell said nothing.

"Rydell?"

Levy came on the line. "He hung up."

"Clear the unis out of there," Saul said.

"We can't do that."

"He's going to kill Jaggar if you don't give him some space. At least make it look like they're packing up. Buy me some time."

"With all the cameras on the scene, we might as well make an ad for kidnapping."

The Audi driver pulled over at the exit for Vermont, hands locked on the wheel. Saul sped past.

"Then clear the media, at least. Say it's for their own safety. Think about how it's going to look with the LAPD standing around while Jaggar gets murdered."

Wayob Takes Parker

Wayob slams the phone down on the counter. Parker does not know. How can he? He cannot. If he knows about the Encanto, if he knows where it is, he would take it for himself. Of course he would take it. He would leave Wayob trapped here in this miserable bright space lined with books, and Jaggar with all his whining.

Jagger is sitting against the semi-circular, white counter centered in the large room, arms tied behind his back with a cord.

"Stand up," Wayob says.

Jaggar glances toward the inner door, beyond which officers are, of course, still lurking, in the main part of the library, in spite of the warning shots Wayob fired. At least the bookshelf he barricaded the door with seems to have held them back so far. And they do not dare shoot through the shades.

The emergency exit, labeled "Alarm Will Sound," is also barricaded with a bookshelf. He'd got it there just in time too, just as police cars flooded the parking lot outside in a chaos of flashing lights.

"I can get you out of this," Jaggar says. "I'll hire you the best lawyers money can buy." He flashes his stupid smile, as though he has power over Wayob.

Above Jaggar's head, the side of the counter is inscribed with the phrase, "*I have answers.*" But Wayob knows the answer, not Jagger. It may seem as though Wayob is trapped here in this hideous tomb of books with no potential vessel sleeping within in range—he has tried to transmigrate, twice —but there is one vessel, one means of escape, so brilliant that it makes Wayob laugh.

"Pay me this, hire me that. You think that I care?" Wayob raises the gun. "Stand up."

Jaggar's eyes widen. He pushes himself up on his knees and rises slowly.

"Do not fear," Wayob says, "I only need you to sleep. Turn around."

Jaggar shakes his head.

"They all want me to set you free," Wayob lowers the gun. "Turn around, and I shall untie you."

Jaggar kicks him in the shin and dances backward.

"You fool." Wayob rubs his shin and raises the gun. But shooting Jaggar would be idiotic when Wayob must be smart to overcome Parker and his minions.

Jaggar lunges forward. Wayob attempts to dodge, but Jaggar head butts Wayob in the side. They topple to the floor. Instinctively, Wayob catches himself with his hand, the hand with the gun, leaving himself vulnerable to Jaggar's next offense, which is unbelievable. Deplorable. Jaggar's teeth sink into Wayob's arm.

"You vile, filthy man," he screams.

As Wayob rolls onto his back, he clutches the gun so hard the metal hurts his hand.

Jaggar, with his arms still tied behind his back, worms onto Wayob's chest.

Wayob slams the butt of the gun into Jaggar's head. "Get off." He slams it again. And again. The metal smacks Jaggar's skull. Something gives.

Jaggar, at last, stops moving.

Wayob rolls Jaggar off him. He scoots backward on the hard, white floor.

Jaggar just lies there on his side, his head facing away

from Wayob, lolling against the floor.

Wayob gets to his feet. He creeps closer. He jabs Jaggar's back with the gun.

No reaction.

Wayob crouches and presses the gun barrel to Jaggar's ear. With his other hand, he slowly reaches over Jaggar's mouth, careful to avoid touching him.

No air coming out. No air going in.

"No!" Wayob leaps around to face Jaggar and falls to his knees.

Jaggar's eyes are open. The life has gone out of them.

"No." Wayob grabs a handful of Jaggar's cheek. The skin is loose, clammy. Jaggar's neck has gone completely limp. His gray-colored hair flops across his forehead, the furrows gone from his brow.

Wayob swallows back the bile in his throat. "No."

He shoves Jaggar away.

The words on the counter practically scream at him. *I have answers.* They mock him. For there are no answers, not anymore. Only one option remains.

Wayob grabs the gun. The officers lurking in the library probably heard Wayob scream, little that it matters now.

Let them gun him down. He shall awaken in some other vessel. Wayob should have allowed them to shoot him an hour ago instead of wasting so much time. This is Parker's fault.

"What are you looking at?" he asks Bob Jaggar. "You are dead already. Easy for you."

Wayob should make a run for it. He should just go. *Go now.* But dying hurts. Dying is utter agony, and worse than the pain is the uncertainty. When shall he awaken in his new vessel? Where? Presumably closer to he who holds the Encanto. But he does not really know. The black-hearted priest banished Wayob to this atrocious existence without explaining a thing. Of course, he probably presumed Wayob would never escape the Encanto. The barbarian, his foul breath and tiny chin.

Blood pounds in the head of this vessel who Wayob must shed himself of but cannot, not here in this awful room with the corpse of Jaggar, who now seems to be smirking.

"Wayob."

It that Jaggar's voice? Jaggar's voice in my head?

"Way-ob."

No, it is Parker. Parker mocking him.

The pounding subsides for a moment. "Rydell?" Parker says. "Open up."

The knocking starts up again. And Wayob realizes it is not in his head.

The phone on the counter blares. From outside, Parker yells again, "Rydell."

Wayob laughs and sprints toward the outer door. *Parker, my savior.*

Wayob drags the bookcase back a foot and peers behind it. Outside the window in the door, Parker's massive trench coat hangs over his stomach and his shoulders on top of which sits Parker's fat face.

"Parker."

"Send Jaggar out," Parker says. "I'll come in."

"No, I shall come out. You shall drive me away from here."

"Whatever you want. Just leave the gun inside."

Wayob laughs. "You think I am a fool, Parker?"

"No one will shoot you if you're unarmed."

"Oh, I know, Parker. I know all too well, all about your fetish for unjustified confinement. But not this time. This time, you drop your weapon and turn your back to the door."

"Not until Jaggar is safe. I'll drop my weapon if you send him out. If I don't surrender, you can shoot us both."

"No. Jaggar stays inside, and if you refuse to comply, I shall end his life."

"Then you'll get the death penalty for sure. If you release him, you'll serve a few years at the most. The guy you shot at his place is going to live."

"I welcome death," Wayob lies. "Just make it quick."

"That's not how it works. You'll be on death row for years. Or... I can get you out of here right now. My car is right there." He points behind him and steps aside, revealing a brown vehicle backed up onto the curb, facing away from the library. Behind it, dozens of police vehicles are fanned out, flashing blue lights, and behind them a crowd of officers with guns all aimed toward Wayob.

Parker steps in front of them. "We'll go together and find the guy you're looking for, I promise."

Parker knows something, Wayob realizes. Not everything, probably, but enough. What if Parker's plan is to have Wayob lead him right to the Encanto?

Wayob slams his fist into the bookcase. *Fucking Parker.* He screams, "I shall shoot Jaggar and then I shall shoot myself."

"Don't."

Wayob should just do it. He should have, earlier, but now he has wasted so much time. "I am counting to ten."

"Be smart, Wayob. Let's work something out."

But Wayob *has* worked it out. "Two." Parker will not wait for a countdown, Wayob knows. The officers will blast their way in here, with Parker leading the charge. "Three."

The phone on the counter starts ringing. Wayob marches to the counter, answers the phone and yells into the receiver, "Four." He slams it down.

"Five," he shouts at the inner wall, then hurries back toward the outer door.

When Parker barges his way in here, attempting to be a hero, Wayob shall take him by surprise. He lays prone by the wall and extends his arms, holding the gun with both hands. He braces his wrists in anticipation of the awful kickback and the noise, hoping only to wound Parker severely. No need to kill him. Wayob just needs to escape.

"Okay," Parker yells from outside. "We'll do it your way."

"Do not be fooled," Wayob says to himself.

"I mean it," Parker says. "I'm unarmed."

Wayob scoots forward and peers out the door. Parker stands there, the back of his giant coat filling the window. *Too easy.*

"Remove the coat," Wayob says.

After glancing around, Parker removes the coat. He

points out that his shoulder holster is now surprisingly empty. He raises his hands. "Okay. Come on out."

Using Parker's immense size, Wayob can easily shield himself from the other officers's guns on the way to the vehicle, at which point Wayob will have to climb in first and duck down, which is probably what Parker is counting on.

Wayob smiles. "What happens when we get to your vehicle?"

Parker removes the handcuffs from his belt and clasps his left wrist. "I'll cuff myself to the wheel." He dangles the other manacle in the air.

"That could work, but first we must get there. Where is your gun?"

"I threw it in my trunk while you were counting."

"You expect me to believe that?"

"I'll show you." Parker's voice has an edge, a certain earnestness. He probably would love to show Wayob the trunk, where there is almost certainly a gun. But is it his only one? *No.*

"Clever, Parker," Wayob says, "but you should know that I have experience dealing with men such as yourself." Wayob cringes at what he is about to suggest. Hard to imagine anything more vile, but Wayob has come too far to allow Parker to outsmart him. "Unfortunately, I must insist that you undress."

Parker's eyes widen. "What?" He steps back, exposing Wayob to the crowd of officers with their guns all aimed toward Wayob.

Wayob lowers himself down from their view. "Undress."

Parker crouches down, exposing Wayob again and causing him to draw back behind the wall. *Will it stop a bullet?* "You are trying to get me shot," he shouts.

"No," Parker says, "I had another weapon. You were right. I'm getting rid of it."

Wayob peers around the wall.

Parker has hiked up one pants leg where, strapped just above his ankle, is a little gun. *Parker, you trickster.*

"What are you doing?" Hernandez shouts. Detective

Hernandez, who had tortured him with her ridiculous questions when he was in the vessel of Saroyan, trapped in that hot little room, is marching towards them. She raises her gun.

Parker removes the gun and slides it away on the sidewalk. "This is the only way." He stands with his back to the door, just like Wayob ordered.

But Parker might have a dozen more guns hidden beneath the voluminous layers of his clothing, and Hernandez is right there, blocked by Parker from Wayob's sight.

"Tell Hernandez to back away," Wayob says.

"Hernandez isn't going to be a problem. Don't worry."

Wayob agrees that Hernandez shall not be a problem, because Wayob shall use Parker to shield himself, and she will not risk her partner's life.

Wayob stands. "But, Parker, you intend to be a problem, as we both know. Remove your clothing."

Parker looks down at his enormous belly. "This is a waste of time. Aren't you in a hurry?"

Wayob clenches the gun in his hand. It would be so easy just to shoot Parker, but then he might as well shoot himself. "You are the one wasting time. Would you like me to shoot you?"

"Go around to the other entrance," Parker says to Hernandez.

Although her response is muffled by the glass, and the massive amount of meat on Parker's body, it's clear from her tone that she is refusing.

Wayob presses the gun barrel to the glass. Time to take charge. If he shoots Parker in the shoulder, just a hole through the fat on his arm, Parker should be able to drive just fine.

"Don't look," Parker says to Hernandez. "There's no way to unsee this."

He faces Wayob and begins unbuttoning his shirt. Hernandez is fortunate to be spared from this agony which Wayob must endure for the sake of his own safety.

Beneath Parker's shirt is another shirt, a tight one, which clings to the immense roll of his belly. Parker unbuckles his pants.

Bile rises in Wayob's throat. The human body is revolting. What has Wayob gotten himself into? He groans.

"Want me to stop?" Parker asks.

Wayob wants to scream, *yes!* But he cannot allow Parker to see him suffer. Wayob swallows back the bile. "Keep going."

Parker's pants fall.

Suddenly, Wayob returns to the most awful night of his life, all those centuries ago, when his bride performed that deplorable act on the odious priest. When Wayob caught them together, the priest banished Wayob to this miserable existence. *Odious fucking priest.*

Nausea overtakes Wayob. His throat burns. Whatever filth Rydell consumed before Wayob took him as a vessel is about to spew up. Wayob bends over, falls to his hands on his knees, and retches. "Enough, enough!"

Obviously, Parker has no other weapon or he would not have undressed down to the thin t-shirt and white garment covering his groin. Whatever awfulness lies beneath it, Wayob cannot bear to look.

"Turn around!" Wayob shouts. For this, he shall take revenge. *Oh Parker, we have just begun.*

Parker glances behind him and then just stands there with his shoulders slumped, looking ridiculous in his awful underwear and his stupid silver watch.

Wayob inhales. "Turn around. I said turn around."

Parker crosses his arms over his belly and attempts to cover his groin with his hands. Finally, he turns around.

Wayob wedges himself between the bookcase and the door and presses the red handle with the "Alarm Will Sound" warning. Hardly matters now.

Wayob shoves the door open. The alarm blares. Wayob covers his ears, the alarm seems to grow louder. So loud it hurts.

Endure. Must endure. Wayob withdraws his hands from his ears and marches out with the gun extended. He presses the muzzle to the back of Parker's head.

"Walk," Wayob says.

Parker lunges forward, and Wayob trots after him.

He must not allow any distance between them for Hernandez and all the other officers who wish to shoot Wayob, though their bullets would almost be easier to endure than the proximity to Parker's body, which Wayob must suffer though because he cannot afford the time it takes to die and find a new vessel. If he waits too long, he who holds the Encanto might turn the dial, trapping Wayob back inside the awful device. And there he would remain, disembodied in the darkness with only his thoughts churning around in the void, and no way of knowing when if ever he shall be released again.

Parker stalls.

Wayob smacks into the awful expanse of his back, just a thin layer of fabric between Parker's flesh and Wayob's face. The nausea returns. Wayob punches the gun barrel into Parker's neck. His finger twitches on the trigger, but right then, the alarm finally ceases.

Wayob shoves Parker forward. "Walk at a steady rate."

Wayob trails Parker the last few steps to the vehicle, staying close. At the rear door, Parker stops and turns unexpectedly.

Wayob's heart slams against his ribs. He cringes back, which exposes him to Hernandez, who stands near the hood of the vehicle, seemingly undaunted by the awful sight of Parker in his undergarments. With one hand she raises her gun while with the other she flips back the mismatched clump of gray hair on her forehead. "Let him go," she shouts.

"Get back." Wayob moves closer to Parker, putting Hernandez out of his sight and therefore Wayob out of hers. If she was going to shoot through Parker, she would have by now.

"If you hurt him, you're dead," she says.

"I doubt that," Wayob says. "Do not attempt to follow us. Or I shall shoot Parker and drive for myself."

Parker motions Wayob to get in the vehicle. Almost too easy.

"I shall ride up front," Wayob says.

"Suit yourself." Parker opens the driver's door. "I assume you'd rather climb across than trust me to walk around."

Wayob backs into the car, keeping his gun trained on Parker while lowering himself to avoid giving Hernandez a shot through the windshield. But when Wayob peeks over the dashboard, she is not even watching. She is staring at Parker. Why? Wayob has to watch Parker for the sake of his own protection, but Hernandez could so easily look away, yet for some reason she is transfixed by Parker's elephantine body, which he is trying to conceal behind the vehicle door, a useless endeavor.

Wayob struggles across the divider between the seats. As soon as there is space, Parker, in his abdominous t-shirt, crams himself behind the wheel and cowers down, a hangdog look on his face. Wayob has won.

Parker starts the engine and cuffs his wrists to the wheel. Wayob does not even have to prompt him.

The exit is blocked by a police vehicle. As Parker accelerates toward it, the officer behind the wheel leaps out to safety.

"What are you doing?" Wayob braces himself for impact.

Just before colliding, Parker swerves up onto the curb. The vehicle plows through some shrubs, over the sidewalk, and bumps down into the road.

"They won't pursue us," Parker says. At the intersection, he swerves left and right at the next. "So, where to?"

Wayob smiles. "I thought you knew."

"Yeah, well, pretend I don't."

"Go north," Wayob says.

They must find a safe place for Wayob to meditate on the sound of the mind who holds the Encanto. But Wayob shall not take Parker to him. *Parker knows something. Perhaps not everything, but enough.* Wayob shall leave Parker restrained in the handcuffs, alone. Let Parker suffer the same torture he inflicted upon Wayob.

"So what's with *Wayob*?" Parker asks. "Is that like a codename?"

Codename? "What do you mean?"

"Someone put you up to this. Tell me who you're

working for and you might not have to serve any time at all."

Working for? Wayob had been afraid for nothing. "You know nothing at all." Wayob laughs.

And he laughs.

Whatever Parker says next, Wayob ignores it. Parker is merely a nuisance. No more than a fly to be swatted away.

And the problem with flies is that you swat them away, and they come back, again and again. They always come back. They keep bothering you until you squash them.

Gray's Painting

The first floor room in the turret has high ceilings, wooden floors, and three vertical windows punched through the curved stone wall. Three cushioned chairs are angled toward one window each. Gray sets the Michaels bag on the wooden desk situated between the windows and the chairs. The desk is barren, and the room is mostly empty space, staged to look like an office even though it seems to serve no clear function at all.

He sets up the easel by the desk. He'd wanted to set up out on Ashley's field-sized lawn, like in his dream, but with her security guy circling the house every ten minutes, probably hoping for another glimpse of Ashley York's boobs—Gray still can't understand how they're his—he can't concentrate. If he could get into the flow, this uneasiness would fade away, as would this feeling of judgment, which seems to fill every room of Ashley York's enormous house, even down here.

Andrea had bought him the art supplies only after asking a lot of questions, apparently doubting he'd ever use them. He should have just gone to Michaels himself. He'd wanted to. He wants to go check on Claire and the kids too, but what if leaving Ashley's is like leaving a dream? What if there's no coming back?

He stares at the canvas.

Where to begin? In his mind, he knows what the fortune teller looks like, but when he tries to picture her face on the canvas, all he sees is white.

A white wall.

He opens the brushes. For some reason, Andrea purchased Beniccis, the most expensive set in the store, instead of the Princeton Select Black Taklons he requested. But they'll do. He pulls out a #2, round and dabs it in raw umber. As he turns toward the easel, the image of a wall returns to his mind. He poises with his brush above the canvas, closes his eyes, and concentrates on the old fortune teller's face….

He sees the wall, bathed in intense light. He has the unmistakable sense of being watched, as if someone is standing behind him. He's afraid to open his eyes… but he has to.

He lowers the brush.

Standing in the doorway, Andrea crosses her arms. "Still haven't started yet, huh?"

"I can't concentrate if you don't leave me alone."

"I was just checking to see if you need anything." She sounds genuine except her eyes flick to the side.

"I'm fine," he says.

She stands there and tilts her head. A lock of hair falls over her left eye.

"What?" he asks.

"It's just… I don't understand why you're starting a new hobby all the sudden? Don't you have that screen test on Tuesday?"

Gray glances down at himself in the body of Ashley York. "Right."

"Aren't you nervous?"

"Maybe I need to take my mind off of it."

"You don't need to rehearse?"

"Tomorrow."

Her eyes bulge almost out of her head. "O-kay." She closes the door.

Here he is with no obligations, no interruptions from Claire or the kids—he can paint all day and all night, if he wants—and yet all he can paint on the canvas is a wall. A blank wall. Here he is in this vast house effectively all for him, with personal staff and a pool, a view of LA and the ocean—the dream of any artist come true—and he is unable to paint.

Why?

Maybe he needs a little lubrication for his creativity. At home, he usually has a Scotch, just to clear his head. Has it gotten to the point that he can't paint without it?

He trots to the living room to check out the wet bar. The cabinet below the bar contains about ten different kinds of schnapps, two tequilas, and one bottle of Pappy Van Winkle. Gray uncorks the Pappy and gulps two swallows, probably four hundred dollars' worth, but it has the same oaky flavor as any other bourbon, the same burn as it slides down his throat.

His shoulders loosen. Ashley's body is feeling more comfortable, more like his own. If there was some way to know for sure that the charm could return him to normal, he could relax. But he couldn't find anything on the internet about the charm or the old fortune teller. He could go looking for her but, he reminds himself as the takes another pull of the Pappy, she doesn't speak English and seemed to want nothing to do with him after she'd given him the charm and told him to destroy it.

On the subject of body switching, Google had only suggested movies in which people trade places by wishing on a star, magic altar, doll, or genie. But Gray had not made any wish. If he had, he'd have chosen someone other than Ashley York to body swap into: maybe her father, since Evan York has all the real money. Maybe he'd wondered, for a brief moment, what Ashley's life was like, but only because Claire is obsessed with her.

From behind the wet bar in the living room, he hears Andrea speaking from somewhere in the back of the kitchen but can't see her. "Ashely thinks she's an artist, all the sudden."

"No way," a male voice responds. The security guy? Gray hadn't seen him circle the house in a while.

Gray carries the Pappy along with him as he sneaks back to the easel. He doesn't have to justify himself to Andrea— he's not even Ashley—but he still has to paint at least one portrait that he's happy with, just to prove to himself that he can.

He stares at the canvas, and there it is again: the wall. He wishes he could punch it. Punch the image in his mind, little good that it would do. He's been stuck before. He just has to get through it, just has to paint something, anything. Anything would be better than standing here staring a blank canvas.

He grits his teeth and traces a curve on the page. A thin line... Suddenly, it comes into focus. The line is edge of a counter. It's not a wall; it's a counter. He sketches its geometry... and slowly it forms as a semi-circular counter inscribed with the phrase, "I have answers."

Weird.

It's as if his hand has a mind of its own. Perhaps he has imbibed too much. That certainly wouldn't be a first for him, but never before has he painted something so specific without first seeing it somewhere else.

Behind him, a voice says, "Hey, that's my Pappy."

Gray whirls around. A short guy with jet-black hair styled into a wave, strides toward him. He looks familiar. He has a chiseled chin and boyish cheeks, and before Gray can resist, the guy's hand is around his waist. He pulls Gray in for a kiss, but Gray doesn't lower his head, so the guy pecks him on the chin.

August Grant, Gray realizes, the Hollywood heartthrob Ashley is dating. Claire would be so jealous. Too bad she'll never believe it.

August steps back, lowers one brow and arches the other, an expression which seems to mean that Gray should explain himself. How did he even get into the house?

"Guess you normally just show up?" Gray asks.

"When Franco's working."

"Franco?"

"I know. You like Sammy better." August grabs the bottle of Pappy from the desk. "But it's demeaning the way Sammy makes me wait while he calls you every time I come over. He knows who I am. It's demeaning. You should get rid of that guy."

August tilts the bottle from side to side, as if it's some big mystery how the level of brown liquid has sunk below the label, which was more than Gray meant to drink.

"Now Franco, he gets it," August says. "He has the gate open by the time I roll up to the booth. All he says is, '*Alright*.' I love the way he says it. *Alright*." August glances around as if something is missing, then fixes Gray with the mismatched brows. "Did you drink from the bottle?"

"So what if I did?" Gray says. Even though it's clearly not something Ashley would normally do, she shouldn't have to take shit from August, not here in her own house.

"You bought it for me." August takes a swallow and returns the bottle to the desk. "Since when do you like whiskey?"

"I'm developing a taste."

August returns the bottle to the desk. "So, what's with the painting?"

"It's just something I have to do." Gray motions toward the door. "And I'd like to get back to it, if you don't mind."

August twists the nearest chair around and plops into it. "'I have answers.' Are you starting an advice blog or something?"

Gray faces the canvas where, instead of the portrait of the old fortune teller he'd meant to paint, his sketch of the counter with the odd inscription almost mocks him. "It's supposed to be art."

But it's not. It's too technical, architectural. He's never painted anything like this before in his life.

"Weird," August says. "It's hard to picture you as an artist."

"Well." Gray inhales deeply. "People change."

"You should paint celebrities—like me. Who wants to look at a painting of words?"

Gray swallows. "I don't know."

"Stick to what you're good at," August says.

Which would be what? Gray wonders. Art is all he has.

August pulls his phone out and motions Gray toward the arm of the chair. "Check this out."

Gray wonders if he can have August removed from the premises. Franco works for Ashley, right? His number must be in her phone.

"Where are you going?" August asks as Gray starts toward the door.

"I need my phone."

"You found it? Wait?"

Before Gray can escape, August is out of the chair and in Gray's face with his own phone. On the screen is a video of the murder Gray nearly witnessed in Venice. The killer, perched on his wheelchair, swings the bat down on the victim's head. Gray grinds his teeth. Someone had been this close and all they did was film it?

Gray backs away, feeling lightheaded.

"They've already hired a screen writer," August says. "You think I should I play the victim or the homicide detective?"

Gray stares at him in disbelief. It's like he doesn't get it. "That was a person—a real person, murdered on the street."

"I know." August steps in close, too close. "If I play the victim, I'll win an award."

Gray steps back and collides with the chair. The armrest catches him behind the knees, and he falls backward into the chair. He swings his legs around, but before he can get to his feet, August leans over him, his hand on the armrest, blocking Gray's escape.

Gray opens his mouth to tell August to back off, but August leans forward and shoves his tongue into Gray's mouth, his two-day-old scruff scratching Gray's lips.

Gray turns his head away and shivers at the abrupt transition from murder to sex. How can August be so detached? It's like he's actually turned on by it.

August starts unbuttoning Gray's shirt. Gray wants to shove him away, but maybe he should try to enjoy this. It might be his only chance to experience sex as a woman, which could be amazing if he can just detach himself from the fact that it's a man who has his knees between Gray's legs.

He closes his eyes. August grabs one of Gray's breasts and with his other hand, guides Gray's hand to the bulge in his jeans, which turns Gray off, probably more due to the abruptness than the male anatomy itself.

He drops his hand, lays his head back, and imagines it's Andrea unbuckling her belt.

At the sound of the zipper, Gray squeezes his eyes shut... and waits.

Nothing happens.

He opens his eyes.

Inches from his face, August's semi-hard snakes out from a bush of black curls.

Gray jerks away and pushes August back.

"What the hell?" August says.

Gray was thinking the same thing, but for the opposite reason. Does Ashley just go to town on August with no foreplay whatsoever?

"Look. Um... I just need to take it slow. Okay?"

"What do you mean 'take it slow'? Look at my face. You're not turned on?"

Gray wants to experience sex as a woman, but not like this. At least, not with August Grant. "I guess not," he says. "Thought I was. Sorry."

August jerks up his pants and snarls his zipper. Slams his belt through the buckle and parades out of the room.

Escape

Before surrendering to Rydell at the library, Saul had activated location sharing with Hernandez on his phone and hid it under the spare tire in the trunk.

Rydell had threatened to kill Saul if anyone followed. Hopefully, since Hernandez could track their location, she would keep the LAPD out of sight long enough for Saul to find out who the hell Rydell was after. He might just reveal the whole plot, so long as he believed he had the upper hand, which obviously he did from the way he was laughing at Saul, leaning against the passenger window and waving his stolen Ruger LCP.

The light turned green, and Saul accelerated up Beverly, both wrists cuffed to the wheel. It was a dangerous game. He'd never have surrendered if he'd known Rydell was going to humiliate him in front of Hernandez. Nothing could have been worse than standing there in his sweat-stained t-shirt, his enormous belly hanging over the waistband of his too-tight tighty-whities, the quarter-sized hole over the left butt cheek, which years ago, his wife (now ex) had insisted he throw out. He'd only kept them to spite her and was only wearing them today because he'd been too busy to do laundry. His chili pepper boxers, or maybe the dachshunds, might have detracted from the awful sight of his sagging belly.

At least now that Hernandez had seen how fat he was, he didn't have to keep wearing the damn trench coat when it was eighty degrees out. Nothing was going to happen between them. Not anymore.

"Par-Par-Parker," Rydell said. He would be handsome if not for the arrogant arch to his brows. His disheveled gray hair shook when he spoke. "Parker-fucking-Parker."

Saul returned his gaze to the road and said nothing.

"So," Rydell continued, "how did you know I would be there last night?"

Saul's heart hammered against his chest. Only Hernandez knew that he'd tracked Aleman's phone. "And where was that?"

"*El dia de los Muertos*," Rydell said with perfect Spanish. "Do not insult me, Parker. I saw you."

"Why were you there?" Saul asked.

Rydell grimaced. "Is this one of your tactics? Pretend to know nothing and see what I say? What did she tell you?"

"Who? Hernandez?"

Hernandez was the only woman Saul had spoken to last night. By the time she arrived, he'd already lost Aleman in the crowd. She'd accused him of inventing the Wayob calls as a way to lure her out for dinner, though she said it with a hint of amusement in her voice, like maybe if he really had, it would be fine—like maybe he should ask her out for real. And he'd planned to, before Rydell humiliated him. Now that she'd seen all that, all he could hope for was pity—and there was no path from pity to love.

Rydell grinned. "You have no idea, do you, Detective Parker?"

"How about you enlighten me?"

"No. Be grateful you know so little. Perhaps now I can allow you to live. If you get me where I need to go and stay out of my way." He waved the Ruger. "Think you can do that, Par-ker?"

"Of course," Saul lied.

"I do not wish to harm anyone," Rydell said, his voice

cracking. "But I have no choice."

Saroyan had said the same thing.

Saul nodded as if the notion made sense. "So then, who's putting you up to this?"

"A sadistic priest. Unfortunately, he died long ago."

What could Rydell possibly gain by blaming his actions on a dead priest? At least he was talking, and maybe if Saul could keep him talking, he'd say something useful. "So why take Jaggar hostage?"

"I needed a vehicle."

Saul turned right on Sunset as if uninterested in where they were going. Rydell fell silent and closed his eyes. The smirk remained on his face.

"You have a Jaguar and a Ferrari," Saul said. "Why bother with Jaggar's car?"

The smirk fell away. "This is exactly what I'm talking about, Parker. No questions."

Saul shrugged. "I was just thinking that if it was some kind of emergency, it might help your case."

Rydell pointed to the right. "Pull over. There in the grass."

"No parking," Saul said. "If I stop here, it'll raise all kinds of attention."

"Then stop somewhere discreet. I do not care where. Just make it fast. You are going the wrong way. I know it."

They crossed Sunset, and Saul turned left into a neighborhood, drove a block, and parked beside the vast lawn of a mansion.

In the passenger seat, Rydell crisscrossed his legs. "I must meditate. Say nothing, or I shall end your life." He rested the Ruger in his lap, aimed at Saul. His finger remained on the trigger as he closed his eyes and leaned back in the seat.

In the rear-view, Saul watched a familiar red Mustang turn the corner and pull to the curb a half-block behind them. Hernandez. She'd acquired the city-owned ride somehow while at Rampart Station and had managed to retain it when she got the bump up to Homicide Special. The other detectives all drove Crown Vics.

Beside Saul, Rydell's eyes remained closed. The corner of his mouth gradually wound back into a smirk.

Meditation required concentration. It required relaxation, especially in the face, Saul knew, because he'd started meditating in the hopes of curbing his near-constant compulsion to stuff food into his face. Acid roiled in his gut. Rydell was planning something. Probably thinking he didn't need Saul anymore, now that they had evaded the police. Rydell was about to make a move.

In the rear-view, all Saul saw of Hernandez was dark hair hanging down from her head. She was probably looking at her phone. *Look up.* Although it went against protocol to confront an armed gunman with a hostage, she would act if she thought Saul was in imminent danger.

Saul glanced at the Ruger in Rydell's hand and back at the rear-view. *Look up. Look up.*

She looked up.

He signaled for her to buzz by them in her Mustang by tilting his head and swiveling it forward. Saul needed Rydell distracted, just for a second, so he could gain the upper hand.

In the rear-view, Hernandez shook her head. She hadn't made sense of his signal.

He repeated the motion.

Through the windshield, she mouthed, *no.*

Maybe she didn't understand what he was asking, but she knew him well enough to assume he was about to try something dangerous.

But he had to. Regardless of Rydell's intentions, Saul needed to gain the upper hand to gain back the respect he'd lost back at the library, along with his clothes. Beauty, after all, was half confidence.

Saul removed the paperclip he kept wound around the band of his watch. He straightened it with his fingers.

Rydell's eyes remained closed. The smirk remained on his face.

With his left hand, Saul slipped the paperclip into the lock on the cuff on his right wrist. He used the lock as a fulcrum to bend the end of the paperclip into a *L*. Pushed it down into the lock. Turned it like a key against the ridges inside.

Rydell's eyes flicked open. His nostrils flared.

Saul jerked his wrist free just as Rydell shoved the Ruger toward his chest—impossible to miss.

Saul couldn't imagine a worse way to die with Hernandez right there to see it. His plus-sized body slumped in the seat. His already sweat-soaked t-shirt stained with blood. Belly hanging out over his tighty-whities, which wouldn't be white anymore after the bullet had pierced his heart and his bowels emptied out. And then the last thing she'd remember about him was the smell of his shit.

Unacceptable.

Rydell squeezed the trigger.

The Ruger didn't fire.

It couldn't fire, because Saul had shoved his finger into the trigger guard and blocked the trigger.

Rydell screamed, wrenched the Ruger to the side and might have broken Saul's finger off in the trigger guard, except Saul, with his other hand, had latched onto Rydell's arm.

Rydell froze.

Saul had to hold onto to the gun, which meant he had to hold onto Rydell, which meant he couldn't leverage his weight advantage. Instead, he pulled Rydell toward him.

Rydell winced. His grip loosened on the Ruger, and for a moment, Saul thought he might just let go.

No such luck. Saul clutched the Ruger with his right hand, his finger still wedged through the trigger guard. With his other hand, he released Rydell's arm and—before Rydell could react—released the Ruger's magazine. He tossed it into the footwell by Rydell's feet. A wasted effort if a bullet was in the chamber. Except, just as Saul had hoped, Rydell followed the motion with his eyes.

Saul pried out the takedown pin. Tossed it over his shoulder. Pulled the slide forward and off the frame. A bullet was in the chamber. Saul shook it loose, reducing the Ruger from a deadly weapon to a harmless piece of metal.

He'd disarmed Rydell, but that was the easy part.

Now he had to find pants. Hernandez hadn't seen him from behind, and he intended to keep it that way. But his pants were back at the library, and Rydell was a size thirty, thirty-two at the most. Even if the geometry worked, there wasn't time for Rydell to strip off his khakis and for Saul to put them on; Hernandez was already out of the Mustang and approaching the passenger side, Glock extended.

Rydell opened the door. So far, he hadn't looked back in Hernandez's direction.

Saul lunged across the divider between the seats, reaching for Rydell's arm. Rydell dodged. Before he could leap from the car, Saul grabbed his belt.

Rydell screamed.

Saul pulled him back. "Relax. Or she'll shoot you."

Rydell clutched onto the doorframe and stared out at Hernandez. She stood ten feet back, on the lawn Saul had parked beside, legs apart, Glock aimed at Rydell.

"Hands on your head," she said. "You have the right to remain silent. Anything you say can and will be used against you—"

"Shoot me," Rydell said. "I dare you."

Hernandez continued mirandizing and kept her weapon trained on Rydell in case Saul lost his grip, which meant it was up to him to subdue him. Which meant Saul—in his underwear, with Hernandez standing right there—had to climb on top of Rydell and pin him against the passenger seat.

He considered letting Rydell charge out of the car so Hernandez could shoot him. She would have to. And Rydell deserved to die.

But Saul couldn't allow it. More and more, he was starting to suspect a third party behind the whole Wayob act, and Rydell likely knew who it was.

So, dreading that Hernandez had to see this, Saul climbed on top of Rydell and pinned him face down in the seat, his belly pressed into Rydell's back.

Rydell screamed.

Heat flooded Saul's neck and face. He clung to the hope that although Hernandez could see his big, hairy back and his shoulders, maybe from where she stood, the roof of the plain wrap blocked her view of his butt.

Saul grabbed Rydell's left shoulder and pulled his arm behind his back. Rydell screamed in Spanish and then in some other language, which Saul had never heard before. Probably just gibberish.

He cuffed his wrist to Rydell's. "We're doing this the hard way," Saul said, "unless you want to tell us who Wayob is?"

With his right arm, Rydell was still trying to pry himself free. Hernandez holstered her Glock and approached. She was going to see.

"Stay back," Saul said. "I've got him."

"You see how Parker tortures me?" Rydell screamed. "I do not deserve such treatment. I was merely defending myself from Jaggar. Look at my arm. See the marks from his teeth?"

"So he bit you," Hernandez said, "and you bashed his head in? Sounds like a great defense you've got there."

Saul pressed forward, grabbed Rydell's right arm, and wrenched it free from the doorframe. But now all he could do was hold it behind his back. He needed another hand.

"Come in through the back," Saul said. "Help me cuff him."

Saul managed to hold onto Rydell while sliding back enough to get his butt down into the driver's seat, out of view, while Hernandez climbed in through the back. She reached between the seats and unlocked the cuff on Saul's wrist.

"Do not touch me, vile woman," Rydell said.

Hernandez transferred the cuff from Saul's wrist to Rydell's other arm. In the mirror, she locked eyes with Saul and brushed the shock of white from her forehead. "I'll drive him downtown," she said, her voice lower than normal, absolute.

She had a thick skin, Saul knew. But whatever her reason was for wanting to drive Rydell, Saul was happy to oblige. It would give him a chance to grab clothes on the way.

Unfortunately, it required him to get out of the car to

cover Rydell while Hernandez escorted him to her Mustang.

"You are wasting my time," Rydell said as he walked. But he climbed right in before she could shove him.

After securing Rydell, Hernandez presented Saul with his clothes. They were in the front passenger seat, folded neatly, suit on top of his trench coat. Saul held the stack over the lower part of his belly in a way that he hoped looked natural, like he wasn't consciously trying to hide it.

"Good work," she said.

"I had hoped Jagger might be alive," Saul said. Although, in truth, he had suspected the real reason Rydell had agreed to the exchange.

"He was dead before you got there. But thanks to you, we got Rydell alive."

Saul nodded. "If he starts talking, call me. Someone else is behind this whole Wayob thing, and I bet he knows who."

"Want to follow me? I'll wait."

No. He wasn't about to let her watch him pull his pants up over his butt, his belly hanging over the belt line. "I'll meet you at the PAB."

"Suit yourself," she said.

Saul chuckled. "Exactly."

As he stood facing her, the stack of clothes in front of his belly seemed to shrink. She got in the car. Sparked the engine. And sat there.

She was waiting for him to move.

But if he turned toward the plain wrap, she'd see his butt, the tear in his too-tight tighty-whities. And if he walked backward, she'd know how awkward he felt. And, probably, he'd fall on his ass.

So he turned. He strolled like he hardly cared that she saw (because beauty, after all, was half confidence). And he vowed to lose the butt—and the belly—whether or not she ever looked at him again.

Back To the Beginning

Ashley swings open the front door to the claustrophobic mid-century where she'd awakened in the body of a stranger, closes it behind her, and leans against it. The nightmare started here, so this is where it has to end.

At Oakhurst Academy, where she'd been shipped off to at age six when her nanny married her father, escape rooms were huge. When you get stuck in an escape room, you have to go back to the beginning and try something else. The obvious thing never works. That would be too easy.

Of course Sammy didn't believe she was trapped in the body of some guy. She wouldn't believe it either. But here she is.

After Sammy had denied her access to her own house, she'd gone to Don's, because she always went to Don, but his gate might as well have been a wall. It was Don's new wife, Connie, who'd answered the intercom. Connie, only two years older than Ashley, gets off on acting superior, like there's any chance she'll be granted some of Don's power and influence in the inevitable divorce.

"I'm sorry, who are you?" Connie had said.

Ashley had looked into the camera mounted above the gate and tried out a disarming smile, like a guy who might be Don's buddy. "I'm a friend of Don's." As soon as she says it, she recalls that Don doesn't have any male friends.

Don's voice booms through the speaker. "Have we met before?"

"Many, many times." If she could look into Don's eyes, maybe she could reach him. "Let me in and I'll explain."

"Explain what?"

"Just let me in."

"I'm hanging up."

No way being Gray Wilson would get her through the gate. She had to work with what she had. "I'm Ashley York. I know, hard to believe—"

"Whoa, buddy. I need you to leave."

"You got me the screen test with Sean Penn for the Kaufman film. Please let me in. Just for ten minutes—"

"Who are you with, *Variety*? I'm not confirming anything."

"No. It's me, Ashley. You said I could count on you—for anything, Don. You said to come to you first. One step at a time, right? Like you always say. Just let me come in and we can talk, you'll see. I need help."

"Look, this is my house. This is where I live. You have no right to be here."

"And how do I know where you live?" she asks, although she knows at this point it's useless. What could Don to do, anyway?

"What's your number?" he asks. "I'll find someone to help."

But he wouldn't. She knew he wouldn't. He just wants the crazy man away from his house.

"I needed you, Don. Remember that." Ashley slams the car in reverse and speeds away, seething through her teeth that when she gets back to her own body, she'll fire his ass and find some other agent.

But how would she get back to normal? She can't drive around forever with no money and no one believing who she is. And, damn it, she's hungry. Going back to Gray's house is basically her only option.

As she grinds through the stop-and-go on Santa Monica

Boulevard, she can't shake this feeling of being watched, which is weird because she's so used to people staring at her. But no one would know her in Gray's body. She's anonymous, now—incognito. The only car behind her is a green Jaguar, two people inside, their features obscured by the reflection of sky on the windshield. Still, she feels something like sinister eyes on her back.

That had given her another reason to return to Gray's. She'd never been alone in LA after dark.

"Is that you, Gray?" a woman shouts from the living room.

Ashley opens her eyes. "That's me." She'll play along. She's an actress, after all. She can fake her way through this.

Ashley parades to the living room, where the TV is on, and the colossal mess of magazines and coloring books have overflowed from the table onto the floor. On the couch, the woman Ashley now knows is Claire, the only favorited contact in Gray's phone, is sporting a faded green t-shirt and sweatpants. In her lap, the baby coos and when Claire ignores it, staring at her phone, the baby coos louder.

"Thanks for the advance notice that I'd be a single parent today," Claire says without looking up.

It occurs to her that Claire might have noticed the real Gray do something out of the ordinary, something to cause Ashley to wake up in his body—something Ashley can reverse. She hopes so. "Sorry about that," she says. "Thank you. I appreciate you."

Claire looks up from her phone. "Huh?"

"I was just wondering, did you notice anything unusual yesterday? I did something weird, right?"

Claire's brows furrow. "What are you talking about?"

That's the problem. She doesn't know what she's talking about.

Claire turns up the TV. An anchor woman with painted-on eyebrows stands before a gate wrapped in yellow police tape. The gate looks familiar. As the camera pans, Ashley recognizes the street. It's Don's street.

"At eleven a.m.," the anchor woman says, "Martin Rydell

stormed through this gate and assaulted Tommy Morello, a food delivery worker. According to a source in the Beverly Hills Police Department, Morello was armed in spite of regulations, and shot and injured with his own gun. Rydell then took Bob Jaggar hostage. We're still learning the details, but sometime after police cornered Rydell at the Beverly Hills Library, he allegedly murdered Bob Jaggar."

"Holy shit," Ashley says, "I could have been killed."

"What are you talking about?" Claire asks.

Ashley doesn't want to go there. Explaining to Claire how she had left Don's probably minutes before the kidnapping is more than she can manage right now. "It just makes you think is all."

"Huh?"

Ashley puts a finger to her lips. On the screen, a montage of Bob Jaggar's career is cut to a soundtrack of cheesy guitar with a raspy male singer. His most notable roles appear to be cheap-looking sitcoms from before Ashley was born. She sure hopes her career sums up to something more meaningful.

The anchor returns to say the police have apprehended Martin Rydell. A mugshot pops up on the screen of an older white man, his skin so pale it looks like he's never seen sunlight.

Ashley shivers.

The news cuts to the police building downtown. A Latina detective with gray bangs promises justice for the senseless killing of a beloved Angelino.

Claire mutes the volume. "Are you making dinner? I did breakfast and lunch."

Ashley hasn't eaten all day. Maybe with something in her stomach, she could think. She's never actually cooked before, but she knows how to heat stuff up.

In the kitchen, she opens the fridge. Its meager contents are all piled onto the middle shelf, as if thrown in with no consideration for arrangement. Bags of wilted green stuff that might have been salad some weeks ago, a block of bright orange cheese, a Tupperware of some white, clumpy stuff that makes her gag. Good thing there's nothing in her stomach to throw up.

She checks the cabinet between the fridge and the pantry. It contains several bottles of brown booze. She moves one aside to see if they have anything good. Behind the booze, at the very back of the cabinet, she spots a round, white stone with a black snake on top. A stone with a spooky, black snake is a strange thing to have. Stranger still to hide it in the back of the cabinet behind a bunch of booze.

She slides the booze aside and snatches up the stone. A pattern of tiny holes spiral from the side to the bottom. The chiseled snake is mounted at the center of its belly. It looks eerily similar to the cave painting her dad showed her on his phone. But how could that be?

If only she could remember his number.

She runs a finger along the S-shaped snake, which seems rigged to turn, but when she applies pressure, it won't move. She tries the other way.

It turns.

A half-turn. Then it sticks, with the snake's forked tongue pointing directly at her.

She shivers. If she believed in magic, which now maybe she has to, this would be just the kind of thing some idiot who should know better would mess with—and mess up her whole life in the process.

Does the stone have something to do with her presence here in Gray's body? If so, and if her dad has any idea of what it can do, then his obsession suddenly makes sense. Evan York doesn't waste his time on anything less than spectacular. That would also explain why he'd refused to tell her what it could do, because who would believe it without seeing proof?

Could this really be one of the artifacts he'd been searching for?

The one he'd bought Friday didn't work, he'd said. What if this one does? What if this was what he'd been searching for all this time, and here she is holding it in her hand with no way to tell him she's found it?

Ashley marches back to the living room. Claire is still on her phone, still watching some crap reality show, a big-haired actress complaining that some bitch tried to slip in the shower with her boyfriend, the bad words bleeped over but obvious.

Ashley stands in front of the screen and holds up the artifact. "How does it work?"

Claire glances up at her. "How would I know? What's it supposed to do?"

Maybe it doesn't do anything at all. "What did you see me do with it?"

"I saw you try to hide it when we came home. How much did it cost?"

Ashley turns it over again, like maybe there's a price tag. "I don't remember. Where did I buy it? I'll check my credit card?"

Claire slaps her phone down in her lap. Her eyes widen. "Are you kidding me? You told me you were going to the bathroom. What's going on?"

Good question. Ashley stares at the snake. She'd woken up this way, so maybe now that she's turned the snake, she just has to fall sleep, and when she wakes up, everything would be back to normal.

Ashley starts toward the bedroom.

Claire shouts after her. "Where are you going? What about dinner?"

In the hallway, out of nowhere, a little girl with cocoa-colored curls ambushes Ashley's legs. Ashley stumbles and throws her hands out reflexively to catch herself on the wall, dropping the artifact. She just manages to restrain herself from shoving aside this girl, who is now clinging to her leg, swaying as she giggles, her curls bouncing.

She's quite endearing. Ashley smiles in spite of herself.

A few feet away on the worn, beige carpet, the artifact is on its side, the snake sticking up at an angle. It looks intact.

From the other room, Claire yells over the din of the TV, "Mindy, you'd better not be out of your room."

Mindy blinks and stares up at Ashley. She has chestnut eyes and surprisingly thick lashes. "But Daddy's home!"

"Do you need to go back to your room?" Ashley asks her.

Mindy frowns, then giggles. "Tickle me."

"What?"

"Tickle me."

"Wait. So, you *want* me to tickle you?"

"No." Still holding onto Ashley's leg, Mindy leans back. She *does* want to be tickled, and if Ashley tickles her, maybe she'll let go.

Ashley bends over and digs her fingers into Mindy's ribs. "Tickle, tickle, tickle."

Mindy releases her leg and falls back on the floor. She rubs her side. "You hurt me."

Ashley's never tickled a kid before. Why did she think she knew how? She squats down beside Mindy and strokes her hair. "I didn't mean to." She really hadn't tickled her all that hard.

Mindy's lip quivers. She turns away and, without another word, goes to her room and shuts the door.

Ashley picks up the artifact. The snake and spindle its attached to are carved from black glass, which could easily have broken, but it seems intact, fortunately.

Ashley returns to the master bedroom and wades through the piles of clothes to the less messy of the two matching pine nightstands. She sets the artifact beside the metal Ikea lamp, lays back on the bed, and closes her eyes.

She inhales slowly. Exhales. "I am in control. I am in control," she repeats again and again like a mantra.

A few minutes later, she feels better. But she's not tired at all. What if she does somehow wake up back in her own body? Will she ever have a chance like this again? That moment with Mindy back there in the hallway, that was a gift. Ashley should have enjoyed Mindy's giggling, the way she was so ecstatic to see Ashley, even though she thought Ashley was her father. Mindy is like the daughter Ashley has always imagined herself having, except instead of blonde hair like Ashley's, Mindy has amazing brown curls, almost begging Ashley to brush them.

It's only Sunday. Ashley still has until Tuesday before the big screen test. And, for all she knows, this could be a dream—a very, very real dream. She hasn't really spent any time exploring what the hell this is. All she did all day was freak out about her body, her whole life lost behind the gates of Beverley Park.

She yanks down the jeans that are not hers and then the awful, black underwear she woke up in. She squeezes the limp sausage… Nothing happens.

She rubs. It is sensitive, but nothing like her clit—her lost clit. *Stop… Be here. Own this narrative.*

She unbuttons the shirt and rubs her abs. They have some potential. Maybe with some manscaping and a training regimen this bod of Gray's could look better than August's, which is too buff for his height. He won't admit it, but she knows the reason he always insists on meeting at wherever they're going out is because he's nearly a head shorter and doesn't want to be photographed walking in beside her.

She sniffs her armpit. Baby powder and man sweat, which she actually prefers to the overpowering deodorants men like to wear.

She cups the sack. Rolls the right ball between her thumb and forefinger and gently squeezes. It hurts. Even with this tiny pressure, it's clear that if she squeezes any harder, the pain will be unbearable. At Oakhurst Academy, her roommate thought squeezing a guy's balls was a huge turn on, and all this time Ashley had believed her, but damn was she wrong. Way, way wrong. Now Ashley understands why whenever she went for August's balls, he pulled her hand away and placed it on the tip.

But something is happening.

A swelling sensation.

She squeezes the shaft. It's growing… getting stiffer. As she strokes, the head becomes more and more sensitive. It feels good.

And at the same time, weird.

This urge to keep touching; it's just too weird. She wrenches the jeans up and belts them over the bulge. Buttons her shirt down over it.

Takes a deep breath. Gets up from the bed.

Solitary Confinement

It was Sunday, so the PAB was mostly empty. On the fourth floor, Saul wheeled a chair from a conference room, dropped his to-go bag into the seat and pushed the chair down the hall. The bag contained two burgers from The Counter, one for him, a half-pounder with provolone and bacon; and one for Hernandez, chipotle turkey with cranberries and jalapeño jack. But it had taken him too long to get here. She was already at the press conference, where the media was going to love her as she exuded competence to all the citizens of LA and demanded justice for Bob Jagger, as if the murder of a once popular TV star mattered more than all the others.

And as thanks for her good performance today, Hernandez could count on more media headaches, and probably, at some point, a promotion. Did she want that? He hated to lose her. She was a damn good detective. And every time she looked at him, something fluttered in his stomach.

But now that she had seen his double-wide butt, the best he could hope for was pity. Maybe it was better if she got promoted. No reason to torture himself by being around her and her pity. He shoved the chair forward. Its wheels skidded on the linoleum.

He yanked his burger from the bag. Tore off the wrapper. Took a big, honking bite. The beef was cold. He hardly tasted it before taking another bite.

As he approached the holding cell, Rydell sat on the bunk and leaned back.

"Par-ker. I knew you would come."

Saul stared at him through the bars and chewed.

Rydell tried to look placid, but his jaw tightened. The slant of his brows betrayed him.

Saul ate the last bite and now that he wasn't focused on himself, he tasted it—Angus beef, cheese, bacon, and bread. Blended together. Perfect harmony. "So." He swallowed. "You're telepathic too?"

"No, I have experience with men like you, Parker. You are like a fly. I swat you away and swat you away, and yet still you return. Only one way to get rid of a fly."

Saul pulled his phone from his pocket and started an audio recording. "Mind if I record this?"

Rydell said nothing. Maybe if he made a clear and credible threat, the DA would add it to the long list of charges.

"It sounded like you threatened me," Saul said.

"It was a promise. Your fault that I am here. Release me now, or I shall have to take revenge."

"And how, exactly, do you intend to carry out this revenge of yours?"

Rydell sat up. "I have the means to free myself. As I have demonstrated to you."

"Are you talking about Saroyan?"

"You are still not seeing me for who I am, Parker."

Saul wasn't sure how to handle this. Maybe humoring him would lead somewhere? "It's hard to see you when you look like someone else, Wayob." Saul tried to follow his delusional line of logic. "So you're saying you escaped from Saroyan's body to Aleman's, and now you're Rydell?"

"He is my vessel, yes."

"Well, it won't happen again. We have ways of preventing your 'escape.' Very uncomfortable ways." Saul hoped Rydell wouldn't call his bluff.

He shrugged. "Chain me to the wall. Go ahead. But soon I'll be free. You should be careful, Detective Parker."

The burger bricked in Saul's stomach. It wasn't Rydell's words. It was the way he spoke that got under Saul's skin.

I'm done with him, Hernandez had said, a fierceness in her voice like Saul had never heard before. She'd asked Saul to book Rydell into the MDC, where, according to protocol, he should be held until arraignment. But Saroyan had nearly died there, and now with Aleman back on duty and somehow involved in whatever the hell this was... *No, I'm not moving him. No way.* Rydell was going to spend the night right here. Saul could count on the watch commander to let it slide.

Now that he had Rydell behind bars, maybe he could press his advantage to make him talk. He rolled the chair up to the bars. Lifted the bag containing the one remaining burger and held it out. Hernandez wasn't going to eat it. After the press conference, she had to get to home to her son.

"What is that?" Rydell asked.

"Turkey burger," Saul said. "Might be good."

"Severed bird flesh and bread. Get that filth away from me."

Saul sat in the chair and looked in the bag. The burger was wrapped in white paper. His mouth watered. He wanted to try it, but he shouldn't. He should give it to the watch commander for keeping an eye on Rydell.

He closed the bag. Rydell's lips stretched into an unnatural grin. A film of dry skin on his upper lip cracked and split.

In the car, Rydell had asked, *What did she tell you?* before he clammed up, no doubt realizing he'd slipped. But now Saul had an idea who this *she* was.

"What did you think she told me?"

Rydell's grin became a grimace. "What are you talking about?"

"You know."

Rydell glanced down and to the right. "Why would I care

what some vile woman told you?"

"Are you talking about Hernandez or Mrs. Luna?"

Rydell said nothing. His face turned from pale to ashen.

"Why did you kill Luis Luna?"

Rydell said nothing.

"Maybe you want to let Saroyan take the blame after all?"

Nothing again, but this time Saul waited him out.

Rydell glanced around the four by ten cell. "I do not know what it is you are talking about."

Without realizing it, Saul had unwrapped the second burger and bitten into it. The turkey was quite tasty, although he would always be a beef man. Since it now had a bite missing, he might as well finish it. No big hurry to get thin now that Hernandez had seen how huge he was. No way she could forget.

He'd eat the rest, but not in front of that smirk and the arrogant arch of his brow. Saul rewrapped the burger, stuffed it in the bag, and stood up.

"Sleep tight."

Rydell leaped up and grabbed the bars. "Hernandez said I must bed down with the worst of your prisoners, like before."

Now Saul had no doubt about keeping Rydell in the holding cell. Maybe a night alone would loosen his tongue. "I decided to spare you."

"Then do not leave me here." Rydell's pitch shot up as he spoke. He pressed his face against the bars, tears welling in his eyes. Crocodile tears. "Please."

Saul dropped the bag in the chair. "I've got work to do."

"You forget your occupation, Parker—serve and protect. I am the victim. I *am* the victim."

"And how is that?"

Rydell's face reddened. "It was the priest." His lip curled. "The odious, fucking priest."

Last time Rydell mentioned the priest, he'd also mentioned the priest was dead, and now Saul had a growing suspicion who had killed him. "What was his name?"

"Ajau Kan Kakzik."

A strange sounding name. Too strange for Rydell to have just made it up.

"Where's the body?"

"I did not kill him," Rydell said. "But you would not blame me if I had, if you knew the torture he had inflicted upon me. He locked me in darkness—for centuries."

"Sounds pretty bad," Saul said. "And also like a load of nonsense."

"Did you speak to the old Luna woman? I am curious why she said her poor son had to die."

Saul's stomach lurched. Mrs. Luna had claimed responsibility. Though there could be a lot of misguided reasons for her to blame herself, she had refused to explain why. She was hiding something. That had been clear. Hernandez had picked up on it, too.

"The way this works," Saul said, "is I ask the questions and you answer them."

Rydell's trademark smirk flickered at the corner of his lips. "She did not tell you anything. Of course. You would be wasting your time to even talk to her, because you know she is senile. Out of her head."

"Where is she?"

Rydell laughed. "You cannot find her? Some detective you are."

"You have anything to do with that?"

The grin vanished. "Do not blame your ineptitude on me."

"She didn't come home last night."

Rydell's brows launched up his forehead. His eyes widened. Maybe he didn't know where the Lunas were, but he knew something. And he was afraid.

"I get a phone call. Do I not?"

Saul shrugged. "Maybe tomorrow."

"I need my call. You cannot keep me here without my phone call."

Technically, he was right. He was allowed a call within a reasonable amount of time. But Saul would get away with delaying it. He had recorded more than enough to justify his concern that Rydell might use his call to place more people in danger.

"You're doing this to yourself," Saul said. "Tell me what's going on and we'll work something out."

Rydell turned his back on Saul. He grabbed the bunk and shook it. It held fast against the wall. "I cannot stay here."

"Then give me some reason to let you out."

"I shall take my revenge. An equal measure to the torture you have inflicted upon me."

"Good luck with that." He had better things to do than to stand here listening to Rydell talk in circles. He had to find the Lunas. He rolled the chair back down the hall.

"Parker. Parker!" Rydell's voice echoed after him. "Parker?"

Saul rolled the chair back to the conference room, and hefted the bag from the chair, the last burger with all but one bite remaining.

"Parker!"

At the elevators, Saul pressed the up button.

"Be careful out there in the fog," Rydell shouted down the hall.

Saul stepped into the elevator and waited as the doors closed. Then he called the watch commander to request a welfare check at the Lunas apartment in El Monte.

Ashley and Mindy

Mindy, now in pink pajamas, pulls a book from the shelf by her little bed and hands it to Ashley. It's *Where the Wild Things Are*. Mindy snuggles under the pink comforter. Ashley sits beside her and starts to read. She finds herself enjoying the story, more than Mindy, apparently, who is frowning.

"What about Prince Spinach?"

Ashley glances at the shelf where books are jammed in and twisted sideways. She moves a stack to her lap and begins shelving them from biggest to smallest. "Help me find it."

"No," Mindy says. "He's a Wild Thing. *You know*."

Ashley wishes she did, but she doesn't. She skims the rest of the story. No hint of Prince Spinach. "Prince Spinach took a vacation," she says. "Hopefully, he'll be back tomorrow." She continues reading where she left off.

"You're reading it wrong," Mindy says.

Of course she is, but what can she say? She's not Mindy's father. She doesn't want to freak Mindy out. She tries reading Carol with a deep, silly voice.

"Quit it. Read it the right way." But Mindy's laughing now.

After Ashley finishes the story, Mindy insists on a second reading, during which she falls asleep. Ashley shelves the book neatly and lays back, her long man-legs draping off the kid-sized bed. She shuts her eyes and listens to Mindy's peaceful breathing beside her, feeling closer than she could have imagined. On some level, Mindy must sense her dad is different, but she doesn't hold back, not at all.

As Ashley moves to get up, Mindy snuggles into her chest. Unconditional trust. Ashley melts back into the bed, not wanting to disturb her innocent sleep and so exhausted, she might soon fall asleep herself.

Her attempt at macaroni and cheese had turned into a trying ordeal. Not because it was hard in and of itself but there were too many distractions from Mindy and Tyler. Tyler had literally cried over spilled milk—screamed, actually—and the juice she'd poured for Mindy had been the wrong kind and needed ice, but not that much ice. The macaroni had almost burned, and then Tyler mushed it around more than he ate it. He'd laughed at Ashley's attempt to wipe his face, raked the macaroni from his tray onto the floor, and started crying again as if some great injustice had occurred. Then, finally, Claire entered the kitchen. Smirking as if *of course* she had to bail Ashley out. That had made Ashley feel better because obviously the real Gray couldn't even handle both kids on his own.

Now she understands that all the help her own dad had employed had nothing to do with him not wanting her. Raising a child is a lot for one person on his own, and with everything else on his plate, especially after the second marriage ended, he had needed the help. No wonder Claire is cranky. She's probably overwhelmed from managing Tyler and Mindy alone all day. She looks exhausted. Her lids are dark and puffy but her eyes have a depth. Maybe if the corners of her mouth weren't tightened down, she would be beautiful. Maybe even more beautiful than Raquel. Maybe, after some rest and a spa-day, Claire would be interesting.

Claire and Sex

Claire is lying on the couch when Gray bursts out of Mindy's room and makes a beeline toward her. She pretends to focus on her phone. As Gray's eyes dart around the mess of magazines she's been meaning to sort through, her body stiffens. Why can't he just leave her alone?

Gray rakes the Legos aside on the floor by the couch and plops down by her head, seemingly unaware of Mindy's drool on his shirt. Claire stares at her phone but it's just the icons on the home screen. She doesn't even know which app to open.

"Are you okay?" he asks as though he might really want an answer this time, his voice lacking the usual, bitter undertone.

"I'm tired," she says, like he couldn't just guess. "If I could just sleep…" If the insomnia would just stop crawling under the covers and itching in hard to scratch places.

"I wish you could," he says. His stoic mask is missing, and behind it, there is no sign of the sadness she knows he's been hiding. If anything, he looks worried, maybe even scared. Probably, he's wondering what she's been thinking. They both know their marriage is crumbling.

"I'm sorry," she says.

"Me too?"

Why is he saying it like a question? Like maybe he isn't sorry for the argument he started last night? She can't even remember what it was about now. She swallows her anger. He is trying to bridge the canyon of crap between them. She should make an effort, maybe even take it a step further, because he is apologizing. Probably he has no idea what she's saying sorry for. "For last night," she says, but she means for everything, for the way they've become. "You didn't have to sleep on the couch."

At least if he hadn't, she wouldn't have stayed awake all night wondering if he'd ever get into bed beside her. She had tried counting backward from a hundred, promising to fall asleep by fifty, then twenty-five. But of course, it didn't work. It never did. When Tyler started crying, it was almost a relief. It gave her a reason to get out of bed.

"Maybe you should have come to get me." He smiles, and his smile seems different, or maybe she just forgot what it looked like. She hasn't seen him smile in so long.

He leans toward her, like he might kiss her, but then he stops.

"What?" she asks, although she knows. "It's too late." She's known it for weeks, months, maybe longer. Yet they keep going through the motions, as if their marriage might suddenly spring back to life.

"No," he says. "It's not like that." An intense mix of emotions swirls across his face as he stares at her, as if deciding which one to react to. He leans over her... and kisses her.

His lips flounder around, like it's their first kiss. She pushes back on his shoulder, but with little effort. She opens her mouth to tell him to stop, to tell him it's too late—it's over—but their tongues touch, and when he pulls back to breathe, she can't say it.

He looks into her eyes, like he is seeing her all over again for the first time.

She wants him to stop, but if he does then it's for sure—their marriage is over. And just by thinking this, she knows it's the last thing she wants.

She climbs in his lap and massages his shoulders. He rubs her neck. His touch shoots electricity up and down her spine. This new way of pressing his fingertips into her muscles is exactly what she needed, after all these years of begging him to try something different, now—finally—he gets it.

And she has been withholding herself, spending all that time on Instagram trying to tune out of her life—their life. That must be why he said he was Ashley York. It was a plea for attention.

He kisses her again. It feels new, somehow, different.

"Maybe we should stop," Gray says.

"No," she says. She might even get some sleep if they have sex. "But, not in here."

She leads him to the bedroom, where in the doorway she pulls her shirt over her head and throws it to him.

He shuts the door. She lays back on the bed, her hands behind her head.

He leans over her, bathed in the rectangle of dim light streaming in through the window. Kisses her nipple. Just the tip. His lips are like tiny sparks, a current she's never felt before.

What was the point she'd been making by giving him the cold shoulder for so many months? Whatever the reason was, it was stupid. What a waste. All this time that she was punishing Gray she was really punishing herself, because she needs this more than he does.

She runs her fingers through his hair. Pulls his head to her other breast. As he takes it in his mouth, she arches her back. Her pulse quickens. The need rises in her body. She slides out of her sweatpants, embarrassed for him to see that she didn't even bother with underwear today. She pushes his hand down. Over her stomach and further down. Presses his fingers into her. *See how ready I am.* She unbuckles his belt.

As he struggles out of his jeans, they tangle at his ankles. He falls to the bed.

It reminds her of college, their first time in her dorm. Just like that night, he now sits on the bed with one foot free and the other still caught in his pants. She swallows a laugh. It's the funniest thing she has seen in weeks.

She flexes her hips. "Hurry up."

When he finally climbs over her, his face looks younger, and the way he touches her, she feels alive. Awake. When he slides inside her, he sighs, and the vibration of his voice resonates all over her. She moans.

He shoves his fingers into her mouth. All she needs right now is for him to keep moving. She arches her back.

His rhythm is uncontrolled. He closes his eyes, and he's off. Gone. Somewhere else. And that's fine. Just don't stop. *Do. Not. Stop. Never stop.*

But then she feels his slickness, and he falls beside her on the sheets.

She throws a leg over his sweaty stomach and straddles him. "Is that it?"

His eyes remain closed.

She pulls on her sweatpants and leaves the room without bothering to turn off the lights.

Death Is No End

Wayob rips a ribbon of cloth from his shirt. There is no way to silence the tearing threads. He cannot stop. Can. Not. Stop. If he stops, he might never start again, and he must—must, must, must—finish before Parker returns.

This is all Parker's fault. All of it. Wayob has to die because Parker—Parker!—has isolated him in this cell and prevented him from taking a new vessel.

Parker thinks he is so smart. Parker has no idea. He suspects. Maybe, Parker suspects, but he does not believe. He shall though, and by then it shall be too late. Wayob will see to that. He shall laugh in Parker's face.

Is Wayob immortal? He certainly feels no different than he did all those centuries ago before the odious priest banished him into darkness, disembodied inside the Encanto.

Egregious priest.

What can stop Wayob from living forever? Not Parker. Certainly not Parker.

Truthfully though, Wayob had not meant to kill anyone.

Jaggar truly was an accident. He did not deserve death any more than Wayob deserves to be locked up. Not his fault. Wayob wishes he could take it back. He would if he could.

He who holds the Encanto was the one who drove away in a vehicle, leaving Wayob no choice but to pursue him. This happened just after Wayob awakened in the vessel of Rydell. He had been trying to meditate on the sound of the mind of he who holds the Encanto—so much harder to hear than Abuela's—when his concentration was broken by someone yelling somewhere outside Rydell's palace. Since it seemed the yelling was not ceasing, Wayob went outside to insist that it did.

And that was when he heard the words of the man. His man. Across the street, he was in a vehicle outside a gate, yelling into a metal box that he was someone else. And then Wayob knew, he was the one who holds the Encanto. He had to be, because when Wayob had felt himself being pulled from the Encanto, he concentrated, really concentrated on the man who holds the Encanto, who Wayob must kill. Though truthfully, he would prefer not to, but kill that man Wayob must. Wayob would kill a thousand times if he had to. The death of one man no more than a grain of sand to the ocean of darkness inside the Encanto, where minutes pass like hours, days like centuries. A torture worse than death—the injustice of the abominable priest. Anyone would kill to save themselves from such agony.

Before Wayob could reach him, the man pulled away from the gate, leaving Wayob no choice but to obtain a vehicle and pursue, and he had previously learned better than to try and drive at the same time. If he had not wrecked, he might have reached Abuela before she gave the Encanto to this man, and Wayob could have spared himself another night of agony disembodied in its darkness.

So he had needed someone else to drive, and he found someone right there at the palace next to Rydell's. But the man with shaggy hair pulled a weapon on Wayob, leaving Wayob no choice. If Wayob had known the delay it would cause taking Jaggar hostage, he would have just shot himself right there and then. Wayob could have found a new vessel. Someone close to the man who has the Encanto.

But no, thanks to Parker, now Wayob is locked in this

filthy cell.

Parker cannot keep Wayob trapped alone like this forever, can he? Wayob will not risk waiting, not this time. If he who possesses the Encanto turns back the dial or gives the Encanto away, Wayob shall be pulled back inside, trapped in an agony much worse than the death he must now inflict upon himself. Total deprivation of all senses. Trapped in rumination with no way out, waiting and waiting and waiting and waiting and waiting for someone to use the Encanto…, Wayob shall go insane.

A magic as strong as Xibalba, as Earth itself. Pity the atrocious priest who banished Wayob to this miserable existence died centuries ago, his flesh no doubt rotted in the jungle along with the whole Mayan Empire. The priest deserved to die a miserable death, which Wayob would have enjoyed carrying out. But Wayob shall still have his revenge when he destroys the Encanto and frees himself forever.

Unfortunately, Wayob must first kill himself. Though not exactly himself—he must not think like this or he will never get it done—only this body that Wayob occupies must die. It will feel like Wayob is dying. Thanks to Parker, Wayob only has this horrible, painful means of escaping this terrible place. But Wayob would die a thousand times before returning to the Encanto.

He knots the cloth strips into a makeshift rope. His hands slow and become unsteady. It is Rydell, his subconscious desire to live impeding Wayob's progress, making Wayob doubt his actions. But Wayob has been through this before. So long as he who holds the Encanto still owns it and still occupies a body other than their own, Wayob shall awaken in a new vessel, another body to control.

Wayob hopes. For he does not really know. Not for sure. It's not like the wicked priest bothered to explain how the Encanto works before banishing Wayob into this tortured existence.

Though Wayob's mind has dominated Rydell's, he is not powerless, and he seems to be awakening, breaking free from the paralysis through which he has witnessed Wayob's actions in his body. Every muscle strains against Wayob's effort to move it. But Wayob shall overcome him. Rydell's life shall end. Pity. This is Parker's fault. Parker killing Rydell. Not Wayob, not really.

Wayob has seen the inside of many minds. He knows that in the reverse situation, Rydell would kill Wayob. For Wayob is no worse than anyone else. In fact, Wayob is better. At least Wayob is honest about his desire.

Not like Abuela, who must have wanted something. She must have had some reason for keeping the Encanto all those years. She is so strong to be able to resist Wayob's whispering for so long, and also smart, Wayob must concede. Somehow, last night, she had known how near Wayob was, for just as he finally fought his way through the mob—his skin crawling from all the many people he had to shoulder past—and her little hut where she performed her fortune-telling-charade was finally within Wayob's sight, she gave the Encanto away. And by doing so, she forced Wayob out of Aleman's body and back into the darkness. The nothingness. Alone.

Does she know what she did? Does she have any idea? Wayob shall tell her—no, he shall show her—that all her effort served only to delay his freedom, and for this she must pay. He does not wish to harm her. Wayob would never harm anyone. No, they bring it upon themselves. They torture Wayob and leave him no choice.

And now Parker—fucking Parker—seems determined to follow in the footsteps of Abuela's dead husband, Sosa. Despite the distance and all the time, so much time. Glacial time. Parker, who hunts Wayob, when Wayob should be helped. Needs to be helped. Why does no one care about Wayob? Wayob does not want any trouble. Does not wish to harm anyone. Wayob is the victim, the one who for centuries has suffered the egregious torture of the revolting priest.

Parker knows nothing compared to what Sosa knew, would know nothing at all if he had not tricked Wayob, angered Wayob into admitting... what? Wayob cannot remember what he said to Parker. No matter, the swine shall suffer. Wayob shall see to that. Wayob shall not let Parker get the best of Wayob again.

With so many obstacles, it is a miracle Wayob can make any progress at all. So many people who care only about themselves regardless of how their actions serve to further Wayob's suffering. Like Saroyan, who almost certainly discovered the power of the Encanto while Wayob was probing his mind for an escape from Parker's false imprisonment. Saroyan's memories were useless, and now, if he knows of the Encanto, he will stop at nothing to gain for himself a new body, one with legs that function as they should. He will try to obtain the Encanto. He will get in Wayob's way.

So now Wayob must go out of his way to put Saroyan down. No choice. Maybe Wayob can take down Saroyan and Parker both in one swoop?

Losing focus. Wayob must do this deed. This time—once he awakens in a new vessel—he shall take care of Saroyan, Parker, and end the life of the man who has the Encanto. Then Wayob shall take the Encanto for himself, ensuring his freedom, forever.

Does he not deserve at least one life to live, maybe two, after all he has suffered? Even Death would be better than the dark, the dark-dark-dark and alone.

Wayob tightens the makeshift noose around his neck, and the other end he ties to the metal bar between the posts of the top bunk. But it lacks enough height. Aside from the bunk, the only other item in the cell is a sink combined with a toilet. So, Wayob must kneel. He must lean forward against the noose, feet back and knees above the floor, in order to create enough pressure to stop blood flow to his brain, to restrict breathing...

It is not working.

Reaching up, Rydell fights Wayob's will. Forcing the arms to pull against the noose.

Stop, Rydell. Stop. Wayob controls your body.

Wayob screams, mustering all his willpower. He twists the knot tighter. Twist. Twist. The bed creaks as though it might topple forward despite being bolted to the wall. Wayob fights Rydell in his mind. Arms release the noose, but now feet come under him, taking his weight.

No. No, no, no. No no no no.

Wayob controls. "You are nothing Rydell. You are powerless," Wayob says through gritted teeth.

Strain. Straining. Strain.

Wayob forces his hands that are Rydell's hands down to his ankles. Wayob lifts his legs off the ground. All his weight held by the torn strips of cloth tied around his neck.

Straining... No. Stay...

Arms locked around legs. Unable to breathe. If he can just pass out, gravity shall take care of the rest. Gravity will help Wayob, unlike everyone else.

And it is not just Rydell fighting to live, Wayob realizes —it is himself. Wayob. His own instinct for self-preservation which must be suppressed.

Think of the freedom. Now, think of the darkness... never again.

Wayob shall be whole—a whole true person, as he once was. Human. Finally and forever free of the Encanto.

Freedom shall come from dying now. His reward. His revenge on Parker. Parker, who has forced Wayob to kill himself. Parker must suffer himself.

Wayob almost smiles as the cinderblock wall before him fades into darkness.

Parker... One more minute. Just one more. Unconsciousness...

Parker. Parker. Parker.

Saul and Marla

Saul parked by the line of palms, trunks like gray pillars rising into the clouds. Using his phone as a flashlight, he found the gate in the hedge. He held his lockpick out and ready... and useless.

His shoulders dropped. He felt suddenly heavy and needed to sit.

He'd found in nothing in Rydell's background to explain his actions. No connection to Saroyan or Aleman or Wayob. Or to anyone. Rydell had no living family or friends. It was almost sad the way the man seemed to move through life with as little impact as possible, subsisting off the fortune he'd inherited from his father's grocery store chain.

Saul would feel better with a guard watching Rydell, but the holding cell wasn't approved for overnights and the cameras were blocked up in court, the ACLU arguing they violated a prisoner's right to privacy. Still, the holding cell beat checking Rydell into MDC where Aleman was on duty and Saroyan had nearly gotten himself killed.

Soon I'll be free. Rydell's voice echoed in Saul's head. So long as Rydell believed himself capable of walking through walls, the threat of prison was useless. Saul had to find some other leverage to make him talk.

His only other leads were the Lunas, who were stonewalling him as badly as Rydell and Aleman were, maybe worse. The uniform who performed the welfare check had put Rosa on the phone, and she had insisted they were fine and claimed they'd simply spent the night with a friend.

"Who?" Saul had asked.

Rosa hesitated. "I can't say."

"Can't or won't?"

"It's just…"

In the background, he'd heard Rosa's grandmother speak harshly in Spanish, and from the determination in her voice, he knew there was more to the story—more than some undocumented 'friend' who was wary of the police. Perhaps a lot more. The old woman had started coughing, and then Rosa said, "I have to go." She'd returned the phone to the uniform, and there was nothing more Saul could ask him to do.

Tomorrow, he would drive to El Monte himself. Maybe if he showed Rosa some photos of Aleman and Rydell, she would start talking. But he doubted it. He needed a lever, some kind of incentive for her and her grandmother to reveal whatever it was they were hiding.

He was too exhausted to think anymore. Tonight, he needed sleep.

He sliced his pick through the air like a wand, wishing it had the power to shatter steel. But as he knew better than anyone, there was no such thing as real magic. The lock remained intact. It glinted obstinately in the light of Saul's phone: a solid steel U hooked through the latch between the gate and the fence, anchored into a fat dial numbered from zero to thirty-five.

The only thing more ridiculous than a grown man of fifty-two years having to break into his own place was that his landlord, Marla, had upgraded the padlock to a combination job.

He had thought they'd come to an understanding that from time-to-time, when he was too tired, he could just sneak in through the back gate. Why choose tonight of all nights to replace the lock? It had been a long day. He was spent, drained, and he just couldn't deal with Marla, not tonight, and whatever 'emergency' she had in mind.

Above him in the fog, something rustled. The palms, probably. The air was still. The fog descended toward him.

He leaned his ear to the lock and turned slowly. Listened hard, imagining the tumblers clicking open.... Turned the dial back and forth. Nothing happened. He was out of patience.

He grabbed onto the gate and lunged up. And couldn't even lift his feet off the ground.

He sighed, backed off and started up the sidewalk. His footsteps fell heavy on the pavement. Fog closed in around him like all the unanswered questions. *"Who is Wayob?"*

The street had almost vanished as he trudged on through the mist, rounded the corner, and took the driveway.

The house was dark space. It loomed ahead in the gray. Floodlights cut through the fog. Saul braced himself and waited for his eyes to adjust. The floodlights were on a motion detector. The house remained dark. Was Marla actually sleeping for a change? He took one hopeful step. Two... A light came on in Marla's living room.

Saul started marching. Beyond the house, at the end of the driveway, was the converted garage where Saul lived. As he passed the house, Marla threw open a window.

Saul froze, wishing he could wrap himself in the fog like a cloak of invisibility. Although the garage wasn't much more than a stucco box with a bed and a shower, it was all he needed. It was close to the Castle. It would be ideal, in fact— if not for Marla.

"Saul," she whisper-yelled.

He was caught in the floodlight. No way to avoid her. She leaned out the window maybe three feet from his face.

"Hey, Marla. I'm beat tonight."

"I need your help."

He gazed longingly toward the darkness beyond the floodlights. His garage apartment waited in the haze. "We'll deal with it tomorrow."

"I think it's a rat," she said. "I can't sleep with that nasty thing in here."

"You have two cats." He had intended to end the conversation there but found himself turning toward her. His shoulders slumped. The rat didn't matter—*if* there even was one—she was just lonely. She'd won this property and two others in a messy divorce, and now it seemed like Saul was the one person in her life who paid her any attention at all.

As he stepped to the window, he surreptitiously slid the rose, which he'd been saving for Hernandez, from the trick pocket in his sleeve.

Marla stood from the couch backed up against the inner wall just below the open window. As usual, she was dressed up, and tonight she wore black, her short hair neatly combed. She hadn't been sleeping; she'd been sitting in the dark, waiting by the window.

"The rat's in the kitchen," she said. "I'll let you in the back."

"Hold on." Saul leaned in through the window. He reached down and made a big show of checking behind a cushion on the couch. He jerked his arm out as if snatching the rat.

Marla screamed, jumped back and landed hard, rattling the window in its frame. She was heavyset, though not as big as Saul.

"It's right here," Saul said. "Right where you were sitting." He flourished his hand, snapped his fingers, and produced the red rose. He held it out to her. "And now your rat is a rose."

Her cheeks brightened. She took the flower and smelled it.

Gray Reversion

The fortune teller's eyes are black holes. Gray cannot look away, not even a glance just to see where they are, before her eyes swallow all the light around them and there is nothing left but darkness. She screams, her breath stale and smelling of death. He reaches out to shove her back—but all there is, is darkness. Darkness so thick he can almost feel it. And when he tries to breathe, the air tastes like ashes. Too thick to breathe. Not air at all.

The sound of gushing water. A familiar sound. The toilet in the master bathroom, in his and Claire's bathroom, in Silver Lake. He'd been meaning to call a plumber about it because every time you flushed it, the toilet practically erupted. Had he actually heard it, or was it just a memory? A sound which had splashed into his nightmare just to let him know he was dreaming. He was only dreaming. As he drifted off toward unconsciousness, now someone was talking.

Claire.

Gray opened his eyes, and it was Claire. She was standing over him. "I can't make breakfast and feed Tyler at the same time," she said, as if nothing at all had changed.

Gray leaped from the bed, which was their bed. The

clothes under his feet were his. And it was his body—
completely naked—and his. He slapped his boring old hips,
his chest. Yes! Him. He was back.

Claire was backing away, brows furrowed, like *what the
hell's wrong with you*, but her right lip was curling toward
her patented wry smile—which he hadn't seen in a long,
long time. He hugged her.

She broke free. "Thanks, but not in the mood, right now."
She wasn't mad, not yet, but she had that spark in her eye
like don't push it or she might be.

"What day is it?" he asked.

She squinted at him. "November… second."

"So, it's Monday?"

"Have you lost your mind?"

He rubbed his temples and glanced around at all the
clothes on the floor, and just above the baseboard were the
little handprints, from when Mindy was a toddler, which
they still hadn't scrubbed off. Their bedroom was the same
as always, only now, somehow, it looked worse.

"I don't know," he said.

"Well, get dressed," she said. "We have to get the kids
ready." She left him standing there.

He pulled on some clothes and sat on the bed. Had he
really been Ashley York? His memory lacked the
indistinctness of a dream. He would check online, though he
was certain she looked exactly like his recollection of her
face reflected in the mirror. He could probably paint the
exact arch of her brow, the slope of her nose, her chestnut
eyes, her lips, her hips.

So, assuming he was actually Ashley yesterday, then had
she been in his body? Or had his body made it through the
day on autopilot, like it seemed to do whenever he drank
past the point of blackout.

Whatever had happened yesterday, he felt more alive
now than he had in months, maybe years. That's when he
saw the eyes. The eyes of the obsidian snake now seemed
beady and cold. It sat on the nightstand, perched on its white
stone, its head—its gaping mouth—pointing directly at him.
He had no memory of placing it there.

After Dia De Los Muertos, he had hit the Scotch pretty hard. His memory had blurred almost to the point of blackout, but he was sure that the last time he'd seen it, the mouth of the snake had been pointing in the opposite direction, toward where the flattened top of the stone came to a rounded point.

Had the snake turned on its own? Like some kind of reset?

He picked up it up and examined it. There was nothing apparently mechanical. The stone was cold and smooth, aside from the spiral of tiny holes that converged at the bottom where something had pricked him and retracted after he turned the snake. The small scab in his palm had healed some, but it was still ringed by red flesh.

He wouldn't have risked turning the snake again. That he knew for sure.

But what if he turned it now. Would he become Ashley York again? It was a crazy notion. And yet, now it seemed possible. But why Ashley? If Claire wasn't following Ashley on Instagram, checking her feed dozens of times a day, Gray would hardly know who she was. Could it relate to one of the recent images of Ashley he'd seen on Claire's phone?

What if he rotated the snake-dial back to the twelve, and instead of Ashley York, he found himself in some horrible life far away and stranded there. Why risk it? He couldn't stand losing Mindy and Tyler and Claire.

The fortune teller had told him to destroy the charm, and maybe he should. It seemed too dangerous to keep around the house, especially with kids. But for now, he decided to hide it in the hall closet, where he kept his clothes.

As he was covering the charm with a pile of old t-shirts, Mindy startled him from behind.

"What are you looking for, Daddy?"

He spun around. *Did she see it?* He didn't think so. Her face was pure innocence and curiosity, her hair tangled from sleep. She looked adorable in her pink nightgown. A sob welled up in his throat. He swallowed it back. "You." He swept her up in his arms. "I missed you."

Her brows furrowed. "Mommy said I have to get ready."

"Yeah. We're late, I guess. Can I help you get dressed?"

"No. I can do it myself."

He put her down. "Better hurry."

She ran to her room and stripped out of her nightgown without closing the door. Gray chuckled to himself.

In the nursery, Claire was swaying Tyler in one arm while with the other she spread a towel on the changing table.

"Let me take him," Gray said.

As she passed Tyler to him, her mouth—though not quite smiling—lacked its usual tightness, and there was a gentleness in her eyes. More like she was sharing rather than dumping off a load she didn't want to deal with.

"So, yesterday," he blurted out as he laid Tyler on the table and began removing his diaper. "What did you think of it?" Awkward. But he couldn't say what had happened. No way she was going to believe that he spent a day as Ashley York.

If Claire reacted at all, he missed it. When he looked up, she was standing in the doorway. She tilted her head, and then a great distance came into her face, as if traveling away. "I'll get Mindy ready," she said as she turned away. "We're running late." She started down the hall.

Gray had to let it go for now because he knew that the more he asked, the less likely she was to answer. He'd have to wait for her to reveal something, which she almost certainly would, if anything odd at all had happened here yesterday.

After dressing Tyler, Gray carried him to the kitchen and belted him into his highchair. Mindy was already eating cereal. "You ready for daycare, pumpkin?" He combed her hair out of her face.

"I've got it from here," Claire said. "You're late for work."

Work was just about the last thing on Gray's mind, but at least in his cube, there would be plenty of time to search the internet. If Ashley's house had a turret like the way he remembered, then he'd know for sure that yesterday was real.

He went into the bathroom, started the shower, and let the hot water stream over him.

Ashley's house had an amazing view, but it was too big, too empty, and he hadn't liked all the people barging in on him. At least Claire knew how to give him some space. And he didn't mind when Mindy interrupted him. She was only five, and yet she was more polite than August Grant showing up out of nowhere and trying to shove his crotch in Gray's mouth.

After experiencing the kind of life so many people aspire to, now Gray knows how little he cares about fame and fortune. The life he'd always wanted was right here where he'd left it. Were there problems? Of course. Who didn't have problems? How many people throw their whole life away for a change they later realize isn't worth it? At least now—thanks to the portrait he'd finished last night at Ashley's—he finally had the confidence to quit his shitty job.

He turned off the shower and got dressed.

In the kitchen, Claire was at the sink. Her back was to him. From the basket beside her on the counter, he grabbed a bagel and said goodbye.

She turned off the water. "Hold on." She dried her hands and, to Gray's surprise, walked him to the door.

She kissed him.

Not a long kiss, but not quick either. Her lips were somewhat dry. They lingered as she withdrew. A hint of a smile brightened her face.

He wanted to say something, more than some platitude like *I love you.*

She turned back toward the hallway.

"I see you," he said.

She didn't react.

He might as well head into work, where he could check on his COBRA benefits and maybe clue Brad into the fact that he was quitting, or, really, he should tell Claire first, but now wasn't the time for a big discussion, because it would make Mindy late for daycare.

Tonight, he would tell her, and he had a good feeling about it. It was going to go better than he'd thought.

He stepped outside into the cool morning air so thick with moisture it tasted fresh. A familiar stiffness in his right knee shortened his stride as he walked down the drive. There was something satisfying about it, like every step he took was spaced exactly the right distance apart.

Sure, he had enjoyed himself in Ashley's body, of course he had—but damn, was it great to be back.

Connection

Saul rolled up to the gate just inside the parking deck below the PAB. He strained his arm out the window toward the electronic box. His card wouldn't reach. He had to back up and pull in closer.

As the gate lifted, he noticed Hernandez's red Mustang backed into the second row. And beneath the glare on her windshield, the profile of her face framed in a shadow of hair crowned by her shock of white.

He nodded to her and rolled past. Though there was a spot right beside her, he parked three spaces down between identical Crown Vics, buying himself a few more precious seconds to come up with what to say. Probably she felt just as weird as he did about her having seen him in his threadbare briefs. If he could joke about it, maybe he could at least salvage their professional relationship.

As he climbed out, she came to meet him. "You're late," she said.

He glanced at his watch. 9:04. He'd meant to arrive at eight, before Hernandez, in order to move Rydell to an interview suite where, he hoped, Rydell would say something useful after having spent the night in the holding cell. He didn't want her to find out about the holding cell, not after she'd specifically asked him to book Rydell into the MDC.

But as he was leaving home, Marla had ambushed Saul with an omelet, pancakes, sausage and potatoes, all setup on the patio outside his garage apartment.

"I had to help my landlord," he said to Hernandez, which was basically true. He had to help Marla eat breakfast. She had the rose he'd given her last night in a glass vase on the table, and then after breakfast, he'd felt obligated to look for the rat she was still pretending was in her house.

Hernandez curled her lip. "When are you going to move out of there?"

"As soon as I find somewhere better," he said. The converted garage was the best he could afford that close to the Castle.

"Let's get coffee." She turned abruptly and started marching toward the elevators.

Saul jogged to catch up, the pancakes ballooning in his stomach. He should check on Rydell. Yesterday, Hernandez said she was done with Rydell, but what if now she wanted to question him too?

It would actually be good for her to see how he was acting, and it would be great to get her input on whatever he said. The truth about the holding cell would go down easier, Saul knew, after she'd had her coffee. And plus, they still had to clear the air.

At the elevators, Hernandez pressed the button and glanced around, her eyes briefly catching his. Awkward silence. Saul studied his shoes. He needed a joke. *You saw me in mine, so now it's only fair you show me yours, right?* Wrong. *Don't piss her off; make her laugh.*

He felt her eyes on him, no doubt picturing him the way he'd looked in his underwear. When he glanced up, she looked away and bit her lip.

He reached behind her and pressed the button again.

"I almost didn't recognize you without your coat," she said.

"I'm kind of trying a new look." He glanced down at his belly, which protruded, in the white button-down, over the belt line his pants. Why the hell did he have to tuck in his shirt? But now that she'd seen him in his too-tighty-whities, the trench coat would only draw attention to what he'd been trying to hide. It wasn't out in the media—at least, not yet. Civilians had been cleared for their own safety before Saul had exited the library. Still, a uniform might have snapped a photo with their phone, which by now would have been forwarded around to at least half of the LAPD.

Hernandez frowned and looked up at him. Brushed back her shock of white. "I liked the way it looked on your shoulders."

His mouth fell open. She held his gaze. Something surged in his stomach. Not hunger, no... She liked the way it looked on his shoulders—*on him*. This was hope. He wanted to run to his plain wrap and get the damn coat right now.

The elevator chimed. The doors whooshed open. He steadied himself, motioned for her to enter first, and followed her in. He stood in the back.

She hit the button marked *L*. "Levy didn't tell you, did she?"

"Chicken shit," she whispered and then louder. "You were right. She's making me lead detective."

Saul nodded. He'd seen it coming, and yesterday when he pressed Levy, she had passively admitted that Hernandez was the lead on the Rydell case, but she'd repeated that it was only because of Saul's personal involvement. But Saul knew the truth.

Over the years, Levy had ostracized a half-dozen detectives under her command by gradually lowering their responsibilities until they had nothing to do. Then she transferred them out of Homicide Special, as if purely due to some lack of work and not at all her opinion of their performance.

Saul couldn't let that happen to him.

"I tried to turn it down," Hernandez said, "but apparently it's not optional."

"I get it," he said. It was all about image. Media relations meant more to the high brass than actual results. "You look better on camera than I do." Even as he spoke, the words ricocheted in his gut.

Lame joke.

Hernandez's eyes widened. Then narrowed. He'd struck a nerve, even though he'd only meant to insult Levy, who was afraid to stand up to the high brass, and himself. Here he was making a self-deprecating joke, which even if she had gotten would have only garnered pity, right after she had just complimented his oversized shoulders. What was he doing?

"No, I, I mean—" he stammered, "Yes— You are great with the press… But, more importantly, you're a damn fine detective. And if that's not Levy's reason for promoting you then shame on her. It's been a privilege—"

Hernandez punched him in the shoulder. "We're still partners."

She smiled.

The doors slid open. Sunlight poured in. Saul shielded his eyes as they stepped out into the lobby. He veered toward the cafeteria. She wasn't beside him.

He squinted and found her silhouette heading for the main exit. She motioned for him to catch up. "Come on."

Saul groaned. "You and your gourmet coffee."

"It's not about gourmet. That sludge in cafeteria is not coffee. It's not even drinkable."

Outside the PAB, Hernandez launched down First. Saul had to almost run to keep up.

"We still make decisions together," she said, "just like always. Levy wasn't even clear if this is a permanent role change or just for this case or what."

"Not surprised." Already, Saul was sweating. Good thing his coat was in the car. He'd wear it again, of course—*I like the way it looks on your shoulders*—but not while they were practically jogging in full sun.

"When she asked me to tell you for her, I nearly lost my shit. I told her she could just go ahead and handle the press briefing by herself."

Saul knew Levy would agree to almost anything to avoid confrontation, especially with Hernandez, and especially right before a press briefing where she was counting on Hernandez to make her look good.

"I'm guessing that ended the conversation," he said.

"Yeah. She said she would, but, of course, she didn't say when."

Hernandez launched across San Pedro, roughly the border between the glass monoliths behind them and the new-old part of downtown where historic buildings were renovated rather than bulldozed. Saul lagged behind in the crosswalk, panting.

Hernandez waited on the curb. When he caught up, she said, "Levy closed the case on Rydell."

Saul shook his head. He shouldn't be surprised—Levy had done the same thing with Saroyan—but still. "We don't have a motive."

"Doesn't matter, according to Levy. We've got him dead to rights."

"Sure, but juries want a reason. They want to know why."

Hernandez flipped back her streak of white. And he saw it in her eyes, how much she hated his need to find the explanation behind every single detail. Levy, too. Saul took longer than anyone else in Homicide Special to close cases. It didn't seem to matter that when Saul closed them, they stayed shut, thanks to his thorough investigation. And now, with Hernandez effectively his superior, he knew what she was going to say....

But he was wrong.

"You're right," she said.

Saul almost fell backward into the street. It was all he could do to contain his shock.

A slight smile brushed her lips. "We should keep digging into it."

She turned and started walking again. Saul bounded after her. His heart hammered in his chest, and not just because of the strenuous pace she was setting but because right now, he loved her. They were on the same page. This was huge.

"I'm thinking there's a third party behind this Wayob thing. I just can't imagine what the endgame is."

"We'll find out," Hernandez said. "Rydell is more than just crazy. You're right about that. Once we have something definitive, then we'll take it to Levy. Who knows? She might be grateful we saved her ass from having to explain to her superiors why she closed the case, prematurely."

"If we can find the connection between Aleman, Rydell, and Saroyan," Saul said, "we'll be on our way. Can you imagine three people less likely to be involved in a conspiracy, or whatever the hell this is?"

"They could be fanatics who saw the same video on YouTube."

Saul was lagging behind again, but they were almost at Starbucks. Next shop on the right. "It's got to be more than that. Rydell knew where I was Saturday night."

Hernandez snorted. "No secret there. One of the unis could have tipped him off."

"But I never made it to the Castle. He knew I was on Olvera."

"Who else knew you were there?"

"You're the only one I told."

She glanced over her shoulder at him. A fiery look in her eyes. "I didn't tell Rydell shit."

"I know," Saul said. "Anyway, this was before you even met him. He must have been there." *But why?*

"What about Aleman? Maybe he saw you."

"That's what I thought, at first, but he seemed confused when I questioned him, like he had no idea where he was Saturday night."

"Like he was lying?"

"No. I don't think so. He was scared. It doesn't make any sense."

"You've got that right." Hernandez blasted past Starbucks and continued down the hill.

Saul shouted after her, "Starbucks not good enough, either?"

"Just a little further," she said. "Race ya."

He wiped the sweat off his forehead. There was instantly more. He was out of shape and she knew it. She was a foot shorter than Saul, yet somehow walking at a pace which

Saul couldn't maintain even at a jog, even though it was downhill. It was so hot. He might as well be wearing the coat. At least it would hide his belly. It bulged against his shirt, threatening to pop a button with every step. Perspiration soaked his pits.

Finally, she stopped (a couple blocks past Starbucks but it seemed further on foot). Heaving to catch his breath, Saul slowed to a walk.

She held open the door to Ground Down, the cafe which had been closed every time Saul had driven past.

"I thought they were out of business."

"Let's pray that never happens," she said.

Affixed to the window, a card listed the hours: "*8 AM to 1 PM, Tuesday–Friday. Closed Saturday–Monday*". Inside, it was packed.

Hernandez ordered Sumatra. Saul asked for the same. She went to get seats. He poured the top inch off his coffee to make extra room for the cream. Hell, he'd earned on the sprint here. He poured it in and sipped... It was good but needed something more. And since he was skipping sugar, he added more cream.

At the high counter by the window, Hernandez had saved him a stool between her and a guy with long hair hunched over a laptop, but the gap had room for maybe half Saul's girth. And after the sprint down here, he needed to sit.

The couch in the corner, the one place he could fit, was occupied by a couple. The girl spoke in earnest as she leaned against the boy, her leg crossed over his, their feet propped up beside crumpled cups that dripped dark remnants on the faded mahogany table.

There must be some kind of etiquette. Once you're done, you should leave.

Saul stood beside the stool he was too fat for, sipped his coffee, and tried to look natural. Hernandez turned sideways to face him. His belly filled the space between them. He backed up.

She held up her phone. "Check this out."

On the screen was a video shot from a traffic cam at the intersection of Beverly and Santa Monica. As the light changed, a silver Camry turned left. A green Jaguar sped after it, ran the red, and careened onto the curb.

"That's Jaggar's Jaguar," Hernandez said. "He was driving, but we assume Rydell had a gun on him at that point. This was just a couple of minutes before the responding officers intercepted and pursued them to the library."

Saul felt his stomach go to work on the cream and the caffeine. This changed everything. He restarted the video. A text notification came up on the screen.

Levy.
Are you with Parker?

He swiped it away. "You get a read on that Camry? Rydell admitted he was pursuing someone."

Hernandez held out a folded piece of paper. She traded him for her phone.

Saul unfolded it. A printout of driver's license. Gray Wilson. White male, thirty-six. Height: 5-11. Weight: 182.

She said, "His silver Camry is registered to the address on his DL."

The first connection was the hardest, and now, thanks to Hernandez, they had it. She was the best partner he'd ever had. When he was stuck, she always found a way through it.

"So let's go talk to him," Saul said. "Maybe he'll tell us what the hell is going on."

She didn't seem to hear him. She was staring at her phone. Her brow furrowed. She dabbed and swiped.

Was she texting with Levy? Saul, looking for an excuse to glance at her screen, reached across the stool to set his cup on the counter.

She blacked the screen. Clipped her phone on her belt. "We have to go see Levy."

"What for?"

Hernandez stood. "Wouldn't say."

Saul chugged the coffee and nearly choked on the thick liquid. After effectively demoting him, Saul had expected Levy to avoid face-to-face at all cost. Whatever the hell she wanted, it must be huge.

"Let's question Wilson, first," Saul said. "Maybe he'll give us something. It might be enough to convince Levy that we need more time instead of just taking whatever she's about to drop on us."

"Takes too long to get to Silver Lake." Hernandez's voice shot up an octave. This was an order, which must have come out harsher than she'd intended because she lowered her voice before continuing. "I mean." She grimaced. "Maybe if I say we're stuck in traffic, we can buy an hour. We could stop by the MDC and see if this video gets us anywhere with Rydell, now that we know who he was chasing."

The coffee curdled in Saul's stomach. He had to tell her.

He started toward the door. "We could split up," he said over his shoulder. "If you want to go see what Levy wants, I'll take a pass at Rydell."

"I wish," Hernandez said. "I'd take Levy over Rydell any day, but I can't show up without you."

Saul pulled the door open and motioned her through. His gut roiled, but what could he do? This was Hernandez. He couldn't refuse. Before this was all over, he had the feeling he'd need her help. Levy was going to drop a new case on them—he just knew it—and there wasn't time. He had to find Wayob.

He stepped out into the sun and stood beside Hernandez. "Rydell's in the PAB."

She blinked rapidly.

"In a holding cell—"

"Shit, Saul. You didn't book him?"

Saul shielded his eyes. "Rydell actually wanted to go to the MDC. You should have heard him. And Saroyan ended up in the hospital the night after we booked him. I couldn't risk it."

"Shit." She tossed back her shock of white. "Well..., I guess now it's easier to have a go at him before Levy."

He nodded and gazed at the daunting hike back up First. Almost certainly, it would land him in the hospital. "Let's Uber it."

"No." She launched up the sidewalk. "Race ya."
Saul sucked in a breath. And trudged after her.

Ashley Revision

Sunlight. Ashley awakened to the warmth on her face. She opened her eyes and squinted at the sunlight streaming through the window. Two windows—no, four. The wall was curved...

Her bedroom! She struggled free from a tangle of covers and felt her face, her hips—it was her body. It worked!

She sprung out of bed. Ran to the dressing room. Stood before the mirror.

Never before had she felt so relieved to find herself in such an awful pair of shorts. She stripped them off and threw them in the trash, like she should have done in the first place after whatever company had sent them hoping she'd wear them. As if. The powder-blue top was not something she would ever wear either. At least it matched her complexion.

Was it a dream? Gray's body? Impossible, right? She must have dreamed about the artifact with the snake after her dad showed her a painting of one like it on his phone.

She found her phone in the bedroom. According to the screen, it was Monday.

It couldn't be Monday.

But it was. On her phone was a day's worth of unread

texts from Raquel. Ashley had never slept through a whole day before, not even that time when she had pneumonia. So if yesterday wasn't a dream, then what was it? If it was like that cheesy movie where Ryan Reynolds switched places with Jason Bateman, then Gray might have been here—in her body. She should have memorized his number. She'd had his phone all day. If she could call him, and he answered, then she would know for sure.

But she *could* call her dad. She could ask him what was really up with the artifact he was looking for. Maybe he would believe that she had spent a day in Gray's body. If it was even real at all.

His phone rang and rang, and then there was a click as the call was transferred. Niles answered right away. He had a big title but basically Niles was her dad's right-hand man, who followed her dad around like a puppy. The fact that it was Niles answering and not some assistant meant that almost certainly something was wrong.

"Where's Dad?" Ashley asked.

"Ashley! Do you have any other way to get in touch with him?"

"What do you mean?" She'd called his personal phone. What other way was there?

"I am not sure," Niles said, "but since he's not answering our calls, I was wondering if his phone is working."

"When was the last time you heard from him?"

"Friday." Niles sounded almost embarrassed.

"Friday? That's two days ago!" *What the hell?* Her dad got busy, sure, all the time. Sometimes she didn't see him for months, but he always took her calls. And he was always, always was in contact with Niles.

"It was a weekend," Niles said. "But now there's this crisis brewing at InGenetics. I need to know how to handle it."

"I can't believe you're worried about that." Ashley marched out of the bedroom. "What if he was kidnapped? Did you call the cops?"

"No. Dimitri saw him at the house yesterday."

"Weird," Ashley said. "So then, he is around?"

"Apparently, but I don't know what's going on."

"Well… tell him to call me."

Whatever was going on, her dad would call her when he could, and she had the feeling that he would call her before Niles.

After ending the call, she descended the stairs, sliding her hand along the redwood rail.

The house was eerily quiet. She stopped and listened… But for what? What did she expect to hear?

Downstairs, sunlight softened by a dissolving layer of cloud streamed in through the windows. On the coffee table, her magazines were all out-of-sorts, and after she had shown Andrea—how many times?—how she liked them fanned out in an arc.

"Andrea?"

No answer.

An intense stillness hung in the air. It was almost lonely compared to the near-constant cacophony at Claire and Gray's.

Down the hallway, the office door, which she always kept closed, was ajar. She peered inside, and almost jerked back. An easel had appeared. Slowly, she approached it. On the easel was a large painting of a man sitting behind a table facing the viewer, his back to a wall. A cheap-looking trench coat stretched over his massive shoulders. He had thinning hair, a boxy head, his brow was deeply creased. And his eyes—they stared right out of the canvas, right at her. It was mesmerizing. The bold lines of the painting seemed to capture the man exactly. Even from a distance Ashley would recognize him in a crowd. It was amazing, really, but also disconcerting. Someone had been in her house.

Could Gray paint like this?

Beside the easel, a disarray of paint tubes, two of them open, were scattered on her desk. They were on a rag, but the rag was thin and the paint could easily soak through to the sandalwood.

A vibration startled her. Her phone, which she'd forgotten was still in her hand. She glanced at the screen.

Raquel.

Ashley declined the call. What could she say to Raquel?

She screwed the caps on the paints. Ten seconds later, Raquel called back. Fuck it. Easier to just to answer.

"Yo biatch," Raquel said. "Where the hell you been?"

Trapped in a man's body, getting busy with his wife. "Long story," Ashley said.

"I got an audition for *Quantum-Man*."

Seriously? "What role?" The real question was why hadn't Ashley heard they were still casting? Some kind of an agent Don was if Raquel got to audition and not Ashley, who was already well known and, in theory, beyond auditions. Maybe her name was hurting her more than it was helping. She needed to change that.

"I did a scene with August," Raquel said. "We really have great chemistry together—on camera, I mean."

"That is so great," Ashley lied. She didn't like the way Raquel flaunted the 'chemistry' she supposedly had with the guy Ashley was supposedly dating. Why was she even friends with Raquel, anyway? And August, he could at least have told her they were still casting for *Quantum-Man*. Even if it was only some bit part, he still could have told her.

"Pretty sure I nailed it!" Raquel said. "You just know when you get it right, you know? Sergei Ratnikov said I have serious potential."

Gratuitous name dropping—nice. Ratnikov was a terrible director and everyone knew it.

"I've got to go," Ashley said.

"Cool, I'll be over later."

"No," Ashley almost shouted into the phone.

"What? Why not?"

Ashley started back toward the living room. It was a bad idea to tell Raquel about the screen test she needed to rehearse for. Raquel would repeat it to the wrong person and somehow ruin it. Deep down, Ashley had always known that Raquel hated her for wealth and her notoriety, which all came from her dad, like she could help it. But now Ashley was going to make her own name for herself. Maybe the

Charlie-Kaufman-Sean-Penn film wasn't destined to be a blockbuster, like *Quantum-Man*, but the role was an almost guaranteed Academy Award nomination.

She couldn't get caught up with what might have happened yesterday, crazy as it was. Whatever explanation existed for everything—the portrait in her office, the disheveled magazines, the dream that she'd spent a day in the life of some guy named Gray Wilson, which had seemed so real—she could only control tomorrow. And the screen test was the best shot she'd ever had. She had to do whatever it took. She had to be better than her best.

"I need to focus on acting now," Ashley said.

"Right, we're actors. So, what are you saying?"

Raquel was a distraction. Worse than a distraction, she made Ashley feel ugly inside. "The other night I was too wasted to go out, but you kept feeding me cosmos. You and your driver practically carried me to the car."

"You're mad about that? You were dying to flash your cooch and you know it."

Raquel would never admit that she had insisted on going to the Standard because she had wanted to be seen there with Ashley, and to be seen looking better than Ashley, with Ashley almost too drunk to stand.

"I told you I wanted to go home."

"Seriously? When?"

Ashley was pretty sure she had said it. Even if she hadn't, Raquel should have known. She must have known.

Ashley sat on the couch and leaned forward. "I need to make some changes in my life. It's time we went our separate ways."

"Seriously? I'm your best friend, Ashley."

"I know," Ashley said, but friends like Raquel were worse than no friends at all. "I can't be around you anymore."

"August told you, didn't he?"

Ashley was curious but knew she didn't have to ask. She just pressed her phone to her ear and waited.

"Put yourself in my shoes," Raquel said. "He was all over me, and it's not like you have an exclusive relationship, right? That's what he said, and I guess I just got caught up in the moment. No big deal. At least not for me. I was one and done—but I think he wants more. I bet he didn't tell you that, though, did he?"

Ashley leaned back into the couch. Was their relationship exclusive? They hadn't discussed it, but she had assumed so. But with her best friend? *Come on.*

She wanted to feel hurt. But instead, it was relief that washed over her. She had known that August didn't care about her. Not really. And she hadn't really cared about him. They were using each other to boost their images, and it seemed to have worked. August had been cast as Quantum-Man, and on social media, Ashley was more popular than ever. Not that she cared anymore. From now on, she was going to make it on her own merit or not at all.

"You still there?" Raquel asked. "So, I'm all you've got. Keep that in mind while you're going around making all these changes." Raquel ended the call.

Ashley tossed her phone on the cushion and began sorting the magazines on the coffee table, which were not nearly so disheveled as the pile at Gray and Claire's, but eventually they would be, if she let it go. It had bothered her before that sorting them in chronological order meant the latest issue of *Vanity Fair* covered her photo on last month's cover, but now it hardly seemed to matter.

Not a Toy

In the nursery, Claire rocks Tyler in her arms. He won't stop crying. His diaper is clean and he's not hungry. By the afternoon, he's usually asleep, so probably he's just crying because he's tired, which Claire can understand. She's tired enough to cry herself despite that she actually slept last night.

Thanks to the sex.

Finally, for the first time since Tyler was born, the first time Gray had so much as touched her since that morning, months ago, when he snuggled up to her under the covers. It was just before dawn, and she, of course, was already awake. They'd started caressing, and just as things were heating up, Tyler started bawling. And she had to get up. She was the only one who could feed him.

Afterwards, she saw herself in the mirror, the dark bags under her eyes, her tangled hair, her saggy breasts. How could anyone want her?

She almost never cries, but that morning she did. And by the time she got it under control, Gray was up, helping Mindy get ready, and neither one of them had tried anything since, not even a kiss, until last night. There just isn't time for sex, and she needs to feel needed.

Like last night.

The way Gray came onto her, like there was no choice. Like he *had* to have her. He was a different person. He'd never turned her over like that before and in the moment it was exactly the right thing. His fingers in her mouth, and she came, and then he came, and she would have again if he hadn't stopped. If he hadn't fallen beside her on the bed and fallen asleep.

Afterwards, she had a nightmare in which Tyler was screaming and she couldn't reach him—couldn't get out of bed because her legs wouldn't move. She called out for Gray, but he wasn't there. She was alone.

But he was right there beside her, mouth breathing, when she jolted awake at three a.m. Tyler was sleeping soundly in his crib.

Now, Tyler's tears have run out and his wail is weakening, like he's forcing himself to keep crying because he knows she'll stop rocking him once he falls asleep. His fat little cheeks are red from the effort, and his eyes are staring up at her, like he's waiting for her to say something.

She keeps rocking him. "What's up with your dad?"

The sex last night was one thing. She wouldn't mind some more of that, and maybe if they did it more often it would last a little longer. But Gray has become such a space cadet lately. When his car got towed this morning, because he'd parked by the hydrant right down the hill from their house, she shouldn't have gotten mad—but come on, she had to drive him to Pomona!

And what's with the new haircut? How did he even have time with all the extra hours he's been working? Or so he said.

Any other man she might suspect of an affair, but Gray is probably just sneaking off somewhere to drink. Or to paint. Probably both.

And she can hardly blame him with how she's been so tired lately. All she can ever deal with is what absolutely must be done in the moment, and she can't even do a good job at that. She can't give him the love he deserves; she can hardly take care of herself. All her energy goes to Tyler and

Mindy, and then there's none left.

But the problem isn't all her. They've been avoiding each other because whenever they go deep, whenever they try to talk about something that isn't immediate, he inevitably asks about the night before he proposed—always wanting to know where did she go. It doesn't matter. Why won't he let it go? It was years ago. It's got nothing to do with anything now. *I need him to trust me.*

But how can she expect him to know what she needs when she never tells him. She hadn't wanted another baby, but did she ever really say it out loud?

That's the problem with insomnia. Thoughts are like little moths always flapping around in her head. Never landing.

Tyler's eyes blink closed. His mouth yawns open. Innocent. She has to stop blaming Gray and just tell him she needs to go back to work.

She lays Tyler in his crib and clicks on the baby monitor. Tonight, she'll talk to Gray—really talk to him.

She'll shower, fix up, make a nice dinner and—*who am I kidding?*—order take out. Once the kids are in bed, she and Gray will sit down, and she'll explain how she needs something outside the house, how she needs to be more than a mom, how it doesn't matter if daycare costs more than her paycheck.

In the hallway, she listens outside Mindy's door. Typical silence. Most likely, Mindy's in there coloring for her usual audience of stuffed animals, which is always entertaining, but right now Claire's so exhausted she's happy to take the quiet as sign that all is well.

She goes out to the garage where, after glancing over her shoulder, she uncovers Gray's easel. She'd half-expected him to have started something new, but the sketch looks the same as Saturday when she breezed past it, pretending not to notice how much life Gray had captured in the stark lines, in this portrait of the man who looks like Charlie's evil cousin. She can already tell it will be amazing if he ever actually completes it. It's a leap above the collection of landscapes he's hidden below the workbench, as if she can't find them there. And even the landscapes have potential—if he'd just finish one.

She should encourage him. It wouldn't kill her to say something positive every now and then. No secret how he desperate he is to hear it. It would be easier if he wasn't always traveling off somewhere inside his head. His body might be right there beside her, but his mind is always off in some secret world he'd rather be painting.

And on top of that, he goes to work every day. He gets to be a software engineer *and* an artist, and meanwhile, what is she?

A mom?

She wouldn't trade Mindy and Tyler—not for the world —but being a mom is not enough. And it never will be.

Once she gets her own job and their marriage is on equal ground, it will be easier to act supportive.

She trudges to the living room, collapses on the couch, and closes her eyes against the sunlight blasting in so bright it almost makes a sound. She could dark it out if they had the curtains the Gray wants, but what good are curtains against the tornado churning through her head?

What to do, what to do? Her old job at Wastewater was better than being trapped here all day, but after wasting so much energy convincing Gray that her job was worse, she can't just capitulate now. So, what else is out there? Who would even hire her after a five-year hiatus?

She needs some kind of a plan before talking to Gray. She'll lay it all out for him such that he'll have to go along. But what's she going to figure out when she can't even think? If she could just get one whole night of decent sleep…

Mindy's laughter reverberates down the hall.

Claire leaps up. Her pulse kicks through the fog in her head.

Mindy's just laughing. What's wrong with that? She's a little girl, and she should laugh more than she does. That's the problem with insomnia: either Claire overreacts or can't react at all.

Outside Mindy's door, Claire stands listening to her daughter laughing. Must be a sugar high. Mindy must have gotten into the desserts again.

But… there's a sharpness, a tone to her laughter that's not quite right. Not quite like Mindy, who as far as Claire can recall has never laughed out loud alone in her room.

The laugher abruptly stops. Mindy whispers.

Claire presses her ear to the door but can't make out what Mindy is saying.

She cackles. Her laughter lacks all sound of fun. It sounds… malicious.

Claire turns the knob… then hesitates. Maybe it's the insomnia. She's not hearing things right.

Mindy screams.

Claire throws open the door, expecting to find her hurt.

Mindy is sitting on her bed, legs crossed, staring down with eyes opened wider than Claire has ever seen them. In her lap is the stone thingy Gray got at the Day of the Dead.

"What happened?" Claire crosses the room and kneels beside Mindy.

Mindy lifts her pale, little palm. A drop of blood in the center. Claire wipes the blood away. A little hole the size of pinprick. The skin surrounding it is red.

She snatches the stone thing from Mindy's lap and runs her thumb over snake's fangs. Too blunt to have pricked Mindy's palm, and the stone is round with a flattened top and bottom. "How did you hurt yourself?"

"I—" Mindy's lip quivers. "I didn't mean to."

Claire sits on the bed and hugs her to her chest. "It's okay." She rubs her back.

Obviously, Gray doesn't know it's dangerous or he wouldn't have left it out for Mindy to find.

After Mindy's stuttered breathing returns to normal, Claire asks what she was laughing at.

"I don't remember."

Claire pulls back and tries to catch her eye.

Mindy looks down.

"You don't remember?" Claire asks.

Mindy shakes her head.

Claire glances around at the usual disarray of Mindy's room. On the floor, a pair of white bears sit in front of a coloring book as if studying it. Nothing odd about that. Nothing surprising at all, aside from the stone thingy with the evil-looking snake, which Claire suddenly wants away from her daughter, out of her house. If Gray wanted a souvenir from the Day of the Dead, why not just buy a sugar skull like everyone else?

"Want a Band-Aid?" Claire asks.

Mindy nods, her mouth small and pouty.

After fetching a pink Band-Aid and applying it to Mindy's palm, Claire carries the stone thingy to the kitchen and opens the cabinet to the trash. Gray won't miss it. Probably, he's already forgotten all about it.

Before tossing in, on a whim, she holds the stone with her fingertips, away from her body, and swivels the snake.

It spins, and some internal mechanism clicks. The snake abruptly stops 180 degrees from where it started. Its head points at her chest.

Weird.

She waits for something to happen…. Nothing does.

She drops it in the trash.

The Key to Your Dreams

What went wrong? After Wayob endured dying, endured killing himself in the awful vessel of Rydell, instead of awakening in the new vessel Wayob deserves, he finds himself here, trapped alone in the black nothingness of the Encanto, his thoughts going around and around. How much time has passed? Hours? Days? A week? There is no sleep, here. No dreams, nothing. Only Wayob, reduced to nothing but a mind.

And why? Because he who held the Encanto had ceased using it. But after he learned of its power, how could anyone lose his nerve?

Wayob would take anything over this disembodied nothing, even Rydell's miserable body, which had always been too hot or too cold, his skin chafed by itchy garments —miserable, so miserable Wayob could retch....

And yet, to have a vessel, to see the world around him, to feel anything other than this.

What Wayob needs is a strong vessel. A body to instill fear in others. *Stand back.* Give Wayob the space he deserves. For Wayob no longer tolerates weakness. Not anymore. Not after what happened with his young bride, after he tried to reason with her when he should have done something the instant he discovered her vile desire—anyone else surely would have—but he was so young himself at the time, so naive, and no one had told him what marriage meant. He had hoped. He had trusted… foolish.

Over his centuries of imprisonment, Wayob has rolled out his hopes again and again, and as always, they got smashed, like berries on a well-traveled path.

Again today, after the little girl took the Encanto for herself, Wayob thought she would free him. Foolish. When Wayob realized she could hear him whispering to her, he had felt almost disgustingly giddy. Never before has Wayob managed to reach the holder of the Encanto so quickly. Even Abuela, who seemed highly attuned to Wayob, only seemed to hear his whispering while asleep.

Of course, Wayob is getting better, but there could be more to it. Perhaps this miserable little girl is special. Perhaps her young ears have a predilection to his whisper, little good that it does Wayob. The brat unlocked the Encanto, but just as Wayob felt its dark magnetism begin to loosen, it tightened again. The little imbecile must have turned back the dial. Why oh why, why would she do that? To open a door just to slam it in Wayob's face. Does she think the Encanto is some toy? This life she is screwing with is Wayob's life.

She shall learn.

Now no one can blame Wayob for slaying this child, who holds the Encanto, for she deserves it.

Wayob concentrates on the sound of her mind. Come closer. Closer. *You want to use the Encanto.*

Useless. She is too far away to hear him.

Wayob must wait. Wait and wait and wait in the darkness. Like always. Sooner or later, she shall give into the temptation to become someone better than herself.

Surely, this child does not possess such willpower as Abuela, who resisted Wayob's whispering for decades. Abuela had heard him—she had to have heard him—but she refused to use the Encanto. Even though it would have returned her sight to her, still she refused. She blames Wayob for the death of her husband, when it was the army who shot him. True, Wayob was using him as a vessel at the time, but Wayob was just trying to escape. Just trying to be free. Does Abuela care? No, she does not care about Wayob.

She ignored him for decades, even after Wayob began whispering while she was in the deepest stages of sleep, when surely it must have seemed like her own idea to destroy the Encanto and Wayob along with it. No way could she have known that destroying it would free Wayob into one final vessel, so why? Why refuse Wayob even this mercy?

Wayob laughs. *Ironic.* After suffering through all the decades of her resistance, it was Abuela's son, Luis, who set Wayob free. All that time, Luis must have lived there with Abuela and within reach of the Encanto, with Wayob so close and yet a million miles away, because despite all his centuries of trying, Wayob can only reach the mind of the one who holds the Encanto.

Stop distracting yourself, Wayob. Concentrate. Must concentrate. Yes, Wayob can whisper. He can and he will. Little brat must want something. Over the centuries, alone in the darkness, Wayob has learned how to hear the desires of she who holds the Encanto—no thanks to the barbaric, fucking priest, who doubtfully had any idea of what Wayob could achieve.

Wayob concentrates on the mind of she who holds the Encanto. She desires to… what? Wayob cannot hear. Focus, Wayob, focus.

Think, my precious holder of the Encanto, why wait to grow up? You can become a princess, right now. You hear me?

Hear me. Come closer. Pick up the Encanto.

The Encanto holds the key to your dreams.

Acknowledgements

Thanks to my amazing editor Marissa Van Uden for reading so carefully and paying attention to every detail. Sharpening this work was no easy feat. Thanks to Lizzie Thornton for proofreading the final draft with such gusto. Thanks to Donn Marlou Ramirez for the amazing cover design. Thanks to the Writers of Sherman Oaks for the two years of critiquing LA FOG, especially Scott Coon who read every single entry. Thanks to Ted Boyke, Aydrea Walden, Ryan Vinroot, and Seth Freedman. Thanks to Matt Marcy for giving me a glimpse into the life of a magician. If you have the opportunity, check out his show. Thanks to Damien Chazelle, James Lee Burke, Michael Connelly, and thank you, dear readers, for taking the time and supporting my work.